"I don't know who I am."

The striking blonde sitting across from Mitch Brody continued. "I don't know my name, where I live, if I have a family, what I'm doing dressed this way at ten o'clock in the morning. For all intents and purposes, I'm not more than a couple of hours old."

"What happened a couple of hours ago?"

"I'm not sure." The woman hesitated. "I...just sort of came to. I had an awful headache. I think I might have been struck with something."

Mitch rose from his chair. Without asking he took her chin in his hand and angled her head for a better view. "It looks like you were struck with a hammer," he said. Despite her grimace, he raked back some strands of blood-soaked hair. "Make that a sledgehammer," he amended. "You need to be seen by a doctor."

"No!" she said emphatically. "No doctor." She frowned. "I know I'm not offering you an easy case, Mr. Brody. But I also know, don't ask me how, that you are the man to help me. I'd stake my life on that."

Dear Reader,

The popularity of our Women Who Dare titles has convinced us that you love our stories about Superromance heroines who do not back away from challenges. So, we're delighted to offer you three more!

For October's Women Who Dare title, Lynn Leslie has created another trademark emotional drama in *Courage, My Love*. Diane Maxwell is fighting the fight of her life. To Brad Kingsley, she is a tremendously courageous woman of the nineties, and as his love for her grows, so does his commitment to her victory.

Evelyn A. Crowe's legion of fans will be delighted to learn that she has penned our Women Who Dare title for November. In *Reunited,* gutsy investigative reporter Sydney Tanner learns way more than she bargained for about rising young congressman J.D. Fowler. Generational family feuds, a long-ago murder and a touch of blackmail are only a few of the surprises in store for Sydney—and you—as the significance of the heroine's discoveries begins to shape this riveting tale.

Popular Superromance author Sharon Brondos has contributed our final Woman Who Dare title for 1993. In *Doc Wyoming,* taciturn sheriff Hal Blane wants nothing to do with a citified female doctor. But Dixie Sheldon becomes involved with Blane's infamous family in spite of herself, and her "sentence" in Wyoming is commuted to a romance of the American West.

Please enjoy our upcoming Women Who Dare titles, as well as the other fine Superromance novels we've lined up for your fall reading pleasure!

Marsha Zinberg,
Senior Editor

Sandra Canfield

PROOF POSITIVE

Harlequin Books

TORONTO • NEW YORK • LONDON
AMSTERDAM • PARIS • SYDNEY • HAMBURG
STOCKHOLM • ATHENS • TOKYO • MILAN
MADRID • WARSAW • BUDAPEST • AUCKLAND

Published October 1993

ISBN 0-373-70568-9

PROOF POSITIVE

ABOUT THE AUTHOR

Although Sandra Canfield has written eight Superromance novels, *Proof Positive* is somewhat of a departure for her. It's the first time she has written a spin-off book. Readers of *Snap Judgement* (Superromance #545) will certainly recognize Mitchell Brody, the hero of this story.

If you missed *Snap Judgement* or any other books by Sandra Canfield, you may order them by writing to us at the following address:

Harlequin Reader Service
P.O. Box 1397, Buffalo, NY 14240
Canadian address: P.O. Box 603,
Fort Erie, Ont. L2A 5X3

Books by Sandra Canfield

HARLEQUIN SUPERROMANCE

213–CHERISH THIS MOMENT
252–VOICES ON THE WIND
278–NIGHT INTO DAY
338–MARIAH
419–TIGERS BY NIGHT
519–STAR SONG
545–SNAP JUDGEMENT

CHAPTER ONE

MITCHELL BRODY, idly lounging in a swivel chair, his tennis-shoe-clad feet propped up on the cluttered desk, was engaged in his favorite sport, that of watching dust collect, when the door of the detective agency opened. He glanced up, saw the woman and immediately felt himself hurled into the midst of the dog-eared Mickey Spillane novel that lay nearby, belly down and forgotten.

"The dame," the novel could have read, "a looker if ever he'd seen one, was classy—real classy, with shapely gams that ran the gamut of a man's erotic imagination. What was such a cultured broad doing in his seedy, second-rate agency? Why was she dressed in a long black evening gown, split from ankle to thigh and clinging like a vine? Why was she wearing diamond pendant earrings in the middle of a Friday morning? Furthermore, who was this paragon of pulchritude?"

"Mr. Brody?" the paragon asked in a voice as soft as the balmy breezes that tiptoed across San Francisco Bay.

As though he'd just been addressed by royalty, Mitch lowered his feet from the desk and straightened his chair, the latter giving off a rather undignified sound reminiscent of a mouse's squeak. He stood, giving full reign to his six feet two and three-quarter inches. His stone-washed jeans, frayed at the pockets and torn at one knee, quickly settled round his lean hips and exercise-firm thighs.

"Yeah, I'm Mitchell Brody. Can I help you?"

"I need to hire a detective, a private investigator, an inspector—" she smiled so tightly that Mitch thought perhaps smiles hadn't come easily of late "—whatever the correct term is."

Mitch returned her smile, motioning her to step forward. "Any of those will do," he said, thinking that he'd been called just about everything there was. In his policeman days, which seemed like another lifetime, but in reality was only a year and a half ago, he'd been called a hero and a credit to the force—until the end, when he'd been called a thief, an officer who'd taken a bribe. After that, words like "*divorced* and *alcoholic*" had described him, along with *struggling private investigator.* Today he was still struggling; his ends never seemed to meet no matter how hard he tried. He was also a recovering alcoholic, and that struggle was the biggest one he'd ever been engaged in. Yeah, he thought bitterly, it didn't much matter what anyone called him. Ten to one, someone had already called him worse.

The woman, far taller than Mitch had realized—she had to be nearing six feet—moved toward him, her hips swaying provocatively amid the sexy song of satin. As she walked, the bodice of the strapless gown waltzed over the generous swells of her breasts in a dance both sexy and proper. From the dress's fashionable slit came tantalizing glimpses of a slender, shapely, black-stockinged leg. The dangling earrings, which one didn't have to be a gem expert to know were flawless diamonds, brushed equally flawless, cream-colored shoulders. Even in the room's dimness, the stones winked flirtatiously but sophisticatedly.

As she approached, Mitch noted some telltale subtleties that he'd missed before: a gaping run in her stockings, the way her hair—long, curly, the definition of butter-blond—scattered about her as though it had seen neither comb nor brush in a long while, the fading makeup on her face. When she sat down, he saw how the side of her black satin shoe had been scraped, leaving an ugly bruise on the delicate fabric. His guess would be that last night hadn't been the best night of this lady's life. That fact intrigued him. Greatly.

"So, how can I help you?" Mitch asked, seating himself again.

The chair, its brown leather padding cracked into deep fissures, groaned another plea for some oil. Doctoring the chair was something he kept meaning to do, but never could spare the time for. Counting dust motes was a bigger job than most people realized. Perhaps in an attempt to make it appear that his agency was more in demand than it was, he picked up a pile of folders and relocated them only inches from where they'd originally lain.

The woman, now elegantly poised on the edge of a bright orange plastic client chair, watched as Mitch shuffled the folders. She also took a closer look around his office; it was small and dark, with broken blinds on the room's single window and an overhead fan moving slowly, hypnotically around in a circle. The desk, old and disordered, held upon it, among other things, a Campbell's soup can—tomato—which contained an assortment of ballpoint pens advertising a variety of companies. Interestingly, none of them appeared to carry the name of the detective agency.

A saucer sat squarely in the desk's middle. It held a rainbow assortment of half-eaten suckers, all of which had melted together into a gooey mess that might have passed as abstract art in one of San Francisco's avant-garde galleries. A pile of detective novels reached from the floor almost to the desk. On the dingy wall behind the desk, someone had tacked up a large calendar. Each Thursday on the calendar was circled in scarlet with AA written into the squares. She briefly wondered if the notation stood for Alcoholics Anonymous and, if so, had he attended last night's meeting?

"Today *is* Friday, isn't it?" she asked suddenly.

Taken by surprise, Mitch frowned. "Yeah."

"June?"

Mitch's frown deepened. "Yeah. June fifth."

She nodded, as though extremely pleased with herself. She was actually pleased on several levels. Primarily, she was pleased that the Brody Detective Agency was pretty much what she'd expected—second-rate and in need of clients.

"You, ah, you want to tell me how I can help you?" Mitch repeated.

Her eyes, as gray as gunmetal, found Mitch's. In his eyes, bluer than the summer sky and twice as warm, she found something she hadn't expected. She found gentleness, caring. She intuitively knew that Mitchell Brody was a nice man. The fact that he was made her feel guilty, because she knew that she was about to complicate his life, perhaps in a major way.

"I'd like to hire you," she said simply. As she spoke, she laid a small, black-sequined handbag on the desk and slowly, methodically, removed the earrings from her ears. These she likewise placed on the littered desk, right next to a photograph of a ten- to twelve-year-old boy. The child had the same sandy-colored hair as Mitch. Without hesitation, she added, "These are all I have to pay you with, but they should more than cover any expenses." As an afterthought, she added, "They're real. At least, I think they are."

Mitch studied the glittering diamonds. He now knew why the woman had chosen his agency. She'd been hoping that he was so desperate for business that her lack of cash wouldn't be a deterrent to his taking on the case. He ought to feel insulted, he thought, and a part of him did, but the truth was that the lady was right on target. He *was* desperate. Furthermore, he was now curious as hell.

Leaning back in his chair, Mitch picked up a yellow sucker, still encased in cellophane, and twirled it. The pose was one of nonchalance, suggesting that he could take her business or leave it, suggesting that he hadn't already received two notices to the effect that his electricity was about to be shut off, both in his office and his apartment upstairs.

"I'm listening," he said.

The woman's attention was drawn to Mitch's hands. The cuffs of his blue-and-white-striped shirt were rolled back, revealing hair-dusted forearms. The hair there was several shades darker than that on his head, brownish-yellow compared to the pale reddish-yellow meticulously cut about his ears and neck. His fingers were long and slender, the veins on the back of his hands pronounced. He had strong hands, masculine hands. He had gentle hands. Gentle eyes, gentle hands. The feeling of guilt intensified.

Suddenly, a bolt of light-headedness, possibly the result of the dull headache that refused to go away, zigzagged through her skull. Ignoring it, she raised her gaze to meet Mitch's. He was clearly waiting for her to speak.

"I—I don't know where to begin," she said.

"How about at the beginning?"

She smiled again, this time enigmatically. "I'm not sure what, where, that is."

"Why don't we make it easy, then? Why don't you begin by telling me your name?"

Something that Mitch could only term fear jumped into the woman's eyes. Carefully, though, and in a way he had to admire, she contained it. Folding one hand over the other, both of which lay in her lap, she tilted her chin bravely. "That's the problem, Mr. Brody. I don't know who I am."

If the striking blonde sitting across from him had just announced that she was queen of a newly discovered planet, Mitch couldn't have been more stunned. "I'm not certain I understand."

"Actually, it's easy to understand. I meant exactly what I said. I don't know who I am. I don't know my name, where I live, if I have a family, what I'm doing dressed this way at ten o'clock in the morning. For all intents and purposes, at least as far as my memory is concerned, I'm a couple of hours old."

"What happened a couple of hours ago?"

"I'm not really certain. I just..." She hesitated, searching for words. Finally, she settled for, "I just sort of came to. I was cowered in the doorway of a building."

"What building?" Mitch interrupted, now making notations on a pad.

The question seemed to surprise her, as did her answer. "I have no idea. I didn't even think to look. It was down on the wharf, though. A warehouse, I guess. I remember boats, the smell of the harbor. I remember some man asking me if I was all right. I remember trying to tell him that I had this god-awful headache, but I don't think I was talking. I think I was only thinking the words."

"Headache? You had a headache?"

The woman's hand went to the side of her head. "Yes. I think I must have been struck with something."

Following the route of her hand, Mitch saw a plump goose egg on the side of her head. Because of the thickness of her hair, it had been concealed.

Rising from his chair and circling the desk, Mitch approached the seated woman. The nearer he got, the more he saw that the plump goose egg looked more like a tennis ball. Maybe even a baseball.

"Good grief! It looks as if you've been struck with a hammer." Without asking, as though he had every right, he took her chin in his fingers and angled her head for a better view. Despite her grimace, he made a thorough investigation, which included raking back strands of hair matted with blood. "Make that a sledgehammer," he amended, adding, "You need to be seen by a doctor."

"No!" she said quickly, emphatically. Obviously realizing how her reply had sounded, she said, "I'm fine. Really, I am. The headache is gone...almost." In a desperate change of subject, she suggested, "Maybe I fell and struck my head."

Mitch backed off his suggestion of the doctor. At least for now. "What makes you think that?"

She indicated her shoe. "It looks as though it's been scraped against something. My knee's also scraped," she said, drawing aside the satin of her gown. Again, hidden behind the black silk stockings was an ugly abrasion.

Mitch made the silent observation that, even though the injury wasn't pretty, it couldn't really detract from the beauty of the leg.

"And my palm," she said, holding her left hand up for inspection. Her long fingernails shone with bright red polish.

Once more, Mitch's mind was busy. He noted that she wasn't wearing a wedding ring—which didn't necessarily mean anything. It did seem a little odd to him, however, that she could have taken a fall under any circumstances and have her inch-long fingernails survive intact. Along with not so much as a blemish to the polish. Then again, what did he know about women's nails and polish? Maybe they were designed to survive a nuclear explosion.

"You still could have been struck, then have fallen and sustained the injuries," he observed logically.

The woman mulled this over. "I guess you're right."

"On the other hand, if you think you fell, then maybe you did. Maybe you're remembering something on some level."

She didn't respond to this, but Mitch could tell she was searching her mind, trying to decide if she had a tucked-away memory of falling.

"So, do you think you fell?" Before she could answer, Mitch prompted her with, "Maybe there was a stairway, maybe there was a crack in some concrete, maybe you tripped over a kid's toy. Do you have a child? Do you have a dog? Did you go out last evening? You're certainly dressed for an evening out. The theater maybe? The opera? A private party? Was it someone's birthday, someone's anniversary?"

With each question, Mitch could see the woman's frustration building until, at last, she raked back her hair with her perfectly lacquered nails, grimacing again when she grazed the bump on her head.

"I don't know," she said hopelessly. "I just don't know."

"What did you do once you came to?" Again, before she could answer, he asked, "Had you been asleep, unconscious, what?"

"I don't know that, either, but once I was aware of what was happening around me, I walked through the wharf section, found a pay phone and looked through the Yellow Pages until I saw the number for your agency."

"And you remember nothing before a couple of hours ago?"

"Nothing," she said, and Mitch could tell that the word had been delivered with the utmost anguish. This time she reminded him not of a Spillane character, but of a heroine from a classical tragedy.

Nodding toward the black-sequined bag on the desk, Mitch asked, "What about your purse? Is there any clue to your identity in there?"

She reached for her handbag, unfastened the clasp and dumped the contents onto the desk, saying as she did so, "I've already thought of that and looked through it, but there's nothing in here that gives me the faintest hint."

Mitch picked up the items one by one: a tube of lipstick in the shade of Razzle-Dazzle Red, an expensive gold compact and a little black book.

As he leafed through this last object, the woman said, "My first thought was that maybe it was an address book, that maybe it contained my name, my family's names, my friends' names, something."

Mitch instantly saw that her hopes had been dashed. The book was certainly no address book, at least not in any conventional sense. In fact, he didn't know what the heck kind of book it was. The same hand, in a bold, perhaps even an arrogant penmanship, had scrawled dozens upon dozens of notations. The only problem was that they seemed to be in some sort of numerical code. Mitch frowned.

"I know," the woman said. "None of the entries make any sense."

"Who or what is Chelsea?" Mitch asked in regard to the only intelligible word he found recorded in the notebook.

"I don't know, but I saw it, too."

Mitch closed the book, turned it over, as though hoping to find some revealing something on the leather cover, then laid the book back on the desk. He

looked over at the woman who wanted to become his client. It was time for bluntness.

"So, why hire me to find out who you are? Why not just go to the police, the press, let someone recognize you, and step forward with your identity?"

The woman didn't dodge the question, but rather met it head-on. "Because I have the feeling that I'm in some kind of trouble. Serious trouble. I think it's possible that someone is looking for me, maybe because of that." She motioned toward the black book.

Smart. The pretty lady was smart. Mitch liked that. The moment he'd seen the cryptically written book, the same thought had crossed his mind. As had the thought that the lady might be in some real danger.

"I know I'm not offering you an easy case, Mr. Brody. I know, too, that I can't offer you the usual form of payment. But I also know, and I'm not certain how I know this, that you're the man to help me. I'd stake my life on that."

What she was saying was tantamount to a declaration of faith in him. Aside from a couple of police officers, aside from a couple of special friends, aside from a son who adored him, people had ceased believing in him a long time ago. Or, more to the point, they believed him to be corrupt. Even his wife had jumped on the Mitch Brody-bashing bandwagon, although, in retrospect, he didn't think she'd needed much urging. He'd known that they'd had problems, but had thought them nothing more than growing pains. Well, the growing pains had split the marriage at the seams. This woman's contrasting faith in him moved him—more than he cared to admit.

"Those are strong words," he said, "considering the fact that you've chosen a two-bit agency which I'm barely managing to keep afloat. Hell, I spend half my time bailing water, and even so, I'm always standing knee-deep in it."

"Your candor is noted, just as I hope mine is. I'm not certain what I'm getting you into, maybe something very ugly, but still I'm selfishly asking you to help me."

Mitch considered his options. The truth was that he might be walking into something he would later wish he hadn't gone near. On the other hand, taking the case promised to be more interesting than counting dust motes, and more lucrative. Plus, when was the last time that someone had expressed faith in him? Reaching for the little black book, he said, "Let's assume that this is important."

"Then you'll take my case?"

Pushing prudence aside, Mitch said, grinning recklessly, "You've got yourself a PI, lady."

The woman reached for the earrings. As she did so, a wave of dizziness again eddied through her skull. This time it was stronger, sharper, like a knife cutting through her consciousness. The dizziness faded as quickly as it had come, however.

"No," Mitch said. "You keep those for now, and I'll keep this." He held up the black book. "Let me give some thought to where to go from here."

The woman nodded, refilling the sequined bag with the compact and lipstick. "When should I check back with you?"

"How about this afternoon?"

"Fine," she said, standing. As she did so, the knife again hacked at her hazy head. She grasped the edge of the desk.

"Hey, are you all right?"

The woman thought that the question sounded as if it had bounced off the metallic walls of a deep tunnel. Over and over, it echoed about her darkening senses. *"Are you all right... all right... all right... ?"*

"Yes," she managed to say, daring to let go of the desk. Picking up her purse, she started for the door, which suddenly looked a very long way off.

She was lying, she mused dimly. She wasn't all right. In fact, unless she was badly mistaken, she was about to faint...faint...faint... She weaved, staggered, saw the floor rising up to meet her. She distantly heard Mitch swear, then sensed more than felt him reach for her. The last thing she thought before the clotted blackness claimed her was that she'd been right: This man *did* have gentle hands.

BLACK GAVE WAY to red—short, bouncy red curls as brilliant as leaping flames.

"Well, hello there," the bobbing red curls said.

The vibrant voice belonged to a woman. Off and on, the voice had penetrated the darkness, along with other voices. Mitchell Brody's voice? Yes, Mitchell Brody's deep, full voice for sure, but another man's as well. This strange man asked a lot of questions in a tone that was authoritative. There had been concern in all three voices, concern that had twirled through the darkness like a runaway toy top. The darkness, though, had ceased to be so dark. In fact, at present it felt a lot like plain old ordinary sleep.

"You awake?" the woman asked, a huge smile curving her full lips and filling her green eyes. Before the patient could answer, she said, "I'm Kelly Stone. I'm a friend of Mitch's."

The woman in the bed cautiously crawled backward to a sitting position. She discovered in the process that she was wearing a man's worn pajama top.

The person who had identified herself as Kelly Stone motioned toward the black satin gown that lay discarded across the back of a chair. "It didn't look all that comfortable, so I took it off of you. Mitch's pajama top is uglier than sin, but it's clean. At least, he swore it was."

The pajama top, although it definitely had seen better days, felt soft and good against her skin. On the whole, she felt pretty good, period. She still had a headache, but it had dulled to the lowest level so far. There was only a single little man pounding away in her skull. Before, there had been a whole sadistic crew of them.

"Where am I?" she asked.

"In Mitch's bed." At the confused look that crossed the woman's silver-gray eyes, Kelly Stone added, "His apartment is above the agency."

She took a quick look around. Like the office, the small bedroom wasn't much to brag about. In fact, it wasn't anything to brag about. It was clean, though— a masculine sort of clean, which meant there were a lot of clothes strewn around. It was also a little dusty. Other than the bed, which had an old wrought-iron headboard on it, the room was sparsely furnished. There was a taupe-colored chair with a sagging bottom, a dresser with a cracked mirror that looked as if it had been bought at a garage sale and a metal locker at the foot of the bed. Again, there were several piles of what looked like detective novels stacked around, along with one lying on the scarred bedside table. A coatrack stood in the corner with a jogging suit hanging from it, along with a jockstrap.

Feeling like an intruder, she glanced away from the intimate apparel and back to the redhead, whom she noticed for the first time was several months pregnant. She wore a T-shirt that had *BABY* printed across the top, with an arrow pointing downward to her basketball-size belly. The mother-to-be looked radiant. In contrast, a sudden aloneness whispered its colorless song in the blonde's ear. This aloneness hurt, and so she mentally turned her back on it, just as she knew instinctively she had done countless times before.

"Did I faint?" she asked, relying on the safety of conversation.

Kelly grinned, displaying an impish look, which the scattered freckles across her nose did nothing to dispel. "Yep, and you freaked Mitch out but good. Here he is, an ex-cop, a private investigator who's seen everything, and you scared him to death with a faint. He made a frantic call to me. Mercy, I thought you'd died on him the way he was carrying on."

"I feel a little like I did die on him." She wasn't certain, but it no longer looked like morning outside the curtainless window. Her guess would be early afternoon. Had she been out all this time?

"Mitch asked me to bring some clothes over," Kelly said, breaking into the blonde's reverie, "but, honest to goodness, how he thought you could possibly wear my clothes is beyond me. You must be at least six feet tall.''

''Five-nine and a half.''

Kelly, who was looking through a grocery sack filled with clothes, glanced up. ''I knew it. Look, some of these T-shirts will fit, but that's about all. These—'' she held up a pair of jeans ''—you won't even be able to get one leg into. You know what?'' she said, heading toward the closet and pulling the dangling cord that turned on the bare light bulb. ''I'll bet Mitch's jeans will fit. You're about the same height.'' She dragged out a pair that looked as though they'd been washed about as many times as the pajama top. ''Yeah, these'll do,'' Kelly said, throwing the jeans over the black satin gown, as though she was accustomed to making decisions. She grinned. ''I don't think you'll catch anything too deadly from them.''

The other woman smiled—feebly. ''What time is it?''

Kelly checked her watch. ''A little after one.''

''Have I been out all this time?''

''You'd come to by the time I got here, but you were exhausted. And heaven alone knows when you ate last. The doctor gave you a sedative—''

Gray eyes flashed with panic. ''Doctor?''

''Yes, doctor,'' Mitch said from the doorway.

He'd been leaning unnoticed against the doorframe for several minutes. In that time he'd made several observations, notably that his new client looked as regal and as provocative—a strange combination, he knew—in threadbare cotton as she did in satin and diamonds, and that, oddly, she remembered a triviality like how tall she was, yet she couldn't remember her name. He also noted that the mere mention of a doctor had sent her into the same tail-spin it had that morning.

"You had to have a doctor," Mitch explained, stepping forward to stand alongside the bed. "I had no idea whether or not you had a concussion, which, incidentally, the doctor doesn't think you do. But if you still have a headache tomorrow, or if you pass out again, he wants to see you in his office."

The sight of Mitch was comforting to the woman, and she couldn't help but remember the gentle way his arms had closed around her when she'd fainted. The memory made her feel warm, although the announcement about the doctor chilled her.

"What did you tell him?" she asked.

"Don't worry. I didn't tell him about your amnesia. I told him that you'd been in a minor car accident and that you hated hospitals."

"He believed you?"

"What reason did he have not to?" Mitch asked. "He gave you something to help you sleep. He said to give you aspirin for your head. Oh, and he bandaged the blisters on your feet."

Mitch didn't mention that the doctor had been surprised at the blisters she'd sustained in the supposed car accident. Initially, the blisters had perplexed Mitch himself. But once he'd thought about it, he'd wondered why she hadn't had more blisters than she did. Even if she'd walked no farther than the distance from the Bay Area to the detective agency, she'd covered a considerable number of miles—and all in heels.

"My headache is better," the woman said, searching her hairline for the injury. She found a bandage taped across the wound. She felt a couple of similar bandages on her feet.

"The doctor said that you were lucky," Mitch said. "A little closer to the temple, and it could have been serious."

With a deep sigh of frustration, the woman wrapped her arms round her bent knees. "I wish I could remember what happened."

"Maybe you *were* in an accident," Kelly said. "That could account for the blow to the head and the scrapes."

The blonde looked over at Kelly, who'd obviously been filled in on Mitchell Brody's new and weird client. She wondered just what the couple's relationship was. Was it his baby she was carrying? The woman wore a wedding ring, while Mitchell Brody did not, but that didn't mean anything. Any more than the fact that the woman had said her last name was Stone. In this liberated age, women often chose to keep their own names. If the woman was married to Mitchell Brody, she was lucky. This the blonde intuitively knew, just the way she knew that Kelly's comment deserved some sort of reply.

"Of course that's possible, but..."

"But what?" Mitch prompted.

"I still have the feeling that I fell." Frustration roamed through her again, this time culminating in anger. "But what do I know? I can't remember anything!"

"That's not entirely true," Mitch said, in an easy tone. Perhaps deceptively easy.

The woman glanced upward, her gaze connecting with Mitch's.

"You remember how tall you are." At his client's frown, he added, "Without hesitation, you told Kelly that you were five-nine and a half."

"Did I?"

"You did."

"How odd."

Mitch shrugged his wide shoulders. "Maybe. Maybe not. But it does tell us that you have some memories."

"What about hypnosis?" Kelly suggested.

At the mention of the word *hypnosis,* Mitch felt the woman tense. No, it was more than a tensing. It was a resurgence of the fear she'd exhibited earlier at the mention of a doctor. He reexperienced the feeling he'd had as he'd held her limp body in his arms. It was the feeling that she was emotionally fragile, that, like a beautiful porcelain doll, she could shatter at the slightest provocation. He'd also felt tremendously protective of her. He'd told himself then, just as he told himself now, that any man would have felt the same way, that any man would feel obligated to come to this woman's rescue.

"That's maybe something to consider later," Mitch said, pushing aside his troublesome thoughts. "Right now what she needs is rest, something to eat, followed by more rest."

"I'll see if I can find something to eat in that vast wasteland you call a kitchen," Kelly said.

"Good idea," Mitch said. "I know there's soup in there if nothing else."

Kelly grinned, cheekily. "Tell the truth. Do you have shares in Campbell's?"

"No, but I wish I did. I'd be wealthy."

Once Mitch and his client were alone, she said, "I can't impose like this."

"It's no imposition. Besides, I'm not offering you that much." He grinned slightly—boyishly, she thought. "I don't know whether or not you've noticed, but these aren't exactly fancy digs. Furthermore, the electric company keeps threatening to cut off the power."

She grinned, too. A least, it was an attempt at a grin. Again, Mitch had the feeling that this woman didn't smile often. Again, he had the feeling that she could be broken with one carelessly flung word, with one thoughtless deed. He knew one other thing: She was too proud to ask for help. It was a sentiment he knew well.

"Your apartment is fine," she said. "But that doesn't change the fact that I can't impose."

"Where do you intend to go?" he asked, stating bluntly, "You don't know where you live, you don't know if you have family or friends in the area, you don't have any money for a room—all of which I should have thought of earlier, but, frankly, you're my first amnesiac client."

"I'm new at this, too," she said.

"So, I repeat, where do you intend to go?"

"I don't know," she said honestly.

"Then it's settled," Mitch said. "You'll stay here."

For a moment, the woman made no response. Finally, in a voice as soft as rainwater, she asked, "Don't you know that nice people are always taken advantage of?"

Mitch thought her question a telling one. Had someone taken advantage of her? And, if so, who?

Fortuitously, the phone chose that instant to ring. It gave him the perfect excuse to hightail it from the room. It gave him the perfect excuse to ignore the protective urge he once more felt for this woman—this woman with the rainwater-soft voice, this woman who had posed such a painfully provocative question.

CHAPTER TWO

"HELLO," Mitch said, answering the phone located in the living room. In the small adjacent kitchenette, he could see Kelly pouring a bowl of piping-hot soup.

"Mitch?"

The voice belonged to Speedy Talbot, Mitch's former partner on the police force. The officer, an ex-track star who'd barely missed making the Olympic team eight years before, was one of the few people on the police force who believed that Mitch hadn't sold his soul for a bribe. Almost everyone else did, which Mitch couldn't entirely blame them for. The evidence stacked against him had been overwhelming. He'd been lucky that he'd been allowed to quietly resign from the force in lieu of facing prosecution. Mitch was no fool. The decision not to prosecute hadn't been for his sake, but rather for the department's. The department could ill afford the black eye.

"Yeah, Speedy, what did you find out?"

As the mystery lady had slept, Mitch had made a call to his old friend, hoping that he could give him some place to start his investigation.

"Nothing you can use. At least, that's what it looks like to me."

Disappointed, Mitch said, "Give me what you've got."

"Last night was a typical night. The usual domestic violence, a couple of nasty shootings, a nastier knifing, some prostitutes pulled in and booked. Oh, by the way, the perps on the shootings and the knifing were all booked, too. None of those incidents involved your lady friend."

"Damn!" Mitch said. "What about auto accidents?"

"Sure, a slew of them, but none with a blond-haired lady who wandered off."

Out of the corner of Mitch's eye, he saw Kelly carry the soup to the bedroom.

"Nothing down on the wharves, huh?"

Before an answer could be forthcoming, Kelly returned from the bedroom, the bowl of soup still in her hands.

"She's asleep," Kelly mouthed, setting the tray back on the kitchen counter.

"Naw. All was quiet on the waterfront last night. I say all was quiet," Speedy amended. "A city councilman drowned when his boat capsized, but I hardly see how that could have involved your client."

"Yeah, you're right," Mitch said with a frustrated sigh.

"Oh, one thing you might be interested in, though here again it's not going to help you out on this case...one of the prostitutes we pulled in last night—excuse me, this lady was a call girl, and a high-class one at that—anyway, we took a look at a listing of her phone calls for the past few months, and guess whose number we found among the oh-so-many."

Mitch's silence was encouragement enough for a man eager to supply an answer.

"John Yen Chang's."

John Yen Chang was to Mitch Brody what Moriarty was to Sherlock Holmes. Unlike Moriarty, however, John Yen Chang appeared to be as pure as the newly fallen snow. Handsome and wealthy, this Eurasian was an active civic leader and patron of the arts. Beneath the philanthropic veneer, however, lay the persistently whispered rumor that he was a Tong leader who had strong ties with the Mafia, particularly racketeering and prostitution ties. Many said that the rumor was a vicious lie, and it was true that nothing had ever been proven against the man. And Mitch had tried to nail him, repeatedly, because he felt that John Yen Chang was responsible for setting him up. At the time Mitch had been charged with bribery, he'd been doing a lot of snooping into Chang's affairs.

At Mitch's second round of silence, Speedy Talbot said, "I knew that would get your attention.

Mitch ignored the hot, tight knot that had jumped into his stomach at the mention of Chang's name. "Yeah, you got it, all right. So how did your high-class call girl explain having dialed his number?"

"Said she didn't, said she must have dialed a wrong number, that she doesn't know a John Yen Chang."

"Yeah, and I'm Cinderella's fairy godmother."

Speedy Talbot laughed, then said, "Well, our call girl has something better than a fairy godmother. She has a fancy, high-priced lawyer who's already got her out on bail."

"Is the department going to pursue the Chang lead?"

"Sure, we'll pursue it, but you know as well as I do that it won't lead anywhere. Look, I've got to go,"

Mitch's ex-partner said suddenly. "Lerner's decided to grace the precinct with one of his impromptu visits."

At the mention of Paul Lerner's name, a name that every San Franciscan recognized as that belonging to the charismatic chief of police, Mitch's stomach turned sour. It was common knowledge that Mitch wasn't overly fond of his former boss. In fact, he was downright hostile toward him, a hostility that had once turned to fisticuffs. It had taken three policemen to pull a foaming-at-the-mouth Mitch off the man, at the end of which Paul Lerner hadn't been smiling his famous three-mile-wide smile. Mitch blamed Lerner for much of what had happened to him; the man had been all too eager to believe in his guilt.

"Give the chief my best," Mitch said snidely.

"Yeah, I will and, look, if you need anything else, let me know."

"Right."

"Watch your sorry rear," Speedy said as a parting remark. It was the way the two men always said goodbye.

"Yeah, watch yours."

As Mitch hung up the phone, Kelly said, "Nothing, huh?"

Mitch looked over at one of the two best friends he had in the whole world. Kelly's husband, Will, was the other. Mitch knew what an odd trio they made—an ex-con, an ex-cop, and a photojournalist who'd won so many awards that her walls were covered with evidence of her successes. Mitch knew, too, that there wasn't anything he wouldn't do for Will and Kelly

Stone, just as he knew that there wasn't anything they wouldn't do for him. In a world that had turned upside down, they were a wonderfully comforting constant.

At the concern he now saw etched on Kelly's face, he said, "*Nada,* but something'll turn up. She has a past. All I have to do is keep looking for it."

"You have a game plan?"

"Yes and no. She came to down on the wharf. Maybe that's significant. Someone down there saw her, talked to her. Maybe he knows something. At least I'm going to work on that assumption." Before his friend could make a comment, he added, "When you come tonight, bring your camera. I want you to take some photos of her."

Every Friday night, alternating apartments, the trio ate pizza and played Scrabble. Mitch knew that it was his friends' way of helping him deal with the weekend. Friday was always the worst night because two long days still loomed before him. It was an ordeal he was never quite certain he was going to get through sober.

"Okay," Kelly said, a frown suddenly curving her lips downward.

"What's wrong?"

She shook her head, causing her tight, corkscrew curls to jiggle. "I don't know. When I first saw her, I thought, Hey, I've seen this woman before."

Mitch grinned. "Don't start that again."

Months before, roughly nine, the three of them had been engaged in clearing Will Stone of murder charges. In the process, one prominent San Franciscan, Edward Andriotti, and a well-known Mexican politician, Rodriqué Echieverra, had been sent to prison for drug trafficking and murder. Before Rodriqué Echieverra's identity had been known, Kelly had insisted that he looked familiar.

Brushing renegade curls from her eyes, Kelly said around a triumphant grin, "I was right, wasn't I?"

Mitch's grin disappeared. "Yeah, you were. So, you really think she looks familiar?"

Kelly gave a deep, contemplative sigh. "I don't know. Maybe she just reminds me of someone. When you've been a photojournalist as long as I have, you've seen thousands of faces. They all begin to blend together after a while." A sudden devilish smile burst upon Kelly's lips. Mitch could have sworn that the half-dozen cinnamon-colored freckles speckling her nose actually danced. "I am certain of one thing, though. She's gorgeous."

Mitch shrugged. "I guess."

"C'mon, Brody, you *know* she is."

Mitch gave Kelly a warning look. "Do not, I repeat *do not*, start your matchmaking again. This woman is my client. Nothing more. Besides, for all we know, she has a dozen husbands."

"That's illegal," Kelly said flippantly as she grabbed her purse and slung it over her shoulder. "And I wish you'd take this godparenting seriously. A child—" here she touched her rounded stomach "—needs a godmother as well as a godfather. I know, I know," she said, stemming his objection, "you're not interested in dating, and I'll be the first to know when you are."

She pranced past her friend, headed for the door.

There, she turned and said, "See you at seven. I put the soup back on the stove, and remember that not all women are like your ex-wife."

Before Mitch could reply, Kelly disappeared out the door. He listened as she took the stairway at what could only be called a cocky clip. As her footsteps grew fainter, he couldn't help but smile. Kelly Cooper Stone was one of a kind, a confident original who didn't know the meaning of the word *failure*. She didn't know what it was like to have a long-standing marriage end. She didn't know the hurt of having a son she seldom ever saw. She didn't know what it was like to turn to the bottle for survival. She didn't know the daily struggle involved in renouncing that bottle.

Mitch sighed and raked his hand through his crisply trimmed hair. He knew she was right about one thing, however. Not all women were like his ex. Not all women would betray a trust, which was what his wife had done by not believing in him. But then, he knew one other thing as well. He wasn't certain that he'd ever have the courage to believe in a woman again—no matter how much the woman could be trusted.

"HELLO."

It was midafternoon and Mitch lay stretched out on the worn sofa, a Mickey Spillane mystery in his hands and a cherry-flavored sucker in his mouth. At the hushed words that feather-floated into the room, he glanced toward the bedroom doorway.

"I, uh, I took a shower," the woman said. "I hope that was all right."

Closing the book, Mitch sat up and placed the wet sucker in an ashtray. "Sure," he answered.

He noted that she'd removed all the makeup from her face and that her hair, obviously only finger-combed, was damp in places, leaving the golden curls to tumble loosely, capriciously. She had put on one of the T-shirts Kelly had brought her, a simple white cotton number that clung in all the right places. As the book he'd just laid aside might have read, "It clung in all the right places, giving a man all the wrong ideas."

For pants, she wore a pair of his faded jeans. Though too large in the waist, she'd belted them with a venetian blind cord that had broken off weeks before. Her feet were bare except for the bandages, revealing beautifully pedicured nails polished in red. Razzle-Dazzle Red? Mitch wondered, too, exactly what word best described the woman now stepping into the room. He decided that Kelly had summed it up best with her choice of *gorgeous*. Even with no makeup and makeshift clothes, this woman was gorgeous enough to drop a man to his knees and make him enjoy being there.

"Did you find a towel and a washcloth?" Mitch asked. "Let me rephrase that," he said with a sheepish grin. "Did you find a clean towel and washcloth?"

The gorgeous blonde smiled. "I did."

"Good."

"I borrowed your jeans," she said, adding, "Is that all right?"

"Sure," Mitch said, thinking that the way they fit was more than all right. He thought, too, that it probably wasn't appropriate for him to notice just how right the jeans fit, and so he said, "How do you feel?"

"A little like Sleeping Beauty. How long was I out this time?"

"A couple of hours. The doctor said that you'd sleep for a while. He said that you needed the rest."

"You shouldn't have baby-sat me. I'm sure you have other clients."

Mitch thought of the only other case he had, a cheat-and-eat case. It was about the only kind of case he ever got. Someone cheated on his or her spouse, which enabled Mitch to eat. It was a vulturelike way to make a living, if that's what you called what he was eking out, but he consoled himself with the knowledge that infidelity had to be present before he could nail anyone.

"I work mostly at night," he said, "and not every night at that."

"I see."

No, she didn't. Not in the least, but Mitch didn't point this out. "How's your head?"

"Better, but still a little achy."

"The doctor said you could have some aspirin."

"That sounds wonderful."

"How about some soup first?"

"That sounds even better."

Mitch pulled to his feet and started for the kitchenette. He turned on the burner beneath the now-cold soup. "I hope you like tomato."

"I guess I do."

Mitch looked up at her. "It must be strange waking up and not remembering anything about yourself or your life." Other than how tall she was, which still struck Mitch as odd.

"It is. It's also very frightening."

"Yeah, I can see where it would be," he said, thinking, however, that there had been many times over the last year and a half when he'd wished he could forget everything. Of course, that would have meant the good along with the bad, and no matter how bad things had been, he would have wanted to remember his friends and his son. Forcing all but the present from his mind, he said, "Make yourself at home."

The woman looked around her. The living area, which consisted of a sofa and a couple of chairs and tables, none of which matched in color or design, was small. The cubbyhole kitchenette was even smaller. Used paperbacks—as in the office and the bedroom—lay everywhere, usually alongside abandoned suckers. She walked to a nearby table, on which sat a lamp with a soiled shade, and picked up the photograph of a young boy. It was the same sandy-haired youngster whose picture reclined on the desk in Mitch's office.

"Is this your son?"

Mitch, a box of crackers in his hand, looked up. "Yeah. He, uh, he lives with his mother in New Mexico. You want milk or soda with your soup?"

The tone of Mitch's voice suggested that he wasn't altogether comfortable discussing his son. The woman respected her host's privacy.

"Milk," she said, replacing the photograph and stepping forward. "You shouldn't be waiting on me. I'm an imposition enough as it is."

"Like I said before, you're no imposition," he said, motioning toward the small dinette table. "Sit down."

The woman did, curling one leg beneath her in a youthful pose, which led Mitch to wonder just how old his client was. His guess would be early thirties. Did she have a husband? Did she have a son of her own? Did she have a family worried sick about her? Was she in the trouble she sensed she was? And what, if anything, was the significance of the little black book?

These questions prompted Mitch to ask, though he suspected the answer before he even did, "You still don't remember anything?"

Frustration once more flitted across the woman's face. "No."

"Nothing?" Mitch asked, setting the steaming bowl of soup before her, along with the crackers and a tall glass of milk. "I mean, I can't imagine not remembering anything. Is your mind totally blank?"

"Pretty much, except for the time after I woke up down on the wharf."

"You said pretty much." Mitch nodded toward the soup. "Go ahead and eat." The woman lifted her spoon as Mitch continued. "Does 'pretty much' mean you have some faint memories, intuitive feelings— what?"

The woman considered his question as she swallowed several spoonfuls of soup. "I think intuitive feelings expresses it best. I have this feeling that I'm in danger. I have this feeling that I'm frightened of something—someone."

Mitch saw this last remark take its toll. It did so with a subtle tightening of her jaw muscles. Even so, she controlled her fear, a fact that Mitch had to admire.

"What about dreams?" Mitch asked. "Did you dream anything while you were asleep?"

Again the woman pondered the question. "I don't think so. At least, I don't remember anything. I'm sorry," she added, as though the whole situation were her fault.

Mitch, who now sat across from her, started to cover her hand with his, but stopped himself from doing so. He wasn't quite sure why he had started to in the first place, except that he had suddenly wanted to very badly. He told himself that it was her vulnerability speaking to the knight in shining armor that came alive in every man when faced with a maiden in distress.

"Hey, don't be so hard on yourself," he said. "We'll get to the bottom of this." He refrained from telling her that his talk with Speedy Talbot had netted nothing of any consequence. Instead, he surprised himself by saying, "I promise."

The woman surprised *her*self by answering, "You don't make promises lightly, do you, Mitchell Brody?"

That she read him so clearly, so thoroughly, startled Mitch. It also caused a warm feeling to start in his heart and to spread outward.

"No, I don't," he replied.

For long moments, for short heartbeats, the two of them simply stared at each other, silver eyes, blue eyes, assessing and being assessed.

Finally, to break the fine tension spinning itself around them, Mitch grinned. "There's one thing I already know about you." At her inquiring look, he said, nodding toward the empty bowl sitting in front of her, "You do like tomato soup."

At the unexpectedness of his comment, the woman smiled, and this time the smile reached all the way to her eyes, making them sparkle more brilliantly than any diamond ever could. The smile also reached Mitch's heart in a way that nothing had in a very long while.

"S-I-N-O-L-O-G-Y," Kelly announced, beaming like a cat who'd just landed in a saucer of rich cream.

"Sinology?" both her husband and Mitch challenged together.

"No way," Will Stone said, his tobacco-brown eyes assessing his wife. "You just made that up."

That the Stones were a very happily married couple was evident the instant the two had arrived. It showed in little ways—in the way they invented reasons to touch each other, in the way they never quite took their eyes off each other, in the way Will was an adoringly overcautious father-to-be. That the red-haired, vivacious Kelly and the brown-haired, quiet Will constituted a classic example of opposites attracting was equally obvious. Strangely, the couple's presence intensified the blonde's feeling of loneliness.

"Yeah," Mitch said, "I have to agree. You're pulling our leg." As he spoke, he placed his partially eaten sucker in the ashtray at his elbow, where it joined other prematurely abandoned suckers.

It had been an interesting evening, at least as far as Mitch was concerned. Despite the chaos in his client's life, he would have sworn that she was actually enjoying herself. Personally, he couldn't remember a time when pizza had tasted so good, nor when companionship had seemed warmer.

"Would I do that?" Kelly asked her partner in this battle of men versus women.

"Of course not," the blonde said, still wearing Kelly's T-shirt and Mitch's jeans. Mitch had found an old hairbrush which she'd used to untangle her hair. It now cascaded over her shoulders and down her back in a wild tumble of sunshine-yellow curls.

"Of course not," Mitch mimicked, trying hard to keep his eyes from those golden curls. They were just about the most perfect curls he'd ever seen. The face they surrounded was no less perfect.

Earlier, Kelly had expressed the same sentiments, this time from a photographer's point of view. As she'd taken some photographs of Mitch's client, according to Mitch's wishes, she'd given a long, slow whistle of appreciation.

"Good grief, lady," Kelly had said, looking through the camera's eye, "the camera loves you. You've got incredible cheekbones."

"Are you challenging us?" Kelly now asked tauntingly, those incredible cheekbones forgotten in the heat of battle, just as she'd forgotten to tell Mitch again that his client looked familiar.

"Yep," her husband said.

"'Fraid so," Mitch agreed, stretching his long jean-encased legs out beneath the dinette table. They grazed the blonde's. Each shifted out of the other's way, though not before Mitch had an impression of softness, the woman an impression of strength.

"That's a real mistake, fellas," Kelly said, reaching for the dictionary and passing it to her husband. "Read it and weep."

"We'll do our weeping after we find the word," Will said, trying to look stern, but managing only to look as though he'd rather be with his wife in bed, playing a game far sexier than Scrabble.

Mitch listened to the teasing banter going on between his two friends. Not for the first time, he envied them. What they had together was very special. Though he loved being with them, observing them sometimes carved out a hollow feeling in his stomach. Like now. He looked away... and right into the gray eyes of his client. Both lowered their gazes.

"What does it say, partner?" Mitch asked, turning his attention from soft silver eyes and back to the game.

"Darn!" Will said. "It *is* a word."

"I told you!" Kelly crowed, adding up her points.

"Another twenty points if you can tell us its meaning," Will challenged her.

"Hey," his wife said, "that's not part of the game."

"You want the extra twenty points or not?" Will asked teasingly, leaning negligently back in his chair.

Mitch again had the feeling that the couple was playing a game other than Scrabble. So did the woman seated beside Kelly. Once more, she felt the oppressive hand of loneliness squeezing at her senses. From the earlier look in Mitchell Brody's eyes, she would have sworn that loneliness was no stranger to him either.

Will turned to his partner. "Do you have any problem giving them twenty more points if they can define *sinology?*"

Mitch, too, leaned back in his chair. He unwrapped another sucker from its package, but, instead of putting it into his mouth, he merely held it. "Absolutely none. Frankly, I don't think they know what it means."

"I never said that I knew exactly what it meant," Kelly said.

"Ah," Will said, "then you don't know what it means."

"I never said that, either," Kelly retorted back.

"Well, what are you saying?" Will said, his brown eyes twinkling.

"I think she's saying that they're going to have to pass on the extra points," Mitch said. "Isn't that right, ladies?"

"Okay, okay—" Kelly began, but was interrupted by her partner.

"Sinology is the study of anything Chinese. You know, art, literature, customs, whatever."

Three pairs of eyes looked over at the blonde. Without exception, all eyes registered surprise.

"She's right," Will said.

"All right!" Kelly said, motioning for her partner to "give her five," which the woman did.

"I'm impressed," Mitch said to his client as Kelly added a whopping twenty extra points to their score. Mitch added the untouched sucker to the others.

The stunning blonde looked as astonished as her fellow players. "I have no idea how I knew that. Do you think it means something?"

"Everything means something," Mitch said. "If nothing else, it means you're bright. You don't have any idea whether or not you attended college, if you have a degree, and, if so, in what? None of those instinctive feelings are telling you anything about a career, are they?"

The woman sighed deeply, heavily. "No," she said, her hand going once more to her head, as if it might be aching again.

"Let's take a break," Kelly said, observing this last gesture. "Beating you guys is making me thirsty." As she spoke, she headed for the refrigerator and started pulling out four cans of soda.

"You need more aspirin?" Mitch asked his client.

She smiled faintly. "No, I'm fine." As though wanting to deflect the subject from her, she glanced over at Will. "How did you two meet?"

From the cabinet, where she was popping tops on the cans, Kelly said, "He took me hostage."

"She asked me," Will said.

"You never tell it right," his wife said, flipping back the crimson curls threatening to obstruct the sight in one eye.

Will looked over at Mitch and shrugged.

Kelly ignored her husband. "He broke out of prison—where he was serving time for murder, I might add—took me hostage, because I'd taken a photograph of him beside the dead body and had testified against him in court, then hauled me all over the country."

"We went to Seattle," Will corrected. "That's hardly all over the country."

"Close enough when you're traveling with a raving maniac," Kelly said, adding, "Mitch showed up—Will had hired him while in prison, but Will had never seen him, so he thought that Mitch was after him—anyway, after a while, the three of us threw in together. We ended up breaking into Anscott Pharmaceuticals, discovered that the drug company was being used for the production of a drug called Delight, and then helped to send the bad guys to prison. All in all, it was great fun."

Will groaned. "You'd think a tornado was fun. Besides, if I'd known the trouble you were going to cause me, I'd have thought twice about hitching up with you."

Mitch noticed that all the talk about murder and mayhem had left the woman sitting across from him a little pale. "Are you all right?" he asked in a quiet voice.

She glanced up and into his eyes. "Yes," she said, but she sounded tired. Tenderly touching her temple, she added, "Maybe I will have a couple of aspirin."

Kelly, who had overheard the exchange, said, "You need to rest. C'mon, honey, let's go home."

"No," the blonde said, "we haven't finished the game."

"There'll be another time," Kelly said, gathering up two cans of soda to take with them. "Look, if you're feeling up to it tomorrow, I'll take you shopping. I suspect you could use a toothbrush, if nothing else."

The woman smiled. "A toothbrush would be nice."

Good-byes were said, with Kelly planting a kiss on Mitch's cheek.

"I need those photographs as soon as possible," Mitch said, kissing his friend back.

"I'll bring them with me tomorrow."

"Thanks," Mitch said. "And take care of my god-child, you hear?"

Will patted his wife's stomach. "She will."

A flurry of waves ensued as Will and Kelly Stone started for the door.

"Kelly?" her Scrabble partner called.

Kelly turned.

"Thanks for everything."

The red-haired woman grinned. "You're very welcome. Just get some rest."

"She's right. You need to rest," Mitch said a couple of minutes later as he walked toward the woman who just stood staring out the window, as though there were answers to be found down among the shadows if she were but clever enough to ferret them out.

Mitch's houseguest took the two aspirin that he placed into her palm and downed them with a generous swallow of soda. Again Mitch noted her long red-lacquered fingernails, her unbroken fingernails.

"I'm sorry the game was called because of me."

Mitch grinned. "I'm not. The two of you were beating the socks off of us."

She started to smile, but her smile never materialized. "I'm so sorry about all of this. I shouldn't be interrupting your life this way."

"Will you stop apologizing?"

"But I shouldn't be taking advantage of you."

"Hey, hey!" he said. "Will you stop it?" He grinned. "I'll kick you out when I'm tired of you."

She started to smile once more, but again, her smile never materialized. "Do you think you can help me?"

Mitch sobered. "All I can tell you is that I'm willing to try."

She did smile then, saying, "That's good enough. What are you going to do with the photographs?"

"I'm going to take them to the wharf area tomorrow and see if anyone recognizes you. I also want you to show me the warehouse, if that's what it was, where you came to."

As though she'd suddenly grown chilled, she folded her arms around herself. Mitch could have sworn that she paled again, just as she had when Kelly was talking about murder.

"Have you remembered anything?" he asked.

"No, I remember nothing. But I just can't shake the feeling that someone is looking for me. You know, as a kid, when you played hide-and-seek, that rush of adrenaline, even fear, you got when someone stopped counting at a hundred and shouted, 'Here I come, ready or not?'"

Mitch nodded.

"Well, that's how I feel now. As though I'm waiting for someone to find me. And I don't think I want to be found."

She hugged her arms more tightly around herself. Far off in the distance, thunder rumbled, indicating that rain was on its way.

Mitch wanted to reach for her, to pull her to him and offer her what comfort he could, and he might have done just that, had not the phone once more saved him.

Relieved, Mitch said, "Excuse me."

In seconds, he'd answered the phone and was listening to a hysterical woman, one of only a handful of clients, tell him that she'd just followed her two-timing husband to a nearby motel, where he was shacked up with his secretary.

Mitch rubbed his hand over his face. "Go home," he said, "and let me handle this."

The tearful client finally agreed, and Mitch hung up the phone.

With obvious regret, he said to the woman who still stood before the window, "I've got to go out for a while. I'm sorry. It's a case I'm following." He didn't say what kind of case, because talking about it would make him feel sleazy by association. "Will you be all right here alone?"

She nodded. "Of course."

"I'll be back in a couple of hours," he said, moving toward the door. "You go on to bed."

"I'll sleep here on the sofa tonight."

"You will not. You'll sleep in the bed." Before she could protest, he said, "Trust me, I can sleep anywhere. Besides, the sofa opens into a bed." He pointed a warning finger at her. "I'd better not find you on the sofa."

The woman's lips curved upward. "That sounds like a threat, Mitchell Brody."

He grinned. "It is. And I can be as tough as nails."

The woman doubted that very much. She suspected that beneath the steel surface lay a lot of silk and satin.

"Go," she said, primarily because these thoughts confused her.

Mitch, too, felt confused, because he didn't want to leave his guest. He told himself it was because she was still fragile, still vulnerable. He told himself that he wouldn't have wanted to leave anyone alone under these circumstances.

But he had to go and so he said, "I'll be back later."

With that, he left.

MITCH COULDN'T SEE the neon name of the motel through the fast-falling rain. It didn't take much to see, however, that the motel was a trashy one. Why did a man and woman choose to make it so obvious that they were cheating? Why did they never choose a decent motel? Well, that wasn't true. Sometimes men did do their cheating at reputable motels. Hotels, even. High-priced call girls, like the one Speedy said had been arrested the night before, did their business in the best motels, hotels and apartments.

What made a woman become a call girl, a prostitute? What made a man or a woman cheat? How could one be so blasé about the vows pledged before God and man? Mitch knew that his lack of answers, especially to this last question, probably made him the most naive man on the face of the earth. *So be it,* he thought.

He had just settled back in the car seat, some one hour and a half dozen suckers into observing room 115, when the motel door opened unexpectedly. Out stepped a man and a woman. Mitch grabbed the camera on the seat beside him. Next to the camera lay the gun that was never far from Mitch's side. All his years as a policeman had taught him that any confrontation could turn nasty. As he aimed the camera and started taking snapshots, he told himself that this assignment was about as routine and nonviolent as you could get.

"C'mon," Mitch whispered, "give me something good and juicy."

As though on cue, the man leaned into the woman, and gave her a long, lingering kiss that no one could interpret as platonic.

"Thanks," Mitch whispered, taking a few more shots. He then watched as the objects of his surveillance got into separate cars and drove off.

He cranked on the engine of his car, turned on the windshield wipers and headed for home. He ignored the fact that, for once, he didn't mind returning there. For once, the apartment wouldn't be empty. For once, the weekend didn't loom interminably before him.

In less than twenty minutes, he pulled his rattletrap of a vehicle into the garage, got out, locked the car door and started up the stairway leading to his second-story apartment.

He'd just inserted the key into the lock on the door when he heard the muffled cry.

CHAPTER THREE

MITCH'S EVERY police instinct kicked into high gear. With a skill that was second nature, he reached for the gun tucked into the waistband of his jeans and quietly, slowly turned the doorknob. Then, in one lithe, cougarlike spring, he rushed into the apartment. His feet apart, the gun anchored in both hands, he crouched to do battle. But with what? Or with whom?

The only things that greeted him were darkness and silence. No, he *did* hear something, something beating fast and loud. Something like his heart? Yes, it was his heart thundering madly in his ears. Above that, he suddenly heard other sounds—a whimper, a sob, another smothered cry. These sounds were coming from the bedroom. Wasting no time, ignoring the leaden hammering of his heart, Mitch headed in that direction. He braced himself for what he might find.

Traces of light that had slipped in between the broken slats of the venetian blinds fell in eerie stripes across the woman in the bed. She was oblivious to this ghostly illumination, as, indeed, she was oblivious to everything except the dream that had so thoroughly ensnared her. Even as Mitch breathed a sigh of relief, the woman moaned.

He stepped toward her, placed his gun on the bedside table, and, after turning on the lamp, eased to the side of the bed.

"Hey," he said, speaking softly in order not to startle her.

Her response was another tormented cry and a thrashing of her head that left golden hair sprawled savagely across the pillow.

"Hey!" Mitch said more firmly, more loudly.

"No," the woman whispered to the demon chasing her. "Please, no!"

Mitch grasped her shoulders. "C'mon, wake up."

The woman fought the dream-demon that had captured her. "No, don't. No!"

Catching a flailing hand, a hand that had just barely missed clipping his chin, Mitch cried out, this time as he shook her boldly, "Wake up!"

On a gasp, the dream fell away and reality hastened to take its place. For an instant, it was plain to see that reality was every bit as frightening as the dream. Mitch didn't even think the woman recognized him. He could see her assessing him, taking in his rain-wet hair, his shadowed chin, his end-of-the-day-tired features. Suddenly, though, just when another cry seemed possible, she went limp with relief.

Mitch released her shoulders, partly because it seemed the appropriate thing to do now that she was awake, partly because he again had the inappropriate urge to take this woman in his arms. One did not take one's client into one's arms, even if said client had had a nightmare, even if said client was in one's bed. Particularly if said client was in one's bed. For a fleeting second, though, he had the feeling that, if he had reached for her, she would have allowed him to hold her. Which was another sterling reason not to reach for her.

"You okay?" he asked instead.

Taking a deep breath, raking back fallen strands of hair from her forehead, she answered, her voice ragged, "Yes. I think so."

Mitch noted that perspiration had dampened her forehead and her upper lip. The dewy drops glistened like the diamonds that had once graced her ears, diamonds that now resided in the safe downstairs. He also noted that his pajama top clung to her moist skin in a way that tantalizingly revealed the full outline of a breast. Mitch tried to ignore this and stood.

"You were dreaming," he said.

"Yes."

"What?"

"I'm not certain. I mean, I remember, but it doesn't make any sense."

"Tell me about it."

The woman sat up in bed, drawing her knees toward her and clasping her arms around her legs. She seemed to be selecting her words carefully.

Finally, she said, "There was this house—"

"Big? Little?" Mitch interrupted. He had seated himself in a nearby chair.

"Big. At least I guess it was big. All I could really see was one room. Actually, it wasn't even a room. It was more like a foyer. Anyway, it had this enormous curving staircase. The wood was white with a gilded edge, and overhead was a huge chandelier. It had hundreds of candle-shaped bulbs that burned so brilliantly they hurt my eyes."

"Was it night?"

The woman considered the question. "I don't know."

"You implied that the chandelier was turned on."

"It was, but I didn't get a sense of day or night."

"It's probably not important," Mitch said, adding, "Go on."

So far he'd heard nothing that should have inspired the fear, the panic, she'd exhibited. But something had, and he meant to find out what that something was.

Frustration streaked across the woman's face. "The dream is hazy, foggy. All I can see is the stairway and the chandelier."

"What were you frightened of?" Mitch asked pointedly.

Even the question seemed to frighten the woman sitting in his bed. He could tell by the way her eyes turned from silver-gray to pewter, and by the way she hugged herself more tightly.

"What frightened you?" Mitch repeated.

The woman hesitated, then said, "I was suddenly out in this field. It was green and open and peaceful. There were flowers—pink flowers, I think—growing everywhere. I felt happy," she said, looking over at Mitch.

Something in the way she announced this last bit, that she was happy, hinted that such contentedness might be rare in her life. If so, it confirmed his earlier observation that smiles were not common occurrences for her.

"So what happened? What caused that feeling of happiness to go away?"

Again she paused. "I, uh, sensed something watching me. I knew that it meant to harm me, so I started running, but my legs felt heavy. They felt bogged down in the pink flowers. It was almost like the flowers had become this beautiful quicksand. The faster I tried to run, the slower I got. It was like a film slowed way down."

"Could you see what was chasing you?"

"Not at first. I just knew that it meant to harm me."

"But after a while you could see what was chasing you?"

The woman's skin became as white as snow.

"Tell me," Mitch insisted.

He could see his client plucking up her courage. Again she seemed reluctant to speak.

"Tell me," he said, this time so softly that her eyes were once more drawn to his. For long moments, they simply stared at each other.

"I don't know what it was," she said at last. "Some sort of creature." A visible chill claimed her, causing her to shiver. "Some sort of hideous doglike creature. It was green. I remember thinking that it looked like stone, and I kept wondering how something made out of stone could be chasing me. It had this horrible face, with fanglike teeth." Here she shuddered, but she found the courage to add, "When it caught up with me, it ripped my throat out . . . and left me to bleed to death on the pretty pink flowers."

At her words, Mitch's gaze lowered to the woman's throat. It was pale and vulnerable, much like the woman herself. The throat was also pretty, much too pretty to be so cruelly sacrificed amidst pink flowers.

As he watched her, Mitch once more felt the woman's fear. It was a tangible thing that knocked upon the door of his heart.

He dragged his thoughts back on to a professional plane. "You don't remember anything else?"

She shook her head. "No. Nothing."

Suddenly, her eyes glazed over with tears, which she fought against shedding. It was a battle she won, a feat that moved him in a way that tears never could have.

"What am I going to do?" she asked in a voice torn with emotion.

Rising from the chair, he walked toward her. He smiled, hoping that he sounded more confident than he felt. "For starters, you're going to let me do the worrying. That's what you're paying me for. Okay?" When she made no response, he repeated, "Okay?"

She smiled faintly. "Okay."

"And now," he said, "you're going to get a good night's sleep." At this, he took the covers in his hands and, much as he might have done with a child, he coaxed her beneath them. "Down you go," he encouraged her as she once more settled into the bed's warmth.

As her head sank into the soft pillow, she sighed heavily, wearily, sleepily.

"Everything'll look better in the morning," Mitch said as he switched off the bedside lamp. The room was plunged into darkness, except for the faint lights from outside once more peeking through the broken slants of the blind.

"Good night," Mitch said, starting from the room.

"Stay with me."

The velvet-soft words stole through the night and, like a lover, entwined themselves around Mitch. He stopped and turned, his gaze finding the woman in the bed. He knew her eyes were on him because he could feel them.

"Stay with me until I fall asleep." With only the briefest hesitation, she added, "Please."

There was no apology for her request, no coy rationalization. The woman was afraid, plain and simple, and she didn't want to be left alone. That kind of emotional honesty was rare. That kind of emotional honesty deserved rewarding, although Mitch knew that even had it not been worthy of reward, there was no way he could have denied this woman's request.

"Go to sleep," he said, easing once more into the nearby chair.

The next few minutes were unlike any Mitch could ever remember spending. Though not a single word was exchanged, a camaraderie, which he could neither deny nor explain, developed between the two of them. The rain had stopped, leaving only the pitter-patter of water as it dripped from roof and eaves. The woman's breathing, the rustle of bedclothes, an occasional sigh, were the only real sounds that intruded on the quiet scene, and yet Mitch heard things unspoken and unsaid. He heard this woman's fear and confusion, heard her frustration, her gratitude to him for staying. As unlikely as it seemed, he even heard her fall asleep.

He told himself that he could leave the bedside now and retire to the sofa in the living room, and yet he didn't budge. Minutes turned into hours and still he stayed, stuffed uncomfortably in the chair that was as worn out as he was. He knew that he was behaving foolishly, but he didn't much care. His mission was an important one: to keep grotesque green dogs at bay.

AT FIRST, the woman didn't know where she was, but, as abruptly as a sneeze, everything came rushing back: the strange bed, the strange apartment, the man who'd sat by her bedside all night. The man himself should have been a stranger—she hardly knew him—but he didn't feel like a stranger. He felt too old-shoe-comfortable for that. She had awakened a couple of times, and each time she'd sensed his presence in the room. She hadn't even opened her eyes to confirm it. She hadn't needed to, any more than they'd needed words to communicate.

Their unspoken communion in the dark of the night had been unlike anything she'd ever experienced. It had been consoling, as had been the sound of his even breathing and the sound of his denim-clad legs brushing together. If their unspoken communication had been consoling, it had also been frightening. She had sensed so much about Mitchell Brody—that he was basically unhappy, that he was a loner, that he didn't know who or what he was. On the other side of that coin, the frightening side of the coin, was the question: What had he sensed about her? Things best left unknown?

Angling her head, she sought out the nearby chair. Mitchell Brody, his large body crammed into the un-comfortable-looking chair, slumped in sleep. His legs, long and lean, stretched out before him, while one arm lay across his broad chest. The other arm dangled over the arm of the chair. Sandy-colored hair lazed about on his forehead, making him look decidedly youthful.

Even as she thought how youthful he looked, her gaze took in his wide shoulders, his hair-dusted arms, biceps that bespoke a muscular power. Well, there might certainly be a lot of the boy in Mitchell Brody, but there was also a lot of the man. This last thought was troubling, and so she crawled out of the bed and quietly disappeared into the bathroom. From there, she headed into the kitchen.

Fifteen minutes later, Mitch stirred. The aroma of coffee wafted beneath his nose, teasing him to wakefulness. He came to with a start. What was he doing asleep in the chair? At the same time that the answer to this question came to him, he glanced over at the bed. The empty bed. For a second, he was ready to panic—maybe the green dog had gotten his client, after all—when he remembered the fragrance of coffee. That most probably meant only one thing.

He found his houseguest just where he suspected he would. What he hadn't expected was for her to look so...*gorgeous*. There was that word again. She once more wore his jeans and Kelly's T-shirt, and, once more, she was barefoot. This time, however, instead of allowing her hair to fall freely about her shoulders, she'd drawn it into a ponytail with a rubber band she'd obviously found lying around. She looked young and girlish, as though she didn't have a care in the world. This last impression was reinforced by her off-key humming.

Suddenly, she turned, gasped, then smiled in relief. "You scared me, Mitchell Brody."

"Sorry," Mitch said, crossing to and leaning across the countertop that separated the kitchenette from the living area. "By the way, call me Mitch."

The woman, a wooden spoon in her hand, considered his request. "No," she said at length. "Mitchell, yes. Mitch, no."

Mitch grinned, reaching for a strip of fried bacon draining on a paper towel. "My mother called me Mitchell. She always said she should have named me Mischievous."

His houseguest whacked his hand with the spoon, saying, "She was right."

"Ouch," Mitch said in response to both the physical and verbal acts.

"Then stay out of our breakfast," she said, turning her attention back to the eggs she was scrambling in the blackened skillet. "Have you ever thought about buying a new skillet?"

"Why should I? That one works fine."

"And I suppose this spoon does as well?" she asked, indicating the wooden utensil that had certainly seen better days.

"It just whopped the daylights out of me, didn't it?"

The woman smiled; Mitch grinned. Both thought it an odd conversation to be having under the circumstances, yet completely natural at the same time. Each could have sworn that this wasn't the first breakfast they'd shared. Nor did it seem the first playful pop she'd ever given him with a spoon, or the first time that they'd stood looking at each other in just this way. Maybe asking someone to sit at your bedside, maybe sitting at someone's bedside, bred familiarity.

She wanted to tell him how moved she'd been by his staying with her the whole of the night, how comforted she'd felt by his being there. She wanted to tell him about the lonely feeling that too often plagued her.

Mitch wanted to tell her how moved he'd been by her asking him to stay, though he was a tad confused about why he'd remained by her side even after she'd fallen back to sleep. He wanted to tell her that the last year and half had been a lonely nightmare.

"Is that coffee off-limits, too?" Mitch asked, filling in the suddenly awkward silence that had crept between them.

Without a word, she turned and poured him a cup, which she handed to him. "Sugar? Cream?"

"No, just black," he said, sitting down at the dinette table and taking a cautious sip. "You didn't have to make breakfast."

"I wanted to," she said, scraping the eggs onto two plates. "It's the least I could do in return for your hospitality." She laid the strips of bacon on the plates as well, along with freshly buttered pieces of toast. Smiling, she said, "I don't do this too often, so enjoy it."

As soon as she'd made the comment, she realized what she'd said. Mitch realized it, too.

"Why don't you do this often?"

She set the plates on the table, her mind clearly distracted now by trying to remember. The effort was almost a visible one. She started to shake her head, indicating that she didn't know.

Mitch stopped her. "Think about it," he said, then tried to jog her memory with a series of questions.

"Do you not usually eat breakfast? Do you sleep late? Maybe you work nights? Maybe you hate cooking? Do you have someone who cooks for you?"

The woman pondered each query—agonizingly. Finally, she said, "I don't know. I just don't know."

At the return of her frustration, Mitch lightened the mood. Once more with a positive attitude he wasn't certain was justified, he said, "There's plenty of time for you to remember." Nodding toward the plate, he said, "Eat. It isn't often that I have a pretty lady cook me breakfast, and that I know for a fact."

They ate and, as they did so, it appeared that both were ravenously hungry. For long minutes, neither spoke. Mitch broke the silence.

"How did you sleep?"

"Fine."

"No more green dogs?"

The fork on its way to her mouth hesitated before she responded with, "No."

"How about other dreams?"

"No," she said, but frowned.

"You *did* dream something else," Mitch said.

The woman laid her fork onto the plate. "Yes, but it wasn't a frightening dream. And it wasn't all that clear. I remember only fragments of it."

"What do you remember?"

"Something about a young woman."

"What about her?"

"I don't remember anything, except that she had this circle of light around her head."

"Circle of light? You mean like a halo?"

The woman weighed this possibility. "Perhaps."

"Only angels have halos. Was she dead?"

Again frustration ruled. "I don't know. I just know that there was nothing frightening about this dream. I felt . . . I don't know, peaceful with her." Just as she had felt with Mitch sleeping only a few feet away, but this she didn't voice.

"How old was she?"

"Early twenties, I guess. No, maybe mid-twenties." Suddenly, the woman grew angry. "I don't know! All I ever have are bits and pieces that make no sense."

"Hey, hey," Mitch soothed her. "Everything's gonna be all right. We're making progress."

"Green dogs and angels with halos are progress?"

Mitch grinned. "It's more than we knew when you walked into my office yesterday morning." Then, before she could say or do anything except marvel at the brilliance of his smile, he nodded toward her plate. "Eat. We have sleuthing work to do."

MITCH'S WORN-OUT CAR, pale blue and with a bevy of pockmarked rust spots, moved slowly through the Saturday-afternoon traffic. It moved slowly because it could move no other way. With more ills than a hypochondriac—the automobile shook violently every time the speedometer rose above sixty—Mitch lived in constant fear of the car's demise and of the mechanic's announcement that there was nothing left worth trying to resurrect.

Glancing over at the woman in the passenger seat, he couldn't help but reflect on how incongruous she appeared in this setting. Again, a royal image came to mind, but in this case her throne had tattered and torn leather. The glove compartment at her knees had been rigged shut with a piece of string, while the dashboard was dented in several places. Yeah, she looked totally out of place. A fish out of water. The question was: Would he ever find the pond she belonged in?

That morning, while he'd put the disgusting end to the cheat-and-eat case he'd collected evidence for the evening before, Kelly had taken his houseguest shopping. She hadn't wanted to accept the money he'd offered her, but he'd known that the wronged wife would cough up the remainder of his fee, which she had. He probably should have paid the electric bill, but what the heck; he always kept a bunch of candles just in case the company got surly and pushed its weight around.

Mitch didn't know much about the shopping habits of women—no man did really—but he knew unequivocally that the outing had been successful... at least, if how his client now looked was any indication. In short, she looked sensational. She'd bought a pair of white jeans that fit her like the proverbial leather glove, plus a toffee-colored T-shirt and matching belt. In addition, she'd purchased a pair of tennis shoes, a couple pairs of white socks, some makeup, and several personal items like a toothbrush, a comb and a few pairs of plain cotton underwear that somehow managed to appear sexy. At least Mitch had thought they looked sexy as they'd peeked out from the woman's shopping bag. He didn't dare think about the present intimate location of one pair of that sexy underwear.

Instead, he let his mind wander back to the comment Kelly had made when they had returned from their shopping spree and his client had been out of earshot. Kelly had just handed him the picture-perfect snapshots she'd taken of the woman the evening before.

"She spent the whole time looking over her shoulder, as though she half expected someone to jump out of the woodwork and shoot her dead. Oh, she tried not to be obvious, but she was scared."

"I can't say her fear isn't justified," Mitch had responded.

"You think she's really in some kind of trouble?"

Mitch had shrugged. "I don't know much about amnesia, but I do know that there's such a thing as hysterical or repressive amnesia...blocking out what's too painful to remember."

"But then again, she's suffered a blow to the head," Kelly said. "Maybe the amnesia was physically induced. I've read about people receiving an injury to the head and wandering around not knowing who they are or where they are."

Mitch hadn't been intellectually equipped to argue the point, which told him that maybe he needed to talk to an authority on the subject. On the other hand, though, he couldn't get beyond the thought that his client was intuitively scared. That had to mean something.

"How did the shopping go?" he now asked her.

The woman, her hair still bound in a bouncy ponytail, looked over at him. "Fine."

"Did you recognize anything? The mall? Any of the stores? Did you have the feeling you'd seen anything before?"

"No."

"Does any of this look familiar?" he asked, indicating the area they were passing through.

"We're nearing the wharf area, aren't we?"

Mitch shot her another glance. "Then you do remember something?"

"Yes, but I think it's only from the other night."

Mitch accepted her reply with disappointment.

Minutes later, she said, "Tell me something about you."

If there was one thing Mitch hated it was talking about himself. In fact, it was something he absolutely refused to do. "Believe me, there's not that much to talk about."

"Are you divorced?"

The question was blunt. "Yeah," he said, hoping that his answer didn't sound short, hoping that nothing more would be required. At the look in the woman's eyes, he knew that something more was expected of him, however, so he added, "For over a year."

"How old is your son?"

If possible, this question hurt even more deeply, simply because any mention of his son reminded Mitch of just how far away New Mexico was and how his son was growing up without him.

"Scott's eleven." Mitch grinned despite the pain. "Going on twenty-one. He's into baseball and model-car racing and loves horses."

Mitch's mysterious client smiled, saying softly, "You miss him."

"Yeah," Mitch responded hoarsely, refusing to look the woman in the eye for fear that the emotion in his own would give his hurt away. That he couldn't do. It was simply too intimate an act.

The woman saw the hurt anyway and thought that she'd been right. Mitchell didn't like talking about his son. Not wanting to seem nosy, she changed the subject. "Your friend, Kelly, said that you used to be a policeman."

Pain pierced Mitch's heart.

"I used to be," he said, thickly, dismissively.

"Did I say something I shouldn't have?" the blonde asked, watching Mitch closely.

"No," he said far more curtly than he'd wished.

"I'm sorry. I didn't mean to pry."

Mitch turned toward his passenger. His face was unusually devoid of emotion. "It's a long story. One I won't bore you with. Let's just say that you might be trying to remember, but I'm trying to forget."

Mitch's comment brought the conversation to an effective end. That and the fact that they'd arrived dockside. In the distance, the bay glistened beneath the bright summer sun. Every conceivable form of seacraft, from the lowliest of rowboats to the fanciest of yachts, lined the wharf, some three-, four- and a half-dozen deep. The smell of sea and sun permeated the air.

For the better part of an hour, Mitch cruised the area in search of the warehouse—his client was pretty well convinced now that it, indeed, had been a warehouse—where she had come to. The effort met with no luck, however.

"You don't recognize any of these as the warehouse?" Mitch asked, unable to keep the disappointment from his voice. Although he was uncertain what locating the warehouse would prove, it was nonetheless a starting point. What intrigued him was why she'd been down by the wharf. As he'd told her, everything meant something. It was simply a matter of discovering what that something was.

The woman beside him heard, sensed, his disappointment. It equaled her own. "No, I don't recognize any of these warehouses."

"Are you sure you would?"

Fingering golden curls that had worked free of the ponytail and clustered around her ear, she admitted, "No, I'm not even sure I would. We might have already passed it. Maybe the building wasn't a warehouse after all."

"Do you have any specific memory of the building? Do you remember anything that would set it apart?"

"No, nothing beyond the fact that it had some sort of overhang where I crouched. Sort of like a small porch over a doorway."

After a few more unsuccessful tries at locating the warehouse, Mitch said, "Let's take a different tack. Let's see if anyone recognizes your photograph. You stay here. I'll be back soon."

For another hour, Mitch questioned everyone he came across, which was a considerable number of people. He spoke with people who worked down on the waterfront, and he spoke with people there only because it was a good sailing weekend. Nobody had seen the woman in the photo. He did confirm, however, what Kelly had said earlier. His client, though she remained in the car, did spend half her time looking over her shoulder. She was definitely afraid.

"Anything?" she asked as Mitch slipped back inside the car. He closed the door with a rickety thud.

"Nope," he said, placing his hands on the steering wheel and simply staring straight ahead.

For a long while, neither Mitch nor his client spoke. There seemed no way to be heard above the loud sound of failure.

"It's not your fault," the woman beside him said quietly.

Mitch glanced over at her and sighed. "Lady, are you sure you didn't just drop out of the sky?"

The blonde smiled. "And land on my noggin?"

He said around a smile that matched hers, "Exactly."

Suddenly, her smile disappeared. "What do we do now?"

"Go home and revamp our plans."

With this, Mitch started the car. The engine whined to life. In seconds he was maneuvering the car away from the wharf and back toward the inner city. A turn to the right, another to the left, and they were passing through the end of the Bay Area. It was a section they hadn't passed through before. A trio of warehouses stood on the seaward side.

"There!" the woman in the passenger seat cried, pointing to the last and the smallest of the three buildings.

Mitch's gaze followed the direction that was indicated. Sure enough, the warehouse had an overhang that would have provided protection to anyone huddled in the doorway.

"There, that's it," the blonde repeated, then added, "I'm positive."

As Mitch slowed the car to a stop, it was obvious that the warehouse was closed for the weekend. Maybe even deserted.

"C'mon," Mitch said, cutting off the engine and throwing open his door, "let's look around."

Mitch couldn't tell how the woman felt about locating the warehouse—relieved? Apprehensive?—but she didn't hesitate at following him to the front door. On it was written the words: Tinsung's Oriental Imports.

"Does the name mean anything to you?" Mitch asked.

"Nothing."

"You're sure this is the building?"

"Positive," the woman repeated.

Without a word, Mitch moved to the side of the building and, finding one long, narrow window, he cupped his hands to the glass and peered in. The woman did the same.

Suddenly, she gasped.

It took Mitch only a fraction of a second to locate the reason behind his client's reaction. Amid boxes and crates crouched the statue of a dog. More frightening than the dog's grotesque snarl was its color, which, unbelievably, was green.

CHAPTER FOUR

"IT'S CALLED a Dog of Fo."

Mitch shifted his gaze from the street and its bustling traffic to the woman sitting beside him. They were headed back to his apartment, a trip that until this moment had been characterized by silence. Mitch understood the source of that wordlessness. His client had been shaken by their find—and still was, if a pair of trembling hands was any indication.

"Such statues actually don't represent dogs at all," his passenger continued, seeming to need to talk now, "but rather Buddhist lions. They're used to guard temples, altars and the home. They flourished from the third century A.D., following the growth of Buddhism. Chinese artists used a lot of different media, but jade, which in an Oriental context refers to nephrite of various colors, has historically been a favorite for depicting these caninelike creatures."

Though surprised by the depth of her apparent knowledge, Mitch managed nonetheless to ask matter-of-factly, "You have no idea why you know so much about these Dogs of Fo?"

The woman stared straight ahead into the Saturday afternoon. She blinked thick-lashed eyelids against the blisteringly bright sun.

"No," she said, "but it's not only Fo Dogs. I think I know a lot about Oriental art in general. I didn't realize it until I saw the dog in the warehouse."

"That would explain your knowledge of the word *sinology*." Before she could reply, Mitch asked, "You're certain that was the green dog in your dream?"

"I'm not certain that particular dog was the one in my dream. As I said, Dogs of Fo are commonplace as far as Chinese art goes, and jade is frequently used."

"Okay. This may not be the exact dog, but the dog in your dream is one like it, right?"

"Right." She sighed. "It seems something of a coincidence, though, that another dog would be involved, doesn't it?"

Unable to argue the point, Mitch simply shrugged. In his experience, coincidence had its roots in the reasonable, the rational, if one only knew how far back to dig. A perfect example of that was his being accused of taking a bribe just when he'd begun sniffing around John Yen Chang. Telling himself that this wasn't the issue at the moment, Mitch forced his thoughts back to the present case. He felt obligated to remind his client, and himself, of one fact.

"You did say that they were fairly common. Maybe it is nothing more than a coincidence."

"Maybe," she agreed.

"And you have no idea if you'd ever seen that warehouse before two nights ago?" he asked.

"None."

"You have no idea why, out of all the places you could have gone Thursday night, you ended up there?"

"No."

"And you don't remember anything about Tin-sung's Oriental Imports? Like if you own it, work there, or maybe just made a purchase from the shop? Like maybe one of those Fo Dogs?"

"I remember nothing." The words were snapped out, as though the woman was angry, primarily with herself, that she couldn't recall anything.

Mitch sensed her frustration. "It's not your fault," he said softly.

This time, as if drawn by the gentleness of his voice, the woman looked over at him. Their gazes meshed and merged, but she said nothing. She simply absorbed some of his kindness before turning her head once more to stare straight ahead. In reaction to the movement, she touched her temple with her fingertips.

Mitch wondered if her headache had returned. He didn't have to wonder if she was tired. She suddenly looked exhausted. More than that, she looked alone. Who was this woman? It was a question that Mitch longed to have an answer to almost as much as the woman herself did.

"Where do we go from here?" his client asked as he pulled into the driveway of his agency-apartment and shut off the engine.

"You're going upstairs to rest," Mitch said as he threw open his door, "and I'm going to pay Tinsung's Oriental Imports a visit. That is, if I can find its address."

Mitch wished that everything about the case was as simple as finding the said address. One look in the telephone directory, and he was on his solitary way to what turned out to be a Victorian-style building in one of the older, ritzier sections of the city. That this particular import shop catered to the elite was obvious not only from its location, but also from its immaculate appearance. The bare wooden floor, off which his footsteps keenly echoed, had been polished until it shone, while embroidered draperies of the finest brocade graced the windows. A hushed coolness dwelled within the small interior, as did the subtle scent of incense. Bolts of fabric lined one wall—in an impressive array of silks and satins.

In addition, there was a small collection of Oriental art. Bronze wares, bells, mirrors and daggers occupied one whole shelf. Next to these items stood a dozen or so terra-cotta vases. On the wall behind them hung a series of landscapes drawn with delicate, featherlike strokes of ebony ink. Pedestals, obviously displaying very valuable pieces, were positioned throughout the room. One bore a blue-and-white vase; another, a bronze horse rearing. A Fo Dog, however, caught Mitch's eye, and it was to this that he walked. Its tag described it: Lion guarding doorway, white marble, height eighty centimeters, Ch'ing Dynasty. It also revealed a price that nearly caused Mitch to choke on the spot.

"May I help you?" a quiet, genteel voice asked. Mitch turned and saw a woman standing in the doorway that led to what he guessed was a back room. Of Chinese descent, the shopkeeper, her hair coal-black and worn in a short, straight bob, appeared as elegant as the store. Though most probably in her late forties or early fifties, she possessed a faultless, alabaster complexion, along with a pair of beautiful almond-shaped brown eyes. Her traditional Chinese dress, royal blue trimmed in gold, fit her immaculately. The dress's slender skirt allowed her to take only tiny steps forward, but these she managed as though she were floating on air.

She smiled, nodding toward the white marble statue. "Lovely, isn't it?"

Mitch smiled back, noting that the woman spoke with only a trace of an intriguing accent. "Yes, but I'm afraid it's a little out of my financial league. No, make that a lot out of my financial league."

"It costs nothing to admire it."

"It's a Dog of Fo, isn't it?" he asked, curious to check out his client's knowledge, curious to see if she was the expert it appeared she was.

"Yes, though it's really not a dog at all, but rather a Buddhist lion, which its tag indicates, I believe."

"It says it's a lion guarding a doorway."

The woman nodded, adding, "Ch'ing Dynasty. Seventeenth century."

"I take it it's the real thing and not a replica."

"It's very much the real thing." She glanced about her, indicating the shop in general. "All of our merchandise is comprised of authentic antiques, except for the fabric, and even some of it dates back to the turn of the century."

Looking back at the sculpture of the dog, Mitch said, "I thought that these were usually carved out of jade."

"I wouldn't say usually, although jade is a common gemstone. Perhaps one of the most common. As a matter of fact, we've just received a jade dog from Canton, although it's still in our warehouse at present." She smiled, apologetically. "But I'm afraid it's going to be even more costly than the marble piece we presently have. The new arrival is from the Ming period—that's the late fourteenth to mid-seventeenth century. Its age alone escalates the price."

"That makes sense," Mitch said, hoping to make his next comment sound nonchalant. "Your warehouse is down on the wharf, isn't it?"

"Yes."

"You, uh, you haven't had any trouble down there of late, have you?"

The woman looked perplexed and instantly cautious. "I'm not sure I understand what you mean."

"There's been no break-in...nothing out of the ordinary?"

"No," the woman said. "Not that I know of."

Mitch could tell that she was growing uncomfortable with his questioning, with him. Reaching into the back pocket of his jeans, he produced his wallet and his identification. "I'm a private investigator."

The shopkeeper perused his card, then said, "I'm afraid that I still don't understand."

Not wanting to reveal any more than was necessary, he said, "I must have made a mistake. I had reason to believe that some trouble may have occurred there Thursday night." He smiled—disarmingly, he hoped. "Wrong warehouse obviously." Before the woman could make any reply, he asked, "Might I ask you to take a look at a photograph?" Producing the photo of his client, he showed it to the shopkeeper. "Have you ever seen this woman?"

Strange, Mitch thought as the woman took the photograph offered her, how people always do what they're asked to do. Stranger yet, Mitch thought as he left the shop, how disappointed he'd been at her negative response. Sitting in his car, he realized that he'd actually expected the woman to recognize the person in the photo. Surely there was a reason that a woman who possessed a wealth of information about Oriental art had ended up at the warehouse of Tinsung's Oriental Imports. And the presence of the green dog in her dream *did* seem more than coincidence.

Yet the jade dogs weren't rare. This he'd had confirmed by both his client and the shopkeeper. Which led to an obvious conclusion: If this wasn't the dog, then perhaps whatever trauma had occurred in his client's life had not happened at the warehouse. And there were facts enough to support that premise, one basic fact, in particular. The mystery lady had dreamed about a chandelier and a gold-trimmed white staircase, neither of which suggested a warehouse. She had also spoken of a foyer. All of this hinted at some posh home somewhere. Mitch frowned. There were posh homes aplenty set in the hillside overlooking the bay. If she lived in one of them, maybe that would explain the presence of only a few blisters on her feet. Maybe, after being spooked by some unknown something, she hadn't had that far to walk to arrive at the warehouse, cutting most of her walking down to the trek she'd made to his agency. But it still didn't answer the question of why she'd selected *that* warehouse.

Mitch sighed, unable to accept the fact that Madame Tinsung—he'd ascertained that the shop was family-owned—did not recognize his client. But she hadn't, and Mitch would have made book on the truthfulness of her reply. One of the first things a cop learned was how to tell when he'd been lied to, and even though he no longer was a cop, even though the department had taken everything they could from him, they couldn't unteach what he'd learned over years of loyal service. No, Madame Tinsung had never seen the woman in the photograph, which left Mitch with the query that had been his constant companion since the paragon of pulchritude had walked into his office the morning before.

Who in hell was this woman? And from what, or from whom, was she fleeing?

MITCH FOUND his houseguest sacked out on the sofa. In sleep, it appeared she had escaped the fatigue he'd earlier seen etched on her face. No dark lines radiated from her eyes. No tightness pulled at her mouth. No demons seemed to dominate her slumber. Instead, she looked blissfully at peace with the world. Golden hair gloriously framed her head, while her parted lips lent her a becoming innocence. To be honest, however, those same innocent-looking lips had a pout to them that suggested a subtle carnality. It was the kind of sexuality that no man could be immune to. Not even him, Mitch mused, allowing the honest admission to defuse any guilt he might reasonably feel. Even so, he reached for a blanket, gently draped it across her—she *was* tall, a fact that caused Mitch to frown when he remembered that she'd recalled her height with total clarity—then he slipped quietly out of the apartment and down to his office.

He checked his phone messages, only to discover that he had none, a blatant confirmation that clients weren't exactly beating down his door. Thankfully, neither were creditors. At least not yet, though the power company was sure to start screaming soon. *Well, let 'em scream,* Mitch thought, crossing to the safe, squatting before it and dialing the combination. Once the thick door was open, he removed the little black book and walked back to his desk. Plopping down in the squeaky chair, he opened the ledger at the first page and methodically thumbed through it. Thirty minutes later, still unable to make heads or tails out of any of the numerical notations, except for the single word *Chelsea,* Mitch sighed and reached for the phone. At the same time, he unwrapped a sucker and stuck it into his mouth.

"Hey, Speedy, ole pal," Mitch said when a masculine voice answered.

"Uh-oh, you want something," the police officer groaned.

"I'm crushed that you think I'd use you," Mitch said, already discarding the sucker.

"Like I said, what do you want?"

Mitch cut to the chase with his friend. "Check around and see if anything unusual has happened recently at Tinsung's Oriental Imports, or rather at their warehouse on the wharf." Mitch didn't think that Madame Tinsung had lied to him, but perhaps she didn't know everything that had gone on, particularly if it was something unsavory.

"What do you mean by anything unusual?"

"Just that. Was the warehouse broken into, were the police called to quell a disturbance, anything."

"I know the answer before I even check, but I'll ask around."

"I'd appreciate it," Mitch said, knowing the answer, too. Nothing had occurred, but anything, everything, was worth a try. Which led him to the real reason for his call. "Do you think Dr. Simpson would talk with me? I'd like to ask her a couple of questions."

Dr. Susan Simpson was the department's resident psychiatrist. Mitch had always liked her. She was bright and personable. Following his being tossed off the force, she'd called him a couple of times offering her shoulder if he needed it. He had, but pride had kept him from saying so. Instead, he'd braved his way through—not well, but enough to survive, and sometimes that was all that one could hope for.

"I'm sure she would. Want me to put you through to her?"

"Yeah, please."

"Hey," Speedy Talbot said, "are we still on for the morning?"

Every Sunday morning, Speedy, Will and Mitch jogged, ironically in the very park in which Will Stone was once accused of murdering a man. Again, Mitch knew that his friends were doing all they could to see that he got through the long, liquorless weekend.

Mitch hesitated answering, then said, "Let's plan on it. I'll call you if I have to cancel."

"How is your client?"

Mitch quickly filled him in on the dream about the green dog, on how they had found a similar dog in Tinsung's warehouse and also about his client's knowledge of Oriental art.

"Interesting," Speedy said. "Maybe she teaches at one of the universities. Maybe art, maybe Chinese studies of some sort."

"Yeah, I'd already thought of that. It's the next thing on my list to check."

"She still can't remember a thing?"

"Nope."

"No luck with the little black book?"

"It might as well be written in Greek."

After a few more comments and the usual admonition for Mitch to watch his sorry rear, Speedy Talbot transferred the call to Dr. Simpson. For the next ten minutes, Mitch asked one question after another about amnesia, dreams and hypnosis, all of which Susan Simpson seemed more than pleased to talk about. Mitch had obviously hit upon some of the areas that most interested the young, zealous psychiatrist.

"In regard to amnesia, you're saying that one's memory can be blocked by either a physical or emotional trauma?"

"Exactly," Dr. Simpson said. "In the case of the latter, one actually rejects remembering. In either case, whether the amnesia is physically or emotionally induced, memory might or might not return."

"And, if it does return, it might be partial or complete?"

"Right."

"What about dreams?" Mitch asked. "How reliable are they in interpreting reality?"

Off and running on this new topic, Susan Simpson said, "Dream interpretation has been a source of controversy for centuries. While there's no denying that dreams are the gateway to the unconscious, it's

prudent to remember that dreams can also be decep-
tive. In fact, the very word *dream,* in a roundabout
way, comes from the German verb *trugen,* which
means 'to deceive.'"

"Interesting," Mitch replied.

"Also," she added, "dreams are rarely literal, but
rather symbolic."

"What do you mean by symbolic?"

"Simply that the green dog you spoke of might
represent any number of things that your client finds
threatening." In the end, clearly intrigued, the psychiatrist said, "Look, if I can help, I'll be glad to.
Perhaps we could find out more if I place your client
under hypnosis."

Mitch knew that Susan Simpson wanted to hypno-
tize his client, but it wasn't his decision to make, and
so he told her the only thing he could.

"Thanks for the offer. I'll be back in touch."

Mitch was once more studying the black book, the
psychiatrist's words still echoing in his ear, when the
door to his office opened. He glanced up, his eyes
meeting those of his houseguest.

"When I saw your car," she said, "I thought I
might find you here."

She looked rested, Mitch thought, but wary, cautious, as though afraid to let down her guard for even
a second. It was a fear he could understand. He hadn't
always been proud of what he was—the drinking had
played havoc with his pride—but he'd always known
who he was. He couldn't imagine losing his identity.
His guess would be that this woman's curiosity about
what he'd learned at Tinsung's Oriental Imports was
the reason she now stood in his doorway.

Mitch met the question in her eyes head-on. "I learned nothing."

"You showed them my picture?"

"I showed Madame Tinsung your photo. She'd never seen you before."

"Was she certain?"

"She said she was."

Disappointment swept across the blonde's face, though even as Mitch watched, he wondered if the disappointment wasn't tempered with a measure of relief. What an irony to fear not knowing who you were, yet equally to fear who you might be or the danger that might be stalking you.

The woman crossed the room and seated herself on the edge of the plastic chair. It was almost an exact replica of the pose she'd assumed on her first visit to his office.

Threading her loose, sleep-tousled hair back from her eyes, she said, "I had thought that maybe..."

She trailed off without specifying exactly what she thought, but Mitch could easily fill in what she hadn't said.

"I know."

Again, her chin tipped to an angle that displayed courage. "So, where do we go from here?" She laughed mirthlessly. "How many times have I asked that already?"

Mitch ignored her questions. "Let me ask you something. And just go with your gut instinct in answering."

She nodded, saying, "Okay."

"Do you think it possible that whatever you fled from occurred in one of the hillside homes overlooking the bay?'' Before she could comment, he added, ''Maybe you live there, maybe you were only visiting there, maybe you were attending a party there. Yeah, maybe you were attending a party,'' he said, as though the thought had just occurred. ''After all, you were dressed to the nines. What do you think?''

''Why do you think it might have been a hillside home?'' ·

''A couple of reasons. First of all, I think it probable that it was a home because homes are usually the location of chandeliers and stairways, and you did mention that those things appeared in your dream.'' He didn't mention that he'd half-expected Tinsung's to have a cut-crystal chandelier and a gilt-trimmed stairway.

The woman nodded in agreement.

''Second,'' Mitch went on, ''although you certainly had blisters on your feet, there really weren't that many, indicating that most of the walking you'd done had been from the Bay Area to my office. Perhaps you didn't have that far to walk before reaching the warehouse. Of course,'' Mitch added, playing his own devil's advocate, ''you could have been taken to the warehouse and dumped. It's even possible, but remote in my opinion, that you drove yourself or took a cab.''

''In regard to walking, I have tough feet. I'm accustomed to standing on them.''

Mitch arched an eyebrow. ''How do you know that?''

The woman frowned. ''I don't know. I have no idea why I said that.''

Her remark led smoothly into Mitch's next question. "Do you think it possible that you're a professor of Oriental studies—possibly Oriental art—in one of the local universities? Professors spend a good bit of time on their feet."

The woman mulled this possibility over. She shrugged. "I suppose it's possible. I *do* seem to know a lot about Oriental art."

"On the other hand," Mitch said, searching for another possibility, "maybe you own or work at another import shop. You'd be on your feet with that kind of job, too."

"Maybe, but..."

"But what?"

"I don't know. I just don't know!"

With this, the woman jumped from the chair and walked like a restless lioness to the dirt-streaked window. Late afternoon was settling in. As the sun's warm rays struck her hair, braiding themselves in and out of its saffron-shaded strands, her hair glimmered as though surrounded by a halo. At least Mitch thought that it did. He also thought she looked very much like the angel she'd dreamed of. *Whoa there, Brody. This line of thinking is getting you nowhere.* Reaching for another sucker, he unwrapped it and stuck it into his mouth. The taste of tart lemon sprinted across his tongue. He longed for the headier taste of Jack Daniel's. Maybe a few licks of the latter would scatter thoughts of flaxen-haired angels.

"I'm sorry," the angel—the woman—said, though she didn't turn from the window. "I shouldn't take my frustration out on you."

"Being the object of client frustration is included in my fee."

The woman cast a glance over her shoulder. A small smile nipped at her mouth. "What fee? You haven't collected a dime yet."

Mitch, a smile at his lips, nodded toward the safe. "I've got the earrings squirreled away. For a rainy day."

His client's smile faded. Her rainy day had already arrived. In her case, the rainy day had turned out to be a deluge capable of swamping Noah's ark.

"I don't remember anything," she said. "Maybe I do live in one of those hillside homes, maybe I am a professor of Oriental studies, maybe I do own an import business. On the other hand, maybe I'm a butcher, a baker, a candlestick maker." Her eyes misted, and this time she didn't try to hide her feelings. That same honesty had led her to ask him to sit by her bedside when the nightmare had grown too large for her to handle alone. "Or maybe I'm a terrible person who's done some horrible thing from which I'm running. Maybe I deserve to be caught and punished."

"I don't believe that," Mitch said with a conviction that he didn't even question.

"But you don't know for a fact, do you?"

"I don't believe you're a terrible person who's done some horrible thing," Mitch repeated.

His client proved every bit as stubborn when she said, "You don't know that."

"Then why don't we find out?" Mitch's suggestion captured his client's full attention, just as he knew it would. "I talked with a psychiatrist a little while ago. She volunteered to help."

A hesitation followed, before she simply asked, "Hypnosis?"

Mitch, too, paused before answering, "Yes."

When Kelly had first mentioned the word, it had inspired fear. Now Mitch saw a rekindling of that fear. This time the woman was unable to keep it at bay.

"I'm afraid."

She spoke simply, in a sweet trembly voice that laced itself around Mitch like satin bonds. Aside from the fact that something—everything—about this woman spoke so primevally, so elementally, to the man in him, what impressed him most was her candor. She was afraid, and unafraid to admit it. How many times over the last year and a half had he been afraid? Too many times to count, but pride—masculine pride—had forced him to keep silent, to pretend, even in the longest, blackest of nights, that he wasn't frightened.

"I don't expect you to understand," the woman said, gently drawing Mitch back to the moment. "A part of me does want to discover who I am. More than anything. After all, that's what I came to you for. But another part of me is afraid of what I'll find." She smiled softly, repeating what she'd said earlier. "I don't expect you to understand."

Mitch stood, discarding the lemon lollipop to the growing heap. He wasn't certain just why, but it seemed important to be near this woman, maybe because he sensed her courage and hoped some of it would rub off on him.

"I do understand," he heard himself saying. "In fact, fear and I are good friends. Not that I understand the fear of not knowing who I am, but then fear comes in a lot of shapes and sizes."

"And what is the shape and size of your fear, Mitchell Brody?"

The question was as simple as any he'd ever been asked. The answer was just as simple, though it wasn't something that could be simply stated. It took courage to say the words, a courage he'd never had before. Oh, he'd said them at the Alcoholics Anonymous meetings. Everyone there did. In the act of group confession lay the promised anonymity. Beyond the doors of the meeting hall, however, he'd never given voice to the condemning statement—not even to his best friends, Kelly and Will. Why then, did he want so desperately to say the words now, to this virtual stranger?

"I'm an alcoholic."

For a moment, he wasn't certain that he'd actually spoken. Maybe the words had only rambled through his mind. Maybe the words had only taunted him and his lack of courage.

"I know," the woman said quietly, then amended her statement. "I didn't actually *know,* but I suspected as much." At Mitch's questioning look, she nodded toward his calendar. "Every Thursday is circled in red, with AA written in."

Despite himself, Mitch had to smile. "Maybe we're missing the obvious here. Maybe you're a detective."

She smiled, too. "No, I think it falls more under the heading of a calculated guess."

In the silence that followed, smiles slipped under the weight of the subject's seriousness.

"How long have you belonged to AA?"

Mitch laughed, mirthlessly. "Not long enough. There's never a day that I'm not scared stiff that to- day is the day I'm going to fall off the wagon. There's never a night that I'm not surprised that I made it though one more day. And I'm sick of suckers—damn but I hate suckers!—and I'm just about as tired of detective novels. Furthermore, I've logged enough miles jogging to put me near Cincinnati."

"But you're making it," she said. "And you'll continue to make it. You're a strong man, Mitchell Brody. I sense this."

Again, her faith in him was touching. No, more than touching. It made him glow within. It left him feeling morally obligated to share one other fact, however.

"My father spent a lifetime going on and falling off of the wagon. I hated him for turning to the bottle. I despised him for never conquering it. I swore I'd never be as weak as he was, but I fell right into his sorry ways the minute my life went sour."

"You will succeed in conquering it," she said, as though she didn't have the slightest doubt. "As I said, you're a strong man."

"You're strong, too," he said, but, even as he said it, he again had the overwhelming urge to reach out and comfort her in her hour of need. Because of that, he drove his hands into the back pockets of his jeans.

"You want me to undergo hypnosis, don't you?" she asked.

"Only if you want to. It might not do any good, anyway. The psychiatrist I spoke with said that you won't remember any trauma that you're not ready to remember."

The woman turned back toward the window.

"Think about it," Mitch said. "You don't have to decide anything right this minute."

His client said nothing, though her "I'm afraid" still rang in his ears. He couldn't say that he honestly knew what he'd do if he suddenly found himself in her place. On the other hand, he knew quite clearly that he felt obligated to protect her from her nameless demons—and that act wasn't usually included in his fee.

CHAPTER FIVE

"FOR HEAVEN'S SAKE, Brody, you're killing me!" Speedy Talbot hollered. As though to prove his point, the trim police officer, halted in midjog and bent forward to rest his hands on his knees. In the quiet morning stillness of the park, his racked breathing sounded loud and labored, especially for a man in superb physical condition.

"He's killing *you?*" Will Stone said, or rather tried to say. Instead, the words tumbled out amid staggered gulps of air as he collapsed to the ground. Despite his comment, this tall, broad-shouldered man who made his living hewing wood into work-of-art cabinets, was a fine specimen of a healthy male.

Mitch, a considerable distance down the path, doubled back. Dressed in red nylon shorts, a white T-shirt with deeply cut armholes and a red sweatband, he continued to jog in place before his two exhausted friends. A pain stitched his side, and his own breathing came hard and fast. Ignoring both the pain and his depleted breath, he asked, "What's wrong? You two wimping out on me?"

"I prefer to think of it as sparing my body," Speedy said.

"'He who doesn't run himself into the ground lives

to run another day,'"' Will said, taking liberties with an oft-repeated quote concerning fighting.

"C'mon, Brody, confess," Speedy said. "Is the devil chasing you?"

Devil? No, Mitch thought. It was more like an angel. The night before, his houseguest had had the recurring dream, the one about a young woman with ethereal lights encircling her head. Though the dream had not frightened his client, it had nonetheless awakened her. Mitch had heard her moving around, had knocked on the door of the bedroom, and had entered without waiting for an invitation. That had been a mistake. A big mistake. Wearing only his pajama top, she had stood at the window. Platinum moonlight bathed her; leaving Mitch to draw but one conclusion: In sunshine and in starlight, she herself looked like an angel, a sexy angel that had captured his breath in a way that his present hell-bent-for-leather run had not. He'd hoped the run would erase her memory from his mind. Instead, it had done nothing but clear his head, making the images of her appear even sharper.

Indeed, his seeing her standing before the window had honed all of his senses to a perfect pitch, to a crystal clarity. His eyes had taken in her silhouette and in so doing had not missed a single subtlety of her sweetly formed feminine body—not the delicately corded length of her ivory neck, not the curves of her shoulders, not the jut of her full breasts, and certainly not the long, bare legs that made a seemingly endless journey to the floor. His sense of smell had been heightened as well. From clear across the room, the clean fragrance of soap and water had wafted over to him, making a far greater impression than the most expensive perfume ever could have. Most important, that within him which defined his masculinity had been awakened. It had been a long while since he'd been so acutely aware of being a man. Maybe the truth was that he'd never been so profoundly aware of it. But he had been then. Painfully aware.

And then there had been the way she'd looked at him, as though taking in his every feature, from his bare, hair-dusted chest to the lazy, indolent way the pajama bottoms, a match to her top, hung low on his hips. He would have sworn that, just as he was aware of her femininity, so, too, was she aware of his masculinity. It had been an odd, out-of-time moment, one that had taken two strangers completely by surprise. They had spoken quickly, simply, he asking if she was all right, she assuring him that she was, that she'd just had a recurrence of the dream. He'd left her then and returned to the sofa, where he'd tossed and turned for the remainder of the night. He'd awakened out of sorts and with a serious restlessness, the kind he desperately needed to run off.

"I'm going jogging," he'd announced over a quiet Sunday breakfast, his tone daring his houseguest to object.

"Fine," she'd said, and Mitch could almost believe that she was relieved at the prospect of being alone.

And so he'd left the apartment, had met his friends at the park and had started to jog—run, actually, as though pursued by a blond-haired angel. It had soon become apparent, however, that the angel was as fleet-footed as he.

"Hey, Brody," Speedy said, "are you all right?"

The sound of his name being called yanked Mitch back to the present. "Yeah, I'm fine," he answered, plopping down on the grass beside Will and reaching to retie a shoelace that really didn't need retying. The action kept him busy, though, and keeping busy seemed important. His restlessness demanded it.

"I thought the devil was not only chasing you, but had caught you," Speedy commented.

"I'm fine," Mitch repeated, but noticed that Will, who lay stretched out on his back in the emerald-green grass, cocked a curious gaze in his direction. Mitch looked away and changed the subject. "So, how's everything down at the precinct?"

Speedy dropped to the grass, too, and started plucking individual blades. "Everything's just hunky-dory. Lerner beams like the Cheshire cat every time the press gets near."

"I saw him on the six o'clock news last night," Will said.

Speedy snorted. "He's *become* the six o'clock news. If he and the city council get any closer, they're going to have to get married."

"He and the mayor are already joined at the hip," Mitch said, adding, "but then our mighty chief sucks up to anyone in authority."

"True," Speedy agreed.

"I guess the Chang thing led nowhere, huh?" Mitch asked.

"Same old dead end," Speedy confirmed. "The only connection we could make came to nothing—his number was on the call girl's phone list, but she swore that she hadn't made the call. Hell, even the phone company couldn't confirm it. They said that with the vast number of calls made on a daily basis, they can't guarantee that every number is posted correctly. Think about it. Haven't you ever been charged with a long-distance call you didn't make?"

"Yeah," Mitch said, "but I don't trust coincidence."

"Maybe one of her johns made the call," Will offered.

"Good point," Speedy said. "Maybe one of her johns knew Chang, which would make Chang guilty of nothing more than knowing a man who partook of a prostitute's favors. That's hardly illegal."

"Maybe Chang is one of her johns," Will suggested. "Maybe she did call him, but only in the line of business."

"Another good point," Speedy said. "One which doesn't leave him lily-white—he *is* a married man—but then again it doesn't make him the kingpin behind the prostitution trade."

"Good Lord, it sounds as if you're ready to bestow sainthood on the man," Mitch barked.

"Not at all," Speedy said, snapping another blade of grass. "It's just...I don't know, sometimes I wonder if maybe he isn't clean. Heaven only knows we've tried to pin enough on him, but we never can. How long can he keep covering his ass?"

"For forever if you guys accept the premise that he's clean," Mitch said.

"I didn't say I knew for sure," Speedy protested. "But I think you have to admit that you're prejudiced."

"Maybe. Maybe not. But there's that cursed coincidence again. I was set up only after I started actively pursuing the guy."

"But even you couldn't pin anything on him, could you?" Speedy asked.

Mitch sighed. "No, I couldn't."

"So we're back to square one," Speedy said. "Maybe he's guilty, maybe he isn't."

"What about the call girl?" Mitch asked.

"You mean the long, cool woman in the black dress?" Speedy asked.

"Isn't that from a song?" Will asked.

"Yeah," Speedy said, "and did she ever look like she'd stepped out of a song. Hell, she looked like she'd just wandered in out of every man's dream. A brunette with big blue eyes that a man could drown in and dressed to the hilt in a long black evening gown that highlighted every curve. And let me assure you that there were plenty of curves to highlight. No, this lady is no ordinary call girl. Strictly top drawer. A class act from head to toe. And no dummy, either. She has a degree in physics from UCLA. Guess she found anatomy more profitable than atoms."

From the moment that Speedy had uttered the phrase "long, cool woman in a black dress," Mitch had been lost in a haunting reverie. As though it were happening right there in the park, superimposed on the sunny morning, he saw his client walking into his office. The words could have equally described her. Oh, not that she was a brunette with big blue eyes, but she had been tall and coolly elegant and dressed to the hilt in black satin. And, to add to the similarities, she, too, was no dummy. No, his client was highly intelligent, with a knowledge of Oriental art that far exceeded the norm.

So, what are you suggesting, Brody? he asked himself. That your client's a high-price call girl? The very thought made him want to laugh out loud. Whatever his client might be, she was not a prostitute—high-class or otherwise. No, the woman who looked like an angel was not a prostitute.

"The really crazy thing was," Speedy said, cutting through Mitch's musings, "that we made the collar only because of an anonymous tip. Some guy called in, gave her address and said to check her out."

This got Mitch's attention. "An anonymous tip?"

"Yeah. Some guy called in, gave us this fancy address downtown—" Speedy mentioned a street that was known as high class "—1492 was the address. I remember because of the Columbus thing you're taught in school. Anyway, it's an old gorgeous Victorian home. We staked it out for a couple of days, saw some suspicious comings and goings and then had one of the vice cops call and set up an assignation with her. Get this, guys, her fee for the night was fifteen hundred bucks."

Will whistled.

Mitch asked, "And so you all busted her?"

"Yeah. In fact, we moved in that night. The assignation with our guy was set up for the following night, but we moved on it. Found her dressed to the hilt for some symphony gala. I told you the lady has class."

"What's her name?" Mitch asked.

"Sarah Elizabeth Etheridge. Even her name's classy, huh?"

"Classy or not," Mitch mused, "Sarah Elizabeth Etheridge has an enemy."

The statement apparently was too obvious for a comment, leaving the three men to fall into a companionable silence. Speedy continued to pluck blades of grass, while Will, still flat of his back, continued to soak up the sun's warmth. Mitch closed his eyes, allowing the sun to soak into him as well. Something hotter than the sun spilled over him, however, and that was the memory of his client standing before the starlight-shadowed window. God, she had looked incredibly sexy.

Get a grip, Brody, he thought, a feeling of restlessness swarming around him once more. He opened his eyes, only to find his friend Will watching him again. Critically, contemplatively watching him.

"Are we here to run or what?" Mitch asked, pushing to his feet.

Both the other men came to their feet.

"Let's run to the crest of that rise and call it quits," Speedy said, starting off for the stated destination. "Last one there buys coffee."

Mitch had just geared up for the challenge when he felt Will step alongside him.

"You okay?" Will asked.

"Yeah, sure. Why?"

"Just wondering. You seem . . . distracted."

"I'm fine," Mitch said, hoping the words didn't sound as false as they felt.

"Kelly wants to do something a little different this Friday night," Will said.

The two men were jogging now, side by side.

"Great. What?"

"You two come over for spaghetti instead of our usual pizza."

You two come over. It sounded natural. Too natural.

"That'll be fine," Mitch said, "although my client might be gone by then. The minute her memory returns or I discover who she is, she'll be going."

"Then come alone."

Alone. Mitch reminded himself that this was the word that best fit him, the way he preferred his life. Alone, he'd never risk another betrayal.

"Sounds great," Mitch said. "I'll—" he deliberately chose the singular approach "—be there."

"Hey, are you guys coming?" Speedy hollered.

In the end, even with Speedy's head start, Mitch reached the crest of the rise first. But then, a man can run fast when he's got an angel chasing him.

THE FOLLOWING WEEK was a failure or a success, depending on Mitch's vacillating mood. He worked with a vengeance to find out the identity of his client, and yet met with no success; however, since success would remove her from his life, he couldn't help but feel relieved. That relief caused him to work all the harder at tracking down her past.

Methodically, he talked to representatives of every Oriental import business in the city, but he found no one who recognized the woman in the photograph. Again, instinct told Mitch that those he'd spoken to weren't lying. He also checked with every college and university in the area. Only two had professors of Oriental studies. Both were men. In desperation, he called around in regard to a cab having delivered a passenger to Tinsung's warehouse. None had. That left only the homes tucked away in the hillside overlooking the Bay Area. Going door to door presented an impossible task. There had to be at least two hundred homes, all set apart in meandering nooks and crannies and exclusive ravines. It would take days, perhaps even weeks, to cover the area.

Another aspect of searching the hillside troubled him. If a home were, indeed, the scene of the trauma the blonde had endured, he in essence would be handing the lamb over to the wolf. She had already indicated that wherever the brightly gleaming chandelier and the gilt-edged staircase were found, it was a place she was afraid of, a place filled with something sinister. Didn't she already feel that someone was chasing her? No, he just couldn't ring a doorbell and present her to the very person who was possibly responsible for her being on the run. Even if it was only in the form of a photograph. As a compromise, Mitch and his client drove—actually, chugged and sputtered—around the area, hoping that she might recognize one of the swank homes. She didn't, however.

"I'm sorry," she said that Friday afternoon as they headed back to Mitch's apartment.

"You did the best you could," he said, glancing over at her. Once more, he felt frustrated. Once more, he felt relieved.

It had been a curious week. Aside from the incident when he'd burst into the bedroom to find her standing before the window, all dripping in drowsy moonlight, aside from the vibrations he thought he'd received from her, aside from the fact she'd appeared relieved to be left alone Sunday morning while he jogged, nothing had seemed amiss in the days that followed. His houseguest had been her usual self, forcing him to conclude that what had occurred that night had been one-sided, and on his side. But, hey, who could blame him? The woman was beautiful, and it had been a whale of a long time since he'd been with a woman. It had only been human nature kicking in, reminding him that he was still alive. Surely that was a good thing to discover. And it had nothing to do with this woman personally. Any good-looking woman wearing only his pajama top would have elicited the same response.

Mitch allowed himself to feel better, to even feel good about the evening that lay before them. "We have to be at Kelly and Will's at seven."

"Why don't you go without me?"

Mitch shot his passenger another look. "Why?" A sudden thought occurred to him. "Aren't you feeling well? You told me that the headaches had stopped."

"They have."

"Then why don't you want to go?"

"It's not that I don't *want* to go. Then again, on second thought, maybe I really don't want to." Knowing that the contradictory sentiments needed an explanation, she said, "When your life's in chaos, it's hard to know what you want—except for the chaos to end."

"I know you're disappointed that we didn't find out anything this week."

"Disappointed and relieved," she said, smiling faintly. "I don't expect you to understand that, either."

"Actually, I think I do," he said, silently adding, *More than you know*. "Look, I'm no psychiatrist, but I think you ought to get out. The more you're exposed to, surely the greater the chances of something jogging your memory."

"I suppose there's some logic to that, but—"

"No buts."

"Yes, there is a but," she insisted. "I've played havoc with your life already. You're entitled to a social life without my tagging along as excess baggage."

Mitch knew what she was alluding to. He responded with candor. "There is no woman in my life and, furthermore, I don't want one."

He could have added, but didn't, that he was afraid to want one, afraid that she'd betray him as he'd been betrayed once before. It also seemed like a good opportunity to remind himself that, under different circumstances, he wouldn't want this woman, either. He'd simply responded to her in an elementally biological way. Nothing more, nothing less.

"I'm sorry that your ex-wife hurt you so badly."

"Yeah, well," Mitch said, unable to keep the hurt, the anger, from his voice.

"You should find someone else."

Mitch grinned suddenly. "You sound like Kelly."

The woman beside him grinned back. "She's right." Then, her smile widening, the blonde said, "At first I thought that maybe you and Kelly..." She trailed off amid Mitch's laughter.

"Kelly and I? Hardly. She's like the sister I never had. Besides, Will would clean anyone's clock who even looked at her."

"He adores her."

"They adore each other." Mitch tacked on the obvious, though he felt uncomfortable doing so. "It's altogether possible that someone adores you, too. And that you adore someone."

The woman shrugged, but made no comment. She suddenly looked sad, as though she couldn't quite bring herself to believe either aspect of what Mitch had just said, leaving him to wonder if she remembered more than she said she did. He respected her privacy by saying no more on the subject.

"Look," he said, "if you don't go tonight, then I don't go."

"Mitchell, you're being stubborn."

"I'll just call when we get home—"

"All right, I'll go."

"...and tell them we—"

"I said all right."

"...can't go."

"I said I'd go!"

Smiling, Mitch glanced over at his passenger. She, too, was smiling.

"You drive a hard bargain, Mitchell Brody."

"And don't you forget it."

Just as he wouldn't forget that she was his client— and nothing more.

THE STONE HOUSE, like so many of the old two-storied structures in the city, was undergoing extensive remodeling. The outside, cream-colored with gingerbread-brown trim, had been finished first, while the inside still had a ways to go. Even so, the downstairs area was homey and comfortable, a feeling the thick multicolored Persian rugs splashed across the gleaming hardwood floors and the white overstuffed furniture helped to create.

"It's lovely," the blond-haired woman said as Kelly showed her through the house.

"There's still a lot to do, of course," Kelly said. "We're doing the work ourselves, and with our jobs, the renovations fall into the catch-as-catch-can category." She grinned her gamin smile. "At the rate we're going, we should have the nursery finished just about the time the kid—" here she spread her hand across her stomach "—goes to college."

The woman beside her smiled. "Mitchell tells me that you travel some."

"Too much," Kelly said. "It was all right when I was single, but now I'd like to slow things down a bit. The baby has helped in that department, but I'm still pretty busy."

In testimony to Kelly's photographic career, one whole wall of the living room had been devoted to her work. Photographs, large and small, black-and-white and color, stared back with a lifelike vividness, along with some very prestigious awards.

"You're good," the blonde said, studying the photos with interest. She moved from one to the other, as though captivated by each. At the end of the tour, she proclaimed, "No, you're not good. You're *very* good."

"Thanks," Kelly said, adding, "C'mon, let me show you the kitchen and what a true artist's work looks like."

Will groaned. "Sounds like you're getting the up close and personal look at our cabinets. Bear in mind that the woman is prejudiced."

"I am not," Kelly said. "I'm only a little in love with the guy. Of course, he *is* the father of my child, but that fact doesn't detract from my ability to recognize genius at work."

With that, she gave her husband a quick kiss. During that brief second, Mitch's eyes went unerringly to his client, while hers went unerringly to his. Both their gazes fell away quickly.

"Want a ginger ale?" Will asked Mitch as the two women stepped into the kitchen.

"Yeah, sure," Mitch answered, walking behind his friend toward the bar in the living room.

Mitch cast one last look at the blond-haired woman before she disappeared. He'd been sorely mistaken if he'd thought that he would be able to keep his professional perspective during the evening. Oh, he'd been as sturdy as the Rock of Gibraltar, as steady as a compass pointing due north—until she'd walked into the living room, wearing her tight jeans and cotton-knit top, her head a mass of organized disarray. Then some damn little voice whispered in his ear again. *You're a man and she's a woman*, the pesky little sucker had said . . . over and over and over again.

"You okay?" Will asked.

"Yeah," Mitch grunted, reaching for the glass of ginger ale and swallowing generously. He wished to high heaven it was something stronger.

By only milliseconds, he'd managed to miss the parting glance the blonde had tossed back at him. She hadn't known why she'd looked back, except that it had something to do with that empty feeling that dwelled in the pit of her stomach. It was always there, an uncomfortable vagueness that gnawed at her. She'd

begun to notice, however, that, while nothing eradi-
cated it entirely, being around Mitchell eased it to a
tolerable level, a sometimes hardly noticeable level.
She didn't understand it any more than she understood exactly what had happened between them that
night when he'd burst into the bedroom. Even now,
she tried not think about how aware of him she'd
been, how easily she could have tumbled into his arms
and buried herself in his gentleness. No, it was best not
to remember. It was best to keep her distance. It was
best to concentrate on the here and now, not on the
then and there.

The kitchen, done in pristine white and royal blue
sparkled with an almost eye-hurting cleanliness. Vibrant green plants grew in profusion, while a display
of antique crockery in white, blue and red resided
within an enormous white breakfront. Everywhere
wafted the aroma of garlic, oregano and simmering
tomato sauce, mixed with the piquant perfume of
blended cheeses and the yeasty smell of freshly bak-
ing bread.

"I am prejudiced, of course," Kelly said, the
wooden floor of the kitchen squeaking a welcome the
way the floors of older homes are wont to do. "But
even if I wasn't, I couldn't be blind to the beauty of
these."

At this, Kelly, her short crimson curls bobbing, indicated the white cabinets that ran both the upper and
lower length of the L-shaped work area. Etchings of
tiny wild flowers, with their leaves and stems entwining, produced a delicately scrolled pattern that bordered the glass-fronted cases. The blonde reached up
to trace the floral design. As though it were braille, she

read it slowly with her fingertips. The feel of finely carved wood whispered through her fingers. The song it sang was sensual, sensual like whisker stubble in the moonlight, sensual like broad bare shoulders filling a doorway, sensual like eyes that seemed to see right through her.

"Pretty, isn't it?" Mitch said at her elbow.

He'd watched the way she touched the wood—no, the way she caressed it—and had been moved by it. There was a sweetness, a softness, about this woman. *A near-combustible sensuality,* the little voice whispered once more in his ear. Mitch took another swallow of ginger ale and tucked his free hand into his jeans pocket, a place it seemed to be spending a lot of time lately, but then it could hardly get into trouble there, could it?

Startled, the woman yanked her hand from the wood. She forced her thoughts into a safe harbor, even as she slipped both hands into the pockets of her white jeans. It seemed the safe thing to do.

"It's gorgeous," she said, then, nodding toward the breakfront, she asked, "Did you do that as well?" She directed the question at Will.

"Yeah," he answered, and the woman made the mental note that her host was a man of few words.

"It's lovely, too," she said.

"Thanks," he said, embarrassed at the compliment.

"You should see the cradle he's carved," his adoring wife said. "But I won't foist that on you until later in the evening." Without the slightest hesitation, she said, "Mitch, why don't you get our guest a drink while Will helps me set the table?"

"I can help you, Kelly," the blonde said, knowing that her offer had less to do with etiquette than it did with the fact that she didn't want to be alone with Mitchell. Being alone with him was all too easy, all too comfortable. It was something she could grow accustomed to and, if she allowed herself to do that, what would happen to her when she left?

"No, indeed," Kelly said.

"I insist."

"You can help me clean up after dinner. How about that?" With reluctance, both Mitch and his client soon found themselves alone in the living room. Mitch stepped behind the bar while the blonde walked to the huge plate-glass window overlooking the bay. Harbor lights cast a ghostly, but beautiful glow across the calm, navy water. In the silence, the television softly rumbled the evening news.

"Ginger ale, root beer, soda?" Mitch offered, trying to ignore the way the woman's blond hair fell around her shoulders in chaotic curls.

The woman turned, trying to ignore the way a pair of extraordinarily broad shoulders filled out a very ordinary shirt. "Ginger ale is fine."

Mitch splashed the bubbly liquid over ice cubes, started toward the woman—she met him halfway—and handed her the glass. She took it, then moved toward the bar. Mitch moved toward the bay window.

The woman took a swallow of the ginger ale.

Mitch took a swallow of his.

The television mumbled the news.

"Nice view," Mitch commented, striving to push aside thoughts of golden curls.

"Yes, it is," his client replied, striving to put away thoughts of broad shoulders. "It's a lovely home."

Mitch turned. "Yes, it is. They've worked hard on it."

"It shows."

Silence, except for the voice whispering in Mitch's ear. He drained his glass of ginger ale. As though she, too, had heard a taunting voice, the blonde emptied her glass as well.

The silence swelled.

"Today, mourners turned out for the memorial service held in honor of Richard Rhincuso," the television babbled. In gratitude for the distraction, Mitch gave his attention to the news announcer. So did the woman. "Mr. Rhincuso, who served two terms on the city council, presumably drowned last week. His yacht was found abandoned just miles from Santa Catalina."

Here, footage of a sleek, expensive yacht filled the television screen. Mitch took it in, surprised that city councilmen made that kind of money, although he believed that the man had had a law practice at one time.

"Richard will be missed," the mayor said solemnly. "He was a real friend of the city, a man who unselfishly gave of himself."

Suddenly, another face leaped to the screen. The man, tall, tanned and dressed in a white suit despite the somber occasion, looked like a movie star instead of the chief of police. At his appearance, Mitch's stomach tightened.

"Richard was a fine man...a fine man. I just can't believe he's gone."

"Think he's going to burst into tears?" Will said at Mitch's elbow.

"It wouldn't surprise me if the son of a bitch did," Mitch said, not even trying to hide his animosity. Mitch snorted. "He's so smooth that I never saw it coming. I was standing out in the cold, my ass fired, before I ever knew what hit me."

Will laid his hand on Mitch's shoulder. "Forget it. It isn't worth remembering."

"Yeah," Mitch said, knowing that he had no intention of forgetting. If it took the rest of his life, he was going to find a way to clear his name.

Kelly, who stood in the doorway and had heard everything, said, "C'mon, let's eat."

Mitch turned, his eyes slamming into those of the blonde. For a moment, he'd forgotten her. Remembrance came back in a rush, along with a new torment, this one the realization that he'd shown himself in another bad light, first as a recovering alcoholic, now as a cop kicked off the force. What the hell? he thought defiantly. This woman meant nothing to him. She was only a client. If she wanted to take her business elsewhere, it was all right with him. In fact, it was more than all right.

"Let's eat," he said. "I'm starved."

Despite what promised to be an inauspicious beginning to the meal, it turned out to be a pleasant affair, perhaps because Mitch was determined to make it so. It was a matter of pride that his friends, and the strange woman that had come into his life didn't see how badly he was hurting. With that as his goal, he kept the conversation alive and lively. He got Kelly to talk about her latest photographic assignment, a portfolio of the homeless. He then engaged Will in a discussion about his volunteer work with the underprivileged children in the city, a program in which he taught woodworking and, more importantly, self-esteem. Mitch even regaled his companions with a tale about his most unusual detective case, that involving an elderly woman who had hired him to find her missing cat.

"Did you find the cat?" the blonde asked, a smile at her lips.

"Yeah. He was four streets over...tomcatting around."

Everyone laughed.

"Okay, you guys," Kelly said after dessert had been served, "you go set up the Scrabble game while we women clear the table. Oh, and by the way," she said smugly, "it's a battle of the sexes. Men against women."

"If you all want to look bad, that's all right with us, huh, partner?" Mitch said to his friend.

"Can't stop a fool from making a fool of him—or herself," Will said, tweaking his wife's nose, which looked as though it had once entertained the thought of turning up, but had abandoned the idea in mid-act.

In return, she playfully swatted his behind with a dish towel.

"You're going to pay for that," Will said on the way out. Again, it sounded like a delicious threat.

When the two women were alone, Kelly said, "You clear the table and I'll load the dishwasher, okay?"

"Sounds fine," the blonde said, beginning to pile the plates. "Dinner was wonderful."

"Thanks. Spaghetti is the only decent thing I can cook. We'd starve if it wasn't for Will."

The blonde smiled as she brought the plates and silverware over. Kelly began to place them in the dishwasher. The iced tea glasses followed.

"May I ask you something?" the blonde said, reaching for the silver server, which still contained several slices of buttered garlic bread.

Something in her tone caused Kelly to abandon her loading chores and turn around. "Sure, what?"

"Why did Mitchell leave the police force?"

For long seconds, Kelly said nothing. Then, with a sigh, she answered, "He was accused of taking a bribe and given the choice of leaving without receiving his retirement benefits, or of facing prosecution. He chose to leave because the evidence against him was overwhelming. Among other things, he didn't want to embarrass his family any more than they'd already been embarrassed."

"But his wife didn't appreciate his noble gesture?"

"Nope," Kelly said, her voice betraying just what she thought of Mitch's ex-wife. With that, Kelly started for the table and, forgetting their division of chores, grabbed the pitcher of tea, which she carried back to the dishwasher and slammed into a slot. "I don't know who I'm angrier at—whoever set Mitch up or his wife for walking out when he needed her most. And for taking their son with her."

"That was when Mitchell turned to the bottle?"

Kelly appeared surprised that the woman knew of Mitch's drinking problem. "Yeah, but he has it under control now. He's been sober for months." Here, Kelly stalked back to the table and picked up the tureen that held what was left of the spaghetti sauce and Italian sausages. When she spoke, her anger was back. "Believe me, he's been to hell and back and for absolutely no reason. He never took a bribe in his life. He never—"

Abruptly, she stopped talking when the tureen, which she had carelessly set too near the edge of the cabinet, seemed to come to life. Its first act of animation was to tumble over the side of the cabinet top.

The blonde watched it fall. Slowly, quickly, it traveled down...down...down... As in a dream, when all time is slowed, the tureen hit the floor, smashing into dozens of jagged fragments even as it spilled forth its contents. The sauce, thick and red, ran like a river over the wooden floor.

"Damn!" Kelly cried.

"Oh, God," the woman said, so softly that it was little more than a whispered prayer, a call to a higher being for help. "Oh, God, the blood...the blood...keep the blood off me..."

With each word, hysteria blossomed in her voice until it rang like a shrill bell throughout the kitchen. The prayer ended abruptly, however, when the woman keeled over in a faint.

CHAPTER SIX

WHEN MITCH LAID the limp, unconscious woman on the sofa, the first thing he noticed was that her face had blanched, causing her to blend right in with the sofa's snow-white fabric. The grim sight sent a wave of anxiety flooding through him. Only her steady heartbeat, which had thudded against his chest as he'd carried her from the kitchen, reassured him that, at least on some level, she was all right. His own hammering heartbeat, however, was another matter. From the instant that Kelly had hollered his name, he'd had a sick, frantic feeling.

"Tell me again what happened," Mitch ordered.

"The tureen fell, sauce went everywhere and she started raving about blood. Something like 'Oh, God, the blood . . . the blood . . . keep the blood off me.'"

Kelly, whose own pallor was such that her freckles stood out more than usual, looked as distraught as Mitch. Instinctively, Will stepped forward, protectively placing his arm around her shoulders. Kelly eased back into her husband's sure embrace.

"Is she all right?" Kelly asked.

In way of an answer, Mitch said, "Get me a wet cloth." As he spoke, he sat down on the side of the sofa. The indentation he made caused the woman's hip to melt into his. He wished that he could absorb all of her into him for safekeeping.

"I'll get it," Will said, slipping from his wife's side and disappearing into a nearby powder room.

"What do you think happened?" Kelly asked.

"I don't know for sure," Mitch said, "but I'd say she's remembered something." He didn't think he needed to comment on how stone-cold serious that something might be.

"Here," Will said seconds later as he handed over a cool, moist cloth.

Mitch took the washcloth and bathed the blonde's face. Up to this point, she hadn't as much as twitched an eyelid. As the cool cloth caressed her, she moaned.

"That's it," Mitch encouraged her. "C'mon back to the land of the living."

When it became apparent that she was still resisting consciousness, Mitch abandoned the cloth for a gentle slap to her cheek. At this, she groaned and raised a hand to brush aside the irritant.

"C'mon," Mitch repeated.

Slowly, the woman's eyelids fluttered open, revealing hazy gray eyes that didn't seem to be focusing. When they finally did, she looked around her. She stared at Mitch, Kelly and Will as though they were total strangers. The room, too, seemed foreign, alien, a place she'd never seen before.

Mitch had the sinking feeling that he'd just lost her to another world, to a set of memories that had finally caught up with her. He wanted to holler, to shout, to shake her.

"Mitchell?" she asked uncertainly.

Relief raced through him so thoroughly that it manifested itself in a tremble. He sighed, smiled and said, "Lady, you're going to have to stop fainting on me."

The word *faint* seemed to take his client by surprise. Suddenly, though, everything fell into place— into alarming place. The woman's eyes widened, and the color that had been seeping back into her cheeks drained from them in one quick rush. She started to sit up.

"Hey, take it easy," Mitch said, taking hold of her shoulders and pushing her back onto the sofa. Frightened, she resisted him. Mitch had the feeling that she was no longer even seeing him. She'd once more slipped into some netherworld where he couldn't reach her.

"I saw the blood. It was everywhere. Don't let the blood get on me!" As she pleaded this, she wiped her hands in Lady Macbeth fashion.

Mitch stilled her hands with his. "There's no blood on you. See?" He held up both her hands, showing her first the backs, then the palms.

Though afraid of what she might find, she nonetheless braved a peek. At what she saw, or rather didn't see, she sighed and closed her eyes.

Mitch felt her heartbeat slowing down, felt her fear dissipating. He sensed that she was traveling some uncharted path that would lead her from that netherworld back to the real world. Seconds later, she opened her eyes to find Mitch staring at her. It was obvious that she wished he hadn't been, that she feared explanations would be required of her, explanations she didn't want to make.

"You want to tell me what happened?"

"I—I thought I saw blood on the floor."

"It was spaghetti sauce," Mitch said. "The bowl it was in fell and broke."

"I know that . . . now."

"What did you remember?" Mitch asked pointedly.

The blonde avoided eye contact. "Not much."

"But something?"

"Yes," she said, and again Mitch sensed her reluctance.

"What?" he prodded, placing a crooked finger under her chin and forcing her gaze to meet his. Curiously, even though he was insisting upon an explanation, he shared her reluctance. He wasn't at all certain he was going to like her response. In fact, he was rather sure he wasn't.

"I saw a man." She hesitated before adding, "He was lying on a floor in a pool of blood."

Yeah, Mitch thought, he'd been right. He didn't want to hear this, but hear it he must. "What man?"

The woman shook her head. "I don't know who he was. I just had this flash of a man lying in a pool of blood. He was . . . dead."

"How do you know that?" Kelly asked. Now that the shock was wearing off, she was her usual inquisitive self.

The woman glanced up at her hostess. Her look said that she'd forgotten that she and Mitch weren't alone. "He had to be dead. The way he was lying there was so unnatural, so unlifelike. He wasn't moving at all. And his eyes . . ." She paused again, apparently garnering the courage to go on. "They were open, wide-open, but glazed. They stared, but saw nothing. No, he was dead. I'd stake my life on it."

"Where was the blood coming from?" Mitch asked.

"His temple." As she spoke, she brought her hand to her own head, ironically fingering her injury. Days before, she'd stopped wearing a bandage, leaving the healing cut to show slightly. "There was this deep gash. I'd never seen a cut that deep. There was blood everywhere," she repeated, as though this single fact was what was most imprinted on her mind.

"How did he get the gash?" Mitch asked.

The question startled the woman. "I don't know— no, wait," she said, as if a vision had materialized from out of nowhere. Her eyes widened once more. "A Fo Dog lay on the floor beside him. A green Fo Dog."

"He'd been struck on the head by a Fo Dog?" Kelly asked.

"Yes." Then, as though remembering something more, she added, "In the house with the bright chandelier and the white, gilt-edged staircase. He was lying at the foot of the staircase."

"Maybe he fell down the stairs," Will offered.

"No," the woman insisted. "He'd been struck with the dog. There was blood all over it."

"Then he'd been murdered," Mitch said, stating the obvious and surprising himself with the calmness with which he did so.

The word sobered everyone present in a way that nothing that had been said so far had. In fact, it hovered in the air, while each one in the room considered its grave implications.

"I—I guess he must have been," the woman said.

"Do you know who killed him?" Mitch asked.

"Oh, God," she whispered. "Maybe *I* killed him."

Mitch wanted to deny what she'd said. He wanted to assure her, and himself, that she hadn't been responsible. He wanted to, but he couldn't. The truth was that, given her dream, given the episode in the kitchen, it was possible—probable, even?—that she'd killed the man.

"Oh, my God," she whispered again.

As she spoke, she drew her hand to her lips, covering them with her fingers. Mitch thought perhaps she was trying to keep the word *murderer* sealed inside. He also thought that her hand was trembling. Yes, her hand *was* trembling. Worse yet, she was trembling all over, a fine shaking that encompassed body and soul. She looked lost, a stranger even to herself. She looked as though she needed someone to find her. She looked as though she needed someone to hold her.

But he wasn't that someone. Finding a stray person was not the same as finding a stray cat. As for holding her, he definitely wasn't the one for that. No, with a capital N-O.

You want to, the annoying little voice whispered in his ear. *You've wanted to ever since you saw her standing in the moonlight.*

Get lost, Mitch told the pesky little dickens.

There wouldn't be any harm in just holding her.

Sure, and I'll bet you'd encourage me to stand in the middle of midday traffic.

Think about what she'd feel like in your arms.

Go away.

Look how she's trembling.

Dammit, go away!

But the damage had been done. He *did* see her trembling and he *did* think about what she'd feel like in his arms, something he *had* wondered about ever since he'd seen her standing in the silver moonlight. Knowing that he might well live to regret what he was doing—hell, there was no *might* about it!—he reached for her and pulled her to him. She didn't resist, but rather settled naturally against him. Her arms crept over his shoulders, her face nestled into the side of his neck, and her breasts, full and firm, cozied against his chest. With a fierceness that suggested he represented her hold on sanity, she dug her hands into the flesh of his back. Mitch reacted by tightening his hold. In that moment, he realized that he didn't care what she had done. He realized one other thing—one other scary thing: In trying to find her, he might well end up losing himself.

THE CAR MOANED and groaned en route back to the apartment. The engine light even flashed red a couple of times, which was just one more new complaint to add to the car's long list of old ills. Mitch couldn't have cared less about the car, however. His thoughts were totally centered on what had happened that evening, and not necessarily what had transpired in the kitchen. No, his thoughts were preoccupied with memories of softness and warmth and of a moist breath beating against the hollow of his throat, memories of a feminine body nestled snugly against him. She had fit him so perfectly, a fact that hadn't surprised him—something had told him all along that she would—but, nonetheless, it had been unsettling. Wonderfully unsettling. Frighteningly unsettling.

Where did they go from here?

Nowhere. They went absolutely nowhere. Because there was nowhere to go. More to the point, she had another world to return to, a world he was professionally obligated to help her find, a world where he was out and quite possibly someone else was in, someone whose body she fit just as perfectly. Mitch wanted to reject this last premise, but refused to let himself. He had to keep it at the forefront of his mind. He had to; it would be the motivation for his keeping his distance. He would never again take this woman in his arms. If he did, he couldn't guarantee that he'd ever let her go.

Unknown to Mitch, the woman beside him was entertaining similar thoughts. She could still remember the chilling way she had trembled, the warming way that Mitchell had held her. Hadn't she known that was how he would hold her? Yes, she'd known it in some way she couldn't explain. Even now, she could feel the breadth of his chest cradling her, the pressure of his arms embracing her. He was the personification of gentleness and kindness, two things she was as helpless as a babe to resist. Self-preservation, however, demanded that she not grow accustomed to those qualities. With that in mind, she vowed to never lose herself in his arms again. There was one other thing she had to do as well.

"Mitchell?"

Her voice captured Mitch's attention with its whispery, whiskey-smooth softness. He glanced over at her. She looked like everything good and kind and pure. She did not look like a murderer.

"I want to undergo hypnosis."

Her statement didn't take him that much by surprise. Not after what had just happened. Nonetheless, he asked, "Are you sure?"

"I don't think I have a choice any longer. I have to know if I . . . if I killed that man."

"As I understand it, hypnosis doesn't guarantee a return of your memory. If you're determined to keep the painful events of that night suppressed, hypnosis will be useless."

"Then again, maybe we'll learn something. Anything will be better than the near nothing I know now."

Mitch saw the pain in her eyes, heard the fear in her voice. "Think about it tonight."

"I've already decided."

Again, Mitch couldn't help but admire this woman. "I'll call the psychiatrist in the morning."

His client said nothing. She simply nodded.

The car pulled into the driveway. Mitch shut off the engine. Curiously, neither passenger made a move to get out. It was as though this closed environment protected them from the real world, a world they didn't care to be a part of.

"If it's any consolation," Mitch said quietly as starlight filled the car, "I don't think you killed that man without a damned good reason. That is, if you killed him at all."

"You know nothing about me, Mitchell Brody. I may be the devil incarnate."

If she was, Mitch thought, he could easily learn to like the hot fires of hell. But she wasn't the devil incarnate. That he'd wager his very soul on, or at least whatever part of his soul he'd managed to hang on to.

"No," he said, "you're not capable of cold-blooded murder."

"And you're not capable of taking a bribe."

The word, as it always did, stopped Mitch's heart cold. Colder yet was the knowledge that this woman knew about his past. But how?

As though hearing his silent question, the blonde responded, "Kelly told me."

"She shouldn't—"

"Don't blame her. I asked her why you'd left the force."

Mitch gave a mirthless laugh. "Well, now you know."

"You aren't guilty," the woman insisted.

"You know nothing about me. *I* may be the devil incarnate."

The blonde remembered the warm feel of his arms. If he were the devil, she'd gladly give herself to his sweet, sinful seduction. But he wasn't the devil. That she knew from the bottom of her heart.

"No," she repeated, "you aren't guilty."

Her implicit faith in him moved Mitch in a way that little in his life ever had. Why should it be that a stranger believed in him when his wife hadn't? And why should it be so damned important to him that this woman do so? It was, though, and that he found frightening, just as he found his need to hold her again—this time for his sake rather than for hers—equally frightening.

Wordlessly, he threw open the car door and started to get out.

His client's soft voice stopped him. He found her face in the ebony night. "It's more important what one knows about oneself than what others think they know about you. You know you aren't guilty. I have to find out if I am.''

Mitch understood the wisdom of her words. He also knew that she was frightened. Her next question proved it.

"Will you be there during the hypnosis?''

"Do you want me to be?''

"Yes,'' she answered unabashedly and without hesitation.

"Then I'll be there.''

That he would if he had to move heaven and earth, if he had to do battle with every dark demon in him, if he had to fight himself and that inner voice that kept telling him that he was playing with a hotter-than-hell fire.

MITCH CALLED Dr. Simpson Saturday morning and, after recounting the incident that had occurred in the Stone kitchen, asked if the psychiatrist was still interested in conducting a hypnotic session. The doctor assured him that she was, stating that, in her professional opinion, the sooner, the better, although, unfortunately, she was tied up for the remainder of that day. How about tomorrow? Mitch asked. Fine, Dr. Simpson answered, and so the following afternoon was agreed upon.

It was obvious to Mitch that the postponement was taking yet another emotional toll on his client. She would have preferred to have it over and done with, as would he have. Though neither spoke of what had occurred the evening before, it nonetheless accounted for the lion's share of their thoughts. Not one single time did she mention the possibility that she might be a murderer, and in her not mentioning it she proved beyond a doubt that the thought that she might be consumed her. Once, Mitch found her simply staring at her hands, as though they had suddenly become strangers that she didn't know, strangers that might have betrayed her in a most gruesome way. As always at those moments, Mitch wanted to comfort her, but wouldn't allow himself to. It was a luxury he didn't feel he could afford.

As restless as he'd ever seen her—it was as though she suddenly had to have answers at all cost—the blonde insisted upon returning to the wharf. While Mitch showed her photograph around, she herself approached total strangers to ask if they'd ever seen her before. No one had, although plenty looked at her as if she'd lost her mind.

"Losing your memory is not losing your mind," Mitch said as they'd climbed back into his car.

"Don't be too sure. I think one might well lead to the other."

From there, the woman insisted upon returning to the warehouse, which yielded nothing even close to another memory. She then asked to be driven by Tin-sung's Oriental Imports on the off chance that seeing the shop might ring a bell. It didn't even cause a tiny tinkling. And so, exhausted, they returned to the apartment after making a quick stop for a bag of fast food.

"Eat your hamburger," Mitch ordered.

"I can't."

"Eat."

The woman smiled. "Yes, sir." The smile drifted away, however. "Why didn't you go to the AA meeting Thursday night?"

"It isn't necessary that I go to every meeting. People miss all the time."

"You didn't go because of me."

"I was busy with the investigation."

"Mitchell, don't let me interfere with your life. I'm not worth it."

"Hey, I don't like the sound of that."

"But it's true."

"We don't know anything for sure yet, so let's not jump to conclusions."

When she would have said more, Mitch silenced her. Nicely, but firmly. Later, they tried to play cards, but neither of their minds was on the game and so they called it an early good night and both headed to bed.

Neither, however, went to sleep. Mitch tossed and turned and listened to sounds that had to be his client doing the same thing. He heard the bed squeaking, he heard her heading for the bathroom a couple of times and he heard her walking around the room. At a little after two a.m., he made a decision. Even as he made it, he knew it might possibly be a wrong one. In fact, he was almost sure that it was.

Throwing back the covers, he went to the kitchen and, after a few minutes of tinkering, he headed toward the bedroom with a mug in his hands. A thin ribbon of light shone beneath the door, confirming that his houseguest was, indeed, restless. He knocked on the door. This time, he waited for a response, because he didn't want a repeat of the earlier scene in which he had found her, half-naked, standing in the moonlight. Or maybe he did and knew that he *shouldn't* want it . . .

"Come in," she called, and Mitch could tell by her voice that he'd startled her.

When he opened the door, he found her sitting on the edge of the bed. She again wore his pajama top, but her legs were thankfully covered by the sheet, except for a couple of toes that peeked out—sexily. Her hair was a wonderful mess. As though sensing this, at least the messy part, she dragged her fingers through the golden curls. Mitch wouldn't have minded tangling his fingers in the same silky thicket.

"I brought you something," he said, indicating the mug. "I have no idea whether warm milk works, but, hey, it's touted as a great cure for sleeplessness."

She took what he offered, smiling faintly. "So, I was keeping you awake, huh?"

Mitch plopped down onto the chair where he'd once spent the night. "Life keeps me awake these days . . . and nights."

The woman sipped at the heated milk. "I know the feeling. You know which memories I miss most?" she asked, once more making it obvious what subject was closest to her heart.

"Which?"

"Memories of my childhood. Where did I grow up? Who are my parents? Are they waiting for me to call? Do I have brothers or sisters? Was I happy?"

Something in the way she said this last once more convinced Mitch that this woman had known little of happiness, at least of late. Then he said, "I don't think you've been very happy as an adult. At least, not for a while."

"It's funny you should say that, because I don't think so, either. I have this empty feeling inside me that doesn't want to go away."

"Empty feelings aren't all that bad," Mitch said, thinking of the hate and self-loathing, the bitterness and shame that all too often filled him.

"No, feeling empty hurts. I'd rather feel anything but empty." She took another swallow of warm milk, as though hoping that it would help to ease the pain of nothingness she'd spoken of. "Tell me about one of your childhood memories. Let me pretend it's mine for a while."

Her request, simple though unusual, moved Mitch. His fingers steepled under his chin, he sorted through his memories, wanting to recall the warmest, the most wonderful. He realized that even with his father's drinking problem there had been many good childhood memories. At last, he settled on one special memory. In fact, it was a memory that in one fashion or another, he continued to dream about occasionally.

He grinned. "Okay, here's my all-time best memory. I was ten—maybe eleven . . . I don't remember—anyway, I was playing Little League baseball. I'd been an average batter all season, but a good pitcher—no a great pitcher—"

"A modest pitcher, too," the woman said, smiling.

Mitch grinned back. "Hey, if you're great, you're great. Now, do you want to hear this story?"

The blonde nodded, looking again like an angel and nothing like a murderer.

"Okay, so a little respect for the great Little League pitcher."

"So sorry. The great Little League pitcher has my respect."

"That's better," Mitch said, observing that she was stifling a laugh just as he was. "Anyway, the other team was killing us, right, but we'd finally managed to get a couple of men on the bases. I had batted out twice before and presently had two strikes against me. I was not looking like a save-the-day kind of guy."

"But you knocked it out of the ballpark, right?"

"There are some who say that ball is still sailing through the air."

The woman's smile grew until it was beautifully wide and sincere. "That's a nice memory. Thank you for sharing it."

"Thanks for reminding me that there was a time when I felt better about myself. I've done a lot of things since then that were more important—" he thought of the two awards he'd received for valor "—but I've never felt better about myself than I did that day on that baseball diamond."

Both Mitch and the woman grew silent. Finally, she said, "I have the feeling, Mitchell Brody, that you've always been, and always will be, a save-the-day kind of guy."

Mitch realized that his client had an uncanny way of clipping him behind the knees with her compliments. "Yeah, well," he said, rising from the chair and taking the near-empty mug from her hands, "I have the feeling that you need some rest."

As he'd done once before, he held the covers while she slipped beneath them. Her hair fanned out across the pillow. Without thinking, Mitch reached to brush a lost strand from her cheek.

He liked the feel of her skin.

She liked the feel of his hand.

"Go to sleep," he said huskily as he turned off the light and started for the door.

"Mitchell?" she called.

He turned, his gaze penetrating the inky darkness.

"I want you to know that regardless of how things turn out, I appreciate what you've done for me."

"Everything's going to turn out all right."

"I also want you to know one other thing." She didn't wait for him to ask what that one other thing was. "The only time I don't feel empty is when I'm with you."

This compliment not only clipped him at the back of the knees, but it also threatened to hurl him down a flight of emotional stairs. He made no response, but then he had the oddest feeling that none was expected.

"YOU'RE GROWING very relaxed," dark-haired, dark-eyed Susan Simpson said in a soft soothing voice. More important, it was a voice that inspired trust. "You're growing very tired, but that's all right. You want to rest. You want to go to that place deep inside yourself where you keep all your memories. It's a safe place. Nothing can harm you there. No memory can hurt you."

Mitch sat silently in a nearby chair. The drapes had been drawn, enveloping his apartment in a dusky darkness even though it was early afternoon. As Mitch watched his client, stretched out on the sofa, breathe steadily in and out, as he watched her eyelids flutter downward, he felt both exhilaration and dread. He desperately wanted to find out about her past, yet he feared what he might hear. He also wanted to take her hand in his, to protect her from any pain she might encounter along the way, but he didn't. He couldn't. After last night, after her admission that he alone could fill her emptiness, he'd felt magnetically drawn to her, yet he knew he had to guard against that very magnetism.

"That's it," the psychiatrist intoned, "you're growing sleepy, very sleepy. You feel warm and safe. You know that nothing you remember will hurt you."

The blonde sighed.

"You've reached a point of perfect relaxation now. All of your memories—your childhood memories, your adult memories—are gathered around you. Can you feel them?"

The patient said nothing.

Undeterred, the doctor moved on. "I want you to go back to Thursday, the fourth of June. I want you to go back to the night before you went to the detective agency."

The blonde whimpered, as though resisting the memories she'd been asked to recall.

"What were you doing that night?" the psychiatrist insisted.

"I can't tell you," the blonde murmured.

"Why can't you tell me?"

"You'll tell him." Before the doctor could comment, she added, forcefully, "He mustn't find out."

"Who mustn't find out?" Dr. Simpson pursued.

As though she'd just encountered her first demon on this perilous mind-journey, the blonde rolled her head to the side. Mitch noted the restless twitching of her eyelids, the flaring of her nostrils.

"He finds out everything," the woman said. "But he mustn't find out what I've been planning. I've been planning this for so long. I've been waiting for just the right time."

The psychiatrist tried a new approach. "What are you planning? Maybe I can help you?"

"No, no one can help me. I'm alone. Always alone. I'm so tired of being alone. It—it wasn't supposed to be this way."

Susan Simpson looked over at Mitch. He had moved to the edge of his seat, poised for what, he had no idea. He knew only that the anguish in his client's voice had cut him to the quick.

"Can you remember your name?" the doctor asked, maneuvering the conversation in yet another direction.

The blonde once more fought some unseen demon. "I don't want to remember my name."

"Why?" Susan asked.

"It was all a lie, a sham."

"What's a lie, a sham?"

"I have to get out. I have to leave." This last utterance produced an agitation that had the blonde, though her limbs were weighed down with a hypnotically induced fatigue, trying to rise from the sofa.

Mitch was halfway out of the chair when the doctor spoke, calmly, as she laid a restraining hand on her patient. At the same time she glanced at Mitch.

"Easy, easy," she soothed, and Mitch had the distinct impression that the words were as much for his benefit as for her patient's. He sat back on the edge of the chair.

The blonde relaxed somewhat, though she continued to mutter, "I have to get out. I have to leave. I owe it to Emily."

At the mention of Emily, both the doctor and Mitch pounced. "Who's Emily?" they asked together.

"Sorry," Mitch mouthed to the psychiatrist.

"Who's Emily?" the doctor repeated.

The blonde's voice lowered when, as though fearful of being overheard, she said, "I'm not supposed to talk about her. He told me never to talk about her."

"Why?" Dr. Simpson asked.

"He's ashamed of her."

"You can tell me about her," Dr. Simpson said. "I'm not ashamed of her."

"No, he'll be angry."

The doctor repeated the question she'd asked earlier. "Who is this man who'll be angry?"

As before, the question couldn't penetrate the blonde's fixation. "I have to go. He's unlocking the safe. I've got to get the book. The plan won't work without the book." She appeared to be reaching for something. "I have to hurry before he comes back."

The psychiatrist frowned and looked over at Mitch. Her expression asked if he knew anything about this book.

"Ask her if it's the little black book," he whispered.

"Is it the little black book?"

"The little black book," the blonde mumbled.

"Ask her what's in it," Mitch said quietly.

"Can you tell me what's in this book?"

"I don't know, but it's important."

"How do you know that?" the doctor asked.

"He keeps it in the safe. I don't know the combination." Then, as though sensing that time was running out, the woman on the sofa said, "I have to get it while I can. I have to go." She seemed to be plucking something from thin air.

"Before you go," the psychiatrist said, "can you tell me about the man lying dead on the floor?"

For a second, the question didn't seem to register. Suddenly, the woman's breathing accelerated. Wisps of air gave way to great gulps. The woman paled.

"He's dead," she whispered. "Oh, God, he's dead."

"Do you know who the man is?"

Again, the question didn't seem to penetrate. Nothing seemed to get beyond the fact that the man was dead. "He's dead—oh, God, the blood; oh, Emily, the blood... I mustn't get it on me. Everyone will see... everyone will know."

The doctor again made eye contact with Mitch. Mitch knew what she was thinking, that she was hearing a confession.

"Ask her if she killed the man," Mitch said.

"With the kind of blocking she's expressing, it isn't likely she'll answer," Dr. Simpson said, her words directed solely at Mitch.

"Ask her anyway."

"Did you kill the man?"

"Oh, God, he's dead... There's blood everywhere, everywhere—look, it's everywhere..." The woman began to swipe her hands down the legs of her jeans, as though trying to remove the crimson stain.

"Oh, God...oh, God...oh, God..." she began to chant.

"It's okay," the doctor comforted her. "There's no blood on you."

"I have to go—now when he's not looking...He's hollering—angry—he's angry...I've got to go now," the woman cried, her head thrashing from side to side, her hands clenched so that her knuckles were chalk-white.

Mitch responded to the woman's fear in the most primitive of ways. Jumping from the chair, he ordered, "Bring her out of it."

"You're never going to learn anything if—"

"Bring her out of it!"

Mitch and the psychiatrist silently squared off like two opposing warriors. In the stillness, the woman on the sofa whimpered, then began to cry. No wounded animal had ever sounded more pitiful.

"Bring her out of it," Mitch demanded, this time with a deadly calm that was more effective than any shout.

Dr. Simpson turned back to her patient. "You're going to leave the past behind now, you're going to leave all your memories behind..."

In minutes, on cue, the blonde opened her eyes. They first focused on Susan Simpson, then, when she remembered Mitch, her gaze flew to him. Her look asked the question, *What did I remember?*

Mitch took in the silver-gray eyes hidden beneath a blur of tears. He remembered the tortured cries that had just swelled in her throat. He wanted to tell her that everything was all right, that he now knew who she was, and that she wasn't guilty of murdering a man. Intuitively, though, he knew that she wanted only the truth. Professionally, he owed her no less. Privately... There was no privately.

"We didn't learn much," he said.

The woman on the sofa sat up, a tear slipping from her eye and running down her cheek. Reflexively, she swiped at it, but didn't seem to pay it much attention.

"Nothing?" the woman asked with obvious disappointment.

"Does the name Emily mean anything to you?" the doctor asked.

The woman considered the name, apparently trying to make it fit a memory. "Emily," she repeated, as though hoping the word might jar loose some hidden thought. "No," she said, finally. "It means nothing. Is it my name?"

"No," Mitch answered. "I don't think so. It's someone else's."

"How do you know?" his client asked, then demanded, "Tell me everything."

Between Mitch and the doctor, they filled her in on the details, few though there were, of the hypnosis session. The woman listened to every word—impassively. When it was over, again with an impassiveness that was notable, she said, "Then it's very possible I did kill that man?"

"Maybe," Mitch said, quickly adding, "but it's not the only possible scenario." Both his client and the psychiatrist waited eagerly for him to proceed. He stood and began pacing the room, as though needing the energy to fuel his thoughts. "Maybe this Emily person was present. Maybe she killed the man. And how do we know that the man you were running from is the same man who was killed? Maybe there were two men. Maybe the one you were running from is the killer."

The psychiatrist's look suggested that Mitch was stretching for an alternative.

His client verbally echoed Dr. Simpson's look, though it was evident that it cost her emotionally to do so. "I appreciate your attempt at finding another possibility but the truth is I'm the most likely candidate."

"No!" Mitch said, then quietly repeated, "It's not the only thing that could have occurred."

Ten minutes later, his client resting off the effects of a mild sedative even though she'd sworn she didn't need one, Mitch walked the psychiatrist to the door.

"She's all right, isn't she?" Mitch asked. He'd noted the way the blonde had begun to tremble once more. The fact had hurt his heart, but not nearly as much as the fact that she'd tried to hide it. It had reminded him of all the times he'd tried to hide his own pain.

"What she's been through this afternoon has been emotionally taxing. What she's been through for more than a week now has been emotionally taxing. Technically, she's all right. She's just emotionally drained." Once at the door, the doctor turned. "For that matter, so are you."

"I'm fine."

"Are you?" Before he could answer, the psychiatrist said, "You're going to have to face the fact that she very likely may have killed that man."

"There are other ways of looking at this. Besides, we don't even have a body."

Susan Simpson shrugged. "Body or not, if there was a murder, she's most likely the guilty party."

"And what are you going to do with that knowledge?" Mitch asked bluntly.

"Easy, Brody. I'm on your side. I'm on her side. Besides, I'm protected by patient confidentiality. But what about you? Aren't you obligated to report a murder?"

Mitch gave a dark laugh. "I played by the rules once. I'll never be that stupid again, and, as I said, we don't know anything for certain."

"Wrong," the doctor said. "We know you've totally lost your objectivity."

Mitch didn't bother with a denial. What would have been the point when the good doctor had spoken the truth?

THE WOMAN LISTENED at the bedroom doorway, straining to hear the exchange between Mitchell and Dr. Simpson. The words she heard swirled with the medication roaming through her veins, producing a surreal sensation. There was something she had to do. She knew that, but she wasn't certain what that something was. Later. She'd think about it later when her head cleared. Right now she had to lie down and close her eyes. Quietly walking back to the bed, she climbed upon its softness, curled into a ball and was asleep almost before her eyelids closed.

CHAPTER SEVEN

THAT NIGHT, the power company made good on its threat. At three minutes to midnight, the electricity went off. Mitch swore, tossed aside his detective novel, and sat up on the side of the sofa. Well, at least he couldn't say he hadn't been warned. He had a pile of correspondence, each letter bolder than the last, promising just this action if a little moola wasn't sent in—and pronto. What galled him, though, was the fact that the power company had been so zealous, they'd done the deed on a Sunday night. What would have been the harm in their waiting until Monday? He started to get up and light a candle, but decided that he'd rather curse the darkness. Doing so fit his dark mood.

He had started out with an amnesiac as a client. That client might now be a murderer, but, as bad as that was, it wasn't the worst of it. The worst of it was that Susan Simpson was right. He was no longer objective as far as this case was concerned, as far as this woman was concerned. He'd once thought that he could easily lose himself in trying to find his client. The truth was that he was already lost.

His houseguest had seemed lost, too, following the session of hypnosis. She'd slept for several hours, then had arisen and silently stalked through the apartment, a caged lioness on the prowl. She'd spoken little, but then so had he. After preparing sandwiches, they ate, again with little conversational exchange. At dusk, his client had excused herself, showered, and, insisting she was tired, crawled back into bed.

From his position on the sofa, Mitch recalled his own struggle with the seemingly endless evening. His mind was a muddle. He didn't know what he thought. He didn't know what he felt. He wanted the woman in his life. He wanted her out of it. He wanted to storm into the bedroom, take her in his arms and promise that he'd let nothing, no one, harm her. And, dammit, he could have sworn that was exactly what she wanted him to do!

Mitch jabbed at his pillow, turned on his side and silently cursed the lumps in the sofa.

SHE THOUGHT he would never go to sleep. Her heart pounding, she'd waited and waited and waited some more. Finally, just when she decided to make her move, the bedside fan quit. Like a cornered mouse, she stood perfectly still. Was it possible that the electric company had grown tired of Mitchell's unpaid bill? Did it really matter what had happened? she thought, reasoning that the darkness could only help her cause.

Slowly, the tennis shoes tied together and thrown over her shoulder, she tiptoed toward the door on bare feet. She turned the doorknob, then, ever so carefully, cracked open the door. She peered out, willing herself to see through the murky sea that rolled before her. With little trouble, she located the sofa. Mitchell's hulking form—hopefully his sleeping form—loomed like a foothill. She waited, watched, then braved a step forward. That step was followed by another, and another, each taking her deeper into the room. She chose a path that gave a wide berth to the sofa, even though it meant prolonging her journey to the apartment door.

Easy, she told herself, her feet digging into the warm, smooth floor. Just take it slow and easy. Cursing the dark, she dodged the chair that jumped from out of nowhere. Next came a stack of books that she sidestepped at the very last moment. *Just keep moving, moving, moving—*

A floorboard creaked.

The woman halted, her heart racing to the rhythm of fear. Too afraid to even look in Mitch's direction, she simply stood rooted in one spot. She waited, listened, then finally dared a backward glance. Nothing. No movement, no sound. She allowed herself a silent sigh of relief before once more starting for the door. She was going to make it. The door was too near for her not to now. All she had to do was reach out and—

"Where are you going?"

Though the voice was quiet, it was also authoritative, commanding. It demanded an answer to a question that was both simple and complex. The woman sighed, although she could have sworn just as easily—at fate, at Mitchell, at her herself. Most of all at herself, for she now knew that a part of her, the weak part of her, had wanted him to stop her. What an idiot she was. What a first-class idiot!

At the realization that this woman was walking out of his life, a cold panic had seized Mitch. It had been all he could do to keep from rushing forward and physically barring her from leaving. Instead, he slowly rose from the sofa.

Minutes before, his client had cursed not being able to see in the dark. Now she cursed how clearly she could see. A pair of jeans hung provocatively low on the hips of the man walking toward her, while nothing, an absolutely splendid nothing, covered his wide, muscular shoulders.

When Mitch stood directly in front of her, his eyes staring deeply into hers, he repeated his question. "Where are you going?"

"Away," she whispered, adding, "Every minute I stay here, I'm putting you at risk."

It crossed Mitch's mind to wonder if she'd overheard his conversation with Susan Simpson. Had she heard the doctor's unspoken reminder that, if he kept silent, he could become an accessory if a murder had been committed by his client? More important, had she heard the doctor accuse him of having lost his objectivity? With a start, he realized that he didn't care about this. Perhaps it was the darkness making him reckless, but he just didn't care. All he cared about was the way golden hair swept about sculptured shoulders, begging him to bury his hands, his face, in it. All he cared about was taking this woman in his arms.

"I'm already at risk," he whispered raggedly, frankly, his hands burning to touch her. God, he wanted to touch her! To keep from doing so, he shoved his hands into the back pockets of his jeans.

His rich, warm voice wrapped itself around the woman, making her feel hotter than the summer night. She remembered well the conversation she'd overheard. She hadn't meant to become attracted to this man. She hadn't meant for him to become attracted to her. Maybe it was the darkness, compounded by his seductive nearness, making her bold. She didn't know. She didn't care. All she knew was that she didn't have the heart for denying the obvious.

"I never meant for this to happen," she said, so softly that the sound danced about the room like ricocheting moonbeams.

Her honesty, her lack of pretense, gutted Mitch's stomach. Both had laid their cards on the table. The only trouble was, both hands were unplayable.

"I know," he replied. "I never meant for it to happen, either."

"I may belong to someone else."

"I know." God, he knew! And how he hated the thought!

She sighed, then gave a soft little laugh. "It would be so easy to give in to your kindness, your gentleness. I'm not sure I've ever known that kind of kindness, that kind of gentleness."

The bleakness in her voice speared Mitch's heart. "What makes you say that?"

"I just feel it. Kindness, gentleness, seem foreign to me. Your arms feel...they feel strange. As though I'm not accustomed to such sweetness."

Mitch took an instinctive step toward her. The hands he'd ordered into his pockets disobeyed. He started to reach for her.

"Don't!" she whispered. "I'm not strong enough to resist you."

Mitch stopped, then gave an out-and-out curse. One hand found the doorjamb, which he used as a prop, while the other hand riffled through his hair. "So, where do you think you're going?"

"I don't know. Somewhere. Anywhere."

"Just away from me?"

"Yes."

"Dammit, you can't go roaming around the city with no memory!"

"Maybe away from you, my memory will return."

Mitch's silence eloquently stated that her comment had taken him totally by surprise. It also suggested that he didn't fully understand the remark. "What does that mean?"

"Maybe I don't want to remember. Maybe I'm too comfortable here." Another silence, this one hers, then, "Maybe I don't want to leave you."

Her words drew Mitch into a warm, honeyed sea and drowned him there in a sweetness he'd never known. He struggled to surface, though, frankly, all he wanted was to sink.

"That's ridiculous," he said, hoping she hadn't spoken the truth, but, in some convoluted way, hoping she had. He wanted her to want to stay. In fact, never in his life could he remember wanting anything more.

"Is it?" When Mitch didn't answer, she went on with, "None of this matters. What matters is that I may be putting you at a legal risk. If I *did* mur... if I am responsible for someone's death, you have the legal responsibility to report your findings to the police."

So she had heard Dr. Simpson. "First of all, quit listening to what any- and everybody says. Second, there is no proof that you killed anyone. Third, I'm legally bound whether you walk out that door or not."

"Go to the police."

"No."

"Then I'll go myself!"

"No!"

"For God's sake, Mitchell, I may have killed someone!"

"I don't care," he said, silently adding, *And I don't care if you belong to one man, to ten men, or to ten thousand. I still want you. Heaven help me, I do.*

The woman made a sound that told Mitch that she was once more fighting tears. That realization devastated him. He swallowed hard, knowing that he had to lighten the mood. If he didn't, he was going to go stark, raving mad.

"You can't go." A slow smile sauntered across his lips as he said, "I'm afraid of the dark."

The blonde heard his desperate attempt to inject a little humor into the gravely serious moment. She also saw his heart-melting smile. Despite herself, she couldn't help but return that smile. "What happened? Did the electric company finally cut off the power?"

Her smile made his heart feel too big for his chest. It made another body part feel too big as well. He cursed himself for his lack of control. Then again, maybe, he ought to congratulate himself on his control. If he didn't have it on a tight leash, verbal communication would have given way to physical communication a long time ago. Yeah, truth was, he probably deserved some kind of medal, just as the woman standing before him certainly deserved some kind of reply.

"Yeah, they have no sense of humor about unpaid bills."

"Take the earrings and—"

"It's okay," he repeated. "Several clients owe me. I'll get the money. Until I do, I've got a slew of candles."

The woman heard the pride in his voice. It was mile-high and valley-deep. It was the ultimate definition of masculine. She wanted—so desperately that it was a tangible thing—to comfort, to console him. She wouldn't, though; to do so would be to court disaster on a grand scale. Just the way that standing here another minute, another second, was courting the same disaster.

Mitch sensed her decision. Another round of panic claimed him.

"Don't go," he said, his voice raw with an emotion he couldn't define. "I'm not asking anything of you except to let me take care of you...until you're able to take care of yourself."

The woman closed her eyes. She mustn't give in. She mustn't listen to her heart. She must ignore the fact that only this man seemed capable of easing the loneliness residing deep inside her. She must go. Now. While she still could. Opening her eyes, refusing to look back, she stepped toward the screened door, which because of the heat, was her only barrier to the freedom she sought.

Mitch hadn't meant to touch her. In fact, he'd meant to do quite the opposite. As if with a will of its own, however, his hand rushed through the darkness, capturing hers just as it pushed at the door. Both were stunned. For long moments, Mitch's palm simply covered the back of her hand. For all its simplicity, the contact was consummately intimate. Her hand felt so incredibly small beneath his, his so large shielding hers. What would she feel like beneath him? What would he feel like sprawled atop her? Each tried to be shocked by the question. Each wasn't, though. Each only longed for an answer. Slowly, Mitch's fingers mingled with those of the woman. It was a tentative mingling at first. That was followed by a desperate entwining.

Don't let go! she seemed to say.

No, I won't! Mitch seemed to answer.

The darkness seductively swirled around them, sanctioning things that the light most certainly would have condemned—things like his drawing their joined hands to his lips, things like the gentle kiss he brushed against her knuckles.

The woman moaned.

Mitch groaned.

Both knew the fire they were playing with.

"Let me go," the blonde whispered. "Please."

"Is that what you want?"

"Yes . . . no . . . but I must."

As she spoke, her free hand found Mitch's bare chest. In the hot summer night, without benefit of even a fan, a fine sweat sheened his skin—a fine, sexy sweat. At her touch, Mitch's breath fled, and his heart began a wild thumping. The woman's own heartbeat crashed in her ears.

At her caress—and it was a caress, whether she'd intended it to be or not—Mitch lost control. Totally.

With a deep, guttural sound, he pulled her to him, fully, completely, fitting her body all along the length of his. His arms folded themselves around her. Her breasts cozied against him as their hips sought to get closer. He was aroused, a fact he didn't bother to hide, though he couldn't have even if he'd tried.

The blonde whimpered at his body's boldness and slid her arms around his neck. His breath was hot at her ear, hers erratic at the hollow of his throat. Slowly, deliberately, she angled her head in a timeless search for his lips. His, too, sought out that which he most wanted.

One kiss, Mitch told himself. *Just one*. He'd be content with that. He'd *make* himself content with it.

If only she could know this man's kiss; she'd ask for nothing more, the woman told herself.

It was impossible to say whose lips found whose. One moment the world was a bleak, lonely place, and the next it shone with rainbows, with promises, with the knowledge that there was at least one other person in the world. Mitch had never been so consumed, so lost in someone else. The past, with all its hurt, seemed to count for nothing. There was only now, and a healing that he had never thought to feel. But feel it, he did. Sighing, wanting more of this healing, he opened his lips wider. Slowly—he made himself go slowly—he urged her mouth to part, to give up all its sweetness. He wanted, needed, all of her, just as he wanted, needed, to give all of himself to her. In fact, he could never remember wanting, needing, anything more.

The woman knew only that the feeling of being alone had disappeared, vanished, as though it had been a long-ago specter. She knew, too, that she was reveling in this man's gentleness, in a tenderness so exquisite that it was painful. When he opened his mouth, when he parted hers, she felt a burning need to be adored, to be protected, to be lost beneath his masculine strength. That strength she felt hard and bold against her. Out of sheer instinct, she stepped into it.

At the beginning of the kiss, Mitch's own need had seemed so simple, so uncomplicated, so elemental. Below the waist, however, that need was growing far too complex. It was growing downright daring, and a recklessness was roving through him that not even the darkness could excuse. The truth was that he was only a man, with a man's needs. On the other hand, this woman had a whole different set of needs. She needed to know who she was before she was asked to make any kind of commitment, especially the physical kind. He could not—would not—further complicate her life. He had a professional and a moral responsibility to her. As for himself, he wasn't strong enough to lose anyone else in his life. Not after all he'd already lost.

With a tortured groan, Mitch dragged his lips from the woman's and stepped from her. He had to have distance if he was to think clearly—if he was to think at all. He moved to the window, trying to gather both his scattered breath and his tattered thoughts.

"I'm sorry," he said at last. "I shouldn't have done that."

The blonde leaned against the doorframe, trying to quell her own runaway emotions. Even though her lips were still wet from his kiss, the lonely feeling had returned.

"I gave you little choice," she responded.

As always, her honesty took him by surprise. He glanced over at her.

"I wanted you to kiss me," she added, destroying the breath he'd managed to catch. "In fact, I might even have kissed you."

"It doesn't matter who kissed whom. The kiss never should have occurred."

"No, it shouldn't have."

A thought, a fear, gripped Mitch. "Are you sorry it did?"

"No," she answered, again with a candor that robbed Mitch of his usual rhythmic heartbeat. "I just don't know what to do now."

"Stay here with me."

"I don't think—"

"Listen to me. You can't just walk out that door with nowhere to go. Stay just a few more days. If I can't come up with a lead, I'll let you do whatever you want." At her hesitation, he added, "No more kisses. I promise."

Time ceased to exist. There was only a man, only a woman, only the certain knowledge that the man and woman had to remain separate entities.

Finally, the woman spoke and Mitch could hear the smile in her voice. "How can I leave when you're afraid of the dark?"

THE FOLLOWING MONDAY night, Kelly took Mitch's client with her to exercise class. That left Mitch and Will to gad about on their own. Because the electricity was still off, the guys went out for the evening. Will had loaned his friend the money to pay the bill, against

Mitch's protestations, but the company was taking its own sweet time turning on what it had taken its own sweet time turning off. Consequently, Mitch and Will decided on a favorite café, where they ordered coffee and pie. Working now under the pressure of time—he remembered all too clearly asking the blonde for just a few more days—Mitch had brought the little black book with him. As he had from the beginning, he felt the answer to his client's mystery lay within the puzzling pages.

"So, that's the book, huh?" Will asked, tearing into a wedge of coconut cream pie with gusto.

"Yeah," Mitch answered, ignoring his own piece of pie in favor of thumbing through the expensively bound volume. "This has to mean something. She confirmed as much under hypnosis. She kept referring to it as important, although even she didn't seem to know quite why."

Mitch had told his friend everything that had transpired during her hypnosis. However, he had not told him about the kiss that had occurred later. What would his friend say if he knew? That he needed a shrink worse than his client did?

"Do you think she doesn't know or is just repressing it?"

Mitch shrugged. "Who knows? The result is the same in either case. She isn't giving me anything to go on."

Mitch could tell that his friend was carefully wording his next comment. "Maybe the dead man was blackmailing her with the information in the book. Maybe she wanted the book to blackmail him with.

Maybe, in either case, things got out of hand and she killed him."

"Why does everyone insist that she's the killer?" Mitch cried, then realized that his voice had carried. Several people glanced his way. Threading his fingers through his hair, he repeated, "Why does everyone insist she killed this guy? There's an Emily person un-accounted for."

"Eat your pie and drink your coffee and listen to me," Will ordered him. When Mitch hesitated, his friend said, "Eat. Drink. Listen."

Mitch sighed and reached for his fork.

"I like your client. I like her a lot. So does Kelly. But the truth is, that we—*you*—don't really know anything about her, except that she seems to be square in the middle of some big mess. For heaven's sake, Mitch, we're talking possible murder here."

Mitch laid his fork down without ever having taken a single bite. Will was wrong. He did know something about his client. He knew she had lips that a man would kill for.

Calmly, Mitch said, "I just don't believe she's a murderer."

"You don't believe it, or you don't want to believe it?"

"C'mon, man, cut me some slack here."

"Cut yourself some." Suddenly, Will looked about as weary as his friend. "Don't you know that I know what's going on here?"

"And just what does that mean?"

"Mitch, you're falling for her."

"I am not!"

"The hell you're not! I'm not saying I blame you. She's gorgeous, she's sweet—"

"She's a murderer?"

Will laid his fork down, his pie now forgotten. "How deep are you in?" When Mitch said nothing, Will added on a sigh, "That deep, huh?"

"She's not a murderer," Mitch insisted.

"Then, you're going to have to prove she isn't."

AN HOUR LATER, back at his apartment, Mitch studied the little black book by candlelight. Kelly and his client had yet to return. Will had left him at the curb with an apology. If he'd upset him, he was sorry. Will had upset him, but only because Mitch knew that everything his friend had said was true. He didn't know anything about the woman who'd hired him to find out who she was. He knew only that he shouldn't have the feelings for her that he did. He knew, too, that caution demanded that he not give a name to those feelings.

Now, leafing through the pages, Mitch forced himself to think only of the book, not of the woman, not of the kiss they'd shared, not of how she'd felt in his arms. What did these numerical notations mean? Why were the entries all so neatly arranged, with each entry occupying three lines, with a single line separating one entry from another? Were the notations addresses, after all? Did the three lines consist of a name, an address and a telephone number? If the third line was a telephone number, it was camouflaged. Instead of the usual seven digits, the number consisted of twelve. Mitch glanced at several of the entries, hoping to recognize any prefixes common to city telephone numbers. He recognized none. Damn! he thought, as he turned to the back page. He frowned.

Chelsea.

What did it mean that everything else in the book had been recorded with precision, yet this word had been carelessly scrawled across the page at an angle? It was the same handwriting as all the other entries, yet someone had not taken the time to enter it neatly. The writer hadn't even bothered to place it on a line. What it suggested, Mitch decided, was that someone had written the word in a hurry and had reached for the first handy thing.

But what did the word mean?

From out of nowhere—why would he think of this now?—came an image of the filmed funeral of the recently drowned city councilman, the footage Mitch had viewed at Will and Kelly's. What was the guy's name? Richard Something-Or-Other. Rhincuso. Richard Rhincuso. As quickly as the image had appeared, it was replaced by yet another image, this one of a smiling chief of police. As always, thoughts of Paul Lerner turned Mitch's stomach, and so he willed his attention back to the book. Flipping to the beginning, he started thumbing through the tiny notebook once more. In minutes, he'd exhausted every boyish code he knew.

Nothing!

He had no earthly idea what the numbers meant, what story they told to one bright enough to read them. Shutting his eyes, Mitch sighed. Where in hell did he go from here? What he needed was an expert on codes, but he didn't know one, except for some ex-military guy who occasionally did some work for the police department. He didn't even remember the fellow's name. Should he or shouldn't he try to find out who the guy was? Mitch opened his eyes and riffled through the book one last time. Yeah, maybe he should give the man a try. Until the code was deciphered, the case was going nowhere. More importantly, there was no way of learning who the woman was. There was no way—

The thought halted in midsentence as a set of numbers jumped out at Mitch. The numbers were familiar numbers, numbers that any elementary-school kid knew by heart. The numbers were 1492.

CHAPTER EIGHT

MITCH COULDN'T HEAR himself think for the sudden roar that blasted through his head. Neither could he quite believe what he was seeing. Because he couldn't, he ran the tips of his fingers across the numbers, as though the act would somehow verify their existence. It didn't. He was left wondering if he was truly seeing what he thought he was. In the end, he had to conclude that he was.

But did it mean anything?

No, of course not. The numbers were commonplace. *In a history book,* Mitch forced himself to admit, but what about in a journal of possible addresses? He picked up the phone.

After dialing, Mitch looked at his watch. It was a little after nine o'clock. Kelly and his houseguest would be returning at any minute, which meant that he had to work fast. Real fast.

"Hello?" came a voice that Mitch immediately recognized as belonging to Speedy's wife.

"Hey, Joan, this is Mitch. Is that slob you're married to around?"

Joan Talbot laughed, a warm, friendly sound. In the background, kids shrieked in play. "Yeah, he's supposed to be watching the boys, but my guess is that he's sacked out on the sofa. You know, keeping it from levitating.''

"Could I talk to him?"

"You bet." She called out to her husband, then, while waiting for him, she said to Mitch, "You haven't been over in a while. How're you doing?"

"Fine," he said, lying through his teeth. Well, actually, he wasn't lying. As soon as he put this coincidence to rest, he was going to feel a whale of a lot better. He was going to feel just fine and dandy.

"Here's the ole man," she announced. "You come see us, okay?"

"Okay." Mitch waited for the telephone to change hands.

"Hey," Speedy said finally, "what's up?"

"Nothing much. Listen, do you remember the name of that cryptanalyst the department uses occasionally?"

"Ye-ah," Speedy answered, drawing out the word as though he was thinking in the process. "Something like Knippe. No, wait, it's Knutson. Roy Knutson. He's in the telephone directory. Want me to look up his number?"

"No, no, I can do that."

"You thinking of having him take a look at your mystery notebook?"

"Yeah, I'm thinking about it," Mitch returned, hoping to heaven he sounded casual. "I figure it can't hurt anything, right?"

"Right, and I think this guy's pretty good. He was in WWII, you know? Deciphering Japanese communiqués and all that nefarious stuff."

"Yeah, I know."

"Give him a call."

"I might," Mitch said, again hoping that what he was about to ask sounded natural enough not to alert suspicion. "Hey, you remember that call girl you guys busted?"

"Sure."

"What was her name? Something high-tone sounding, wasn't it?"

"Yeah, mighty high-tone sounding. Ms. Sarah Elizabeth Etheridge."

"She lives at 1492 Mendoza Avenue, right?"

"Yeah, over in fancy-smancyville." The slightest of hesitations followed, during which Mitch heard the question coming. "Why are you asking?"

Mitch asked forgiveness for the lie even as he was uttering it. "No real reason. Will and I were just talking."

"I would remind you guys that Will Stone is a happily married man, and you, my friend, would have to take out a loan to afford the lady."

Mitch laughed, again trying to appear normal. "No, I'd have to take out a couple." Before his friend could say more, Mitch added, "Well, look, I'll let you get back to holding that sofa down."

"Okay, stay in touch and—"

"Watch my sorry rear," Mitch finished.

Mitch hung up to the strains of Speedy Talbot's, "You got it."

No, he didn't have it at all, Mitch thought as he simply stared at the receiver, now resting comfortably back in its cradle. In fact, he didn't have even the foggiest idea what was going on. Getting up from his chair, he began to pace the candlelit room. Shadows played bizarre games on the walls, but then, they were no more bizarre than the mind games he was playing.

Abruptly, he halted, grabbed the telephone directory and looked up Sarah Etheridge's number. He compared what he found to the twelve-digit number. It didn't take long to determine that all of the seven-digit number was contained within the twelve, except it appeared out of order. Mitch sighed, wanting to feel better, but not being quite able to.

What if this entry did relate to this Etheridge woman? In and of itself, it didn't matter. It mattered only in the context of one question: What was his client doing with a book that contained the name, address and phone number of a call girl?

Mitch wasn't certain what he hoped to prove, but he grabbed the phone and dialed the Etheridge number. On the sixth ring, the answering machine picked up.

"Hello," a velvet-throated voice intoned. "You have reached the Etheridge residence. I can't come to the phone right now, but, if you'll leave your name and number..."

"This is Michael Smith." *Good Lord, Brody, couldn't you have thought of something more original!* "I, uh, I'm in town for a couple of days and I'd like to see you. Could you give me a call? Thanks." He started to hang up, then realized his error. "Oh, my number is..."

He gave the agency number, replaced the receiver and wondered what in the hell he'd just done. First, she might not even call him back, considering the legal trouble she was in and, second, what did he hope to learn if she did? He could hardly ask point-blank if she was listed in this book. Furthermore, if she did call back, it might not be for ages, and his client was due home any minute.

"C'mon, Sarah, call. Now!"

Mitch sighed, twirling a pencil. When it bounced to the floor, he ignored it and reached for another. The phone rang in midstretch. Mitch's heart rolled over.

Letting the phone ring a couple more times, he picked up the receiver and tried to sound casual when he said, "Hello?"

"Is this Michael? Michael Smith?" came the velvet voice.

Thank you, God! "Yeah, this is Michael."

"This is Sarah."

"Hi, Sarah," Mitch said, his heart pounding so loud he could hardly hear himself speak.

"Hi. So, you're in town for a few days."

"Yeah, I thought we could...you know, get together...or, uh, or something. You know, whatever."

Sarah Etheridge laughed—prettily. "You mean, like go out to eat?"

"Yeah, right. Go out to eat."

"How did you get my name, Michael?"

He was afraid she was going to ask this! "You know, I don't remember the guy's name. Douglas, I think. I met him when I was in San Francisco several months ago. He's in real estate, I think. I'm sorry, I just don't remember his name, but he remembered yours. He said that you were the best—at going out to eat."

Sarah laughed again. "I think I like you, Michael."

"I think I like you, too."

"Look, I have a little bit of a problem right now. I can't go out to eat for a while. When will you be in town again?"

He was losing her. The call had been for nothing. "A couple of months."

"Call me then, huh? I promise to make the wait worth it."

"That's a long time to wait to eat."

"I know, but it just whets the appetite." Her voice had gone from sweet to sultry. "Let me give you my number."

Even as she spoke of her number, Mitch wondered why she'd give him something that he obviously had. "I have your number."

"No, no, what I'm going to give you is my identification number. It means you're a regular or we've talked and I like you." Again, her voice was sultry when she said, "For my preferred customers. Got a pen and paper?"

At the phrase *identification number,* Mitch's heart went wild. Was it possible that the number was a five-digit number that was mingled in with her telephone number? *C'mon, Sarah, don't disappoint me.*

When Sarah called out the number, Mitch felt like shouting. Though they weren't in the same order, the numbers matched the five remaining numbers in the twelve-digit number written in the notebook.

"Call me, huh? I really like eating out."

"I'll just bet you do," Mitch said.

"Hey, Michael. Tell me something. Is Smith your real name?"

"Swear to God," he said, hoping a bolt of lightning didn't strike him dead.

"Imagine that," the velvet voice said. A dial tone followed.

Mitch had grown so excited at tying the book entry to Sarah Etheridge that the implication of his doing so had momentarily escaped him. That implication returned with a vengeance, making him feel as if that bolt of lightning had, indeed, struck. He heard nothing beyond the roaring accusation that his client was somehow connected with a book that had a call girl's name in it. What in hell did that mean? What in—

"Mitchell?"

He glanced toward his client who stood in the doorway. Her look said that she might have called his name more than once.

"Ah, yeah," Mitch said to the dial tone, "let me get back to you."

When he hung up the telephone, the woman asked, "Are you all right?"

"Yeah," he said quickly—too quickly. "Just a case."

The woman looked unconvinced, but said no more on the subject. Instead, she stepped into the room.

Mitch couldn't keep the words of the song Speedy had quoted from traipsing through his mind: "long, cool woman in a black dress." While it was true that the woman was currently wearing jeans, a T-shirt and a ponytail that left sassy, sweat-damp tendrils coiling around ears and neck and that she looked nothing like the woman the song spoke of, Mitch was nonetheless reminded of the first time he'd seen his client. He was reminded, too, that Speedy had used the song's description in reference to a call girl, a prostitute, a woman who sold sexual favors. Mitch shook his head, dislodging the ugly thought that had settled there.

". . . said to tell you hi."

"What?"

"Kelly said to tell you hi." The blonde smiled one of her rare smiles. It was uncommonly lovely. "She also said to tell you that I must be a jock."

"How so?"

"I did one hundred push-ups and wasn't even winded."

The woman looked so inordinately proud of herself, so innocent, so unlike a call girl, that Mitch told himself that he was a fool for even entertaining the notion. There could be a dozen reasons why she had the book in her possession.

He grinned. "A hundred push-ups? That's pretty impressive."

The blonde's smile disappeared. "What is it? What's wrong?"

"Nothing."

The woman walked toward him. By the candle's glow she was beautiful enough to take any man's breath away. Every nuance, every subtlety of her face represented perfection—from her gunmetal-colored eyes to her high cheekbones to even the thin layer of sweat that had formed across her upper lip because of the apartment's warmth.

"You've learned something, haven't you?"

Mitch toyed with the idea of telling her the truth, but he couldn't bring himself to do that. He excused his action by telling himself that he couldn't tell her what he didn't know, and the truth was that he didn't know what the truth was. That much wasn't a lie.

"No, I haven't learned anything." *Please, don't ask me again.*

The woman didn't. Even so, as though it had a will of its own, her gaze stayed glued to his. She tried to ignore the way his own eyes peered deeply into hers. She also tried to ignore the dark hair peeking out from the rolled-up sleeves of his shirt, and the way the shirt hung sloppily, but seductively, outside his jeans.

"I, ah, I think I'll shower and go to bed. It's been a tiring day."

"Yeah," Mitch said, not bothering to point out that they were wearing themselves out trying to avoid each other. Right now, he just longed to be alone... for more than one reason.

Mitch listened for the start of the shower and, when he heard it, he walked to the telephone and made another call, this one to Roy Knutson, with whom he made an appointment for the following day at one o'clock. He then stripped his shirt off—damn, but the apartment was hot!—and, blowing out the candle, flopped down on the sofa. He didn't even bother to make it out into a bed, mainly because he knew that he wouldn't sleep tonight under any conditions.

In minutes the shower went off. Tiny muffled noises followed. Mitch imagined the blonde drying off and slipping into his pajama top. Would she wear those sexy cotton panties with it? Probably not, considering the heat. The very thought of her *sans* panties made him break out in an even deeper sweat. He moaned, cursed and jabbed at his pillow. Thankfully, in a short while, the glow of her bedroom candle went out, casting the entire apartment into cavelike darkness. Mitch was relieved. Maybe in the dark his imagination wouldn't be so vivid. But it was. Not only did he conjure up every sensual image he could, but he also summoned up every sordid possibility that Etheridge's name in the book might imply.

As the hour approached midnight, Mitch was certain that he was approaching insanity. Because of that, he was almost relieved when he heard the cry coming from the bedroom. Anything was better than the nightmare he was living. *Nightmare.* It became abundantly clear upon entering the bedroom that the woman was immersed in another nightmare. Even as Mitch crossed to her, she cried out again. Just as before, her head thrashed around on the pillow, while one of her hands fought an unseen demon at her throat. Her clipped breathing cleaved at the silence . . . and at Mitch's heart.

Stepping to the side of the bed, he called, "Hey!"

The woman responded with a pitiful moan.

Without thinking, acting only on instinct, Mitch eased to the side of the bed. He reached for the hand at her throat, calling again as he did so, "Hey, wake up!"

With a gasp, the woman came instantly awake. Mitch sensed this, just as he realized that, despite the heat, her hand was ice-cold.

"Mitchell?" she whispered, sucking in great draughts of air.

He squeezed her hand reassuringly. "Yeah, it's me." Then, trying to treat the subject lightly, he asked, "Is that green dog back?"

She attempted a smile, but it never materialized. Instead, with a fevered desperation, she threw herself into his arms.

"Hold me," she pleaded.

She took Mitch totally by surprise. With his guard down, he did what came naturally. He put his arms around her and hugged her tightly to him. The pajama top, drenched in perspiration, clung to her breasts. He could feel one breast resting just at that place where his heart beat. Her breath, rapid and rough, was warm against his bare shoulder.

"Don't leave me," she begged him.

"No," Mitch whispered, uncertain whether she pulled him down on the bed or whether he pulled her. All he knew was that he found himself stretched out beside her, still clutching her. One hand moved down her back and past the fabric of the pajama top. It was then that he knew with utter certainty that she wasn't wearing the cotton panties. He knew one other thing as well. No matter who or what this woman was—sinner or saint—he wanted to be her lover.

"THE BOOK contains *what?*" Will screeched two nights later.

Mitch had called his best friend and had asked if he could come over, that there was something he wanted to talk to him about. Alone because his wife was on a nighttime photographic shoot out at the marina, Will hadn't hesitated. Not that he would have, anyway. There had been something in Mitch's voice—a certain tone? Perhaps the lack of any?—that had told him Mitch needed a friend. Badly. And so the two men now sat in Mitch's office—in light, thanks to the newly turned-on electricity—the fragments of the bombshell Mitch had just delivered still falling all around them.

From the squeaky chair behind his cluttered desk, Mitch corrected Will. "I said that the little black book *may* contain the names of call girls. More precisely, it *may* contain twenty-three names. Without question, it contains the name of one call girl."

"Sarah Elizabeth Etheridge?"

"That's right."

"And just how did you reach this conclusion?"

"I was leafing through the book, saw the numbers 1492 and..."

Mitch went on to relate all that had transpired Monday night—the call to Speedy, the call that got Sarah Elizabeth Etheridge's answering machine, the call to Roy Knutson. He followed with a description of his meeting with the cryptanalyst. Exactly twenty-four hours after that meeting, the mystery of the book lay unraveled.

"Once he had the Etheridge entry to work with, it was a fairly simple matter to figure out the code," Mitch explained.

Will looked as though he'd been struck by an eighteen-wheeler. Even so, he had the presence of mind to phrase his next words carefully. "So, you think this *may* be a listing of call girls. Let me ask you this. If the names aren't those of call girls, then what do you think they're names of?"

Mitch heard the real question that his friend was asking. How could you be so stupid as to believe they're anything else?

"They could be any number of things," Mitch said.

"Name one."

In exasperation, Mitch raked his fingers through his hair. "It could be some social organization. You know, one of those elite groups of rich women who are out to conserve this and preserve that. Maybe it's a political group. Maybe..." Mitch trailed off, hearing how lame everything he was saying sounded. It angered him that he couldn't come up with a believable alternative. "I don't know! Maybe it's the local bridge club!"

"Do you honestly believe—"

"Dammit, I don't know what to believe!"

But he did know what to believe. There really was only one thing to believe. Mitch picked up a sucker, unwrapped it, then threw it down on the desk.

"God, I want a drink!"

"Don't even think it," Will said.

Mitch made no reply. He merely stood and walked to the window. Night had closed in hard and fast, stamping the sky with a three-quarter moon and a twinkling accompaniment of crystal stars. He wondered what the woman upstairs was doing? He'd left her reading with the excuse that he had work to do. What a joke. He couldn't have concentrated on work if his life had depended on it. The only thing he could concentrate on was the list of names in that damned book. No, that wasn't quite true. He was all too willing to concentrate on how the woman upstairs felt in his arms.

"Mitch, listen to me," Will said. "Use a little common sense. Benign organizations—political, social, or any other kind—don't use a code to list their members." When Mitch said nothing, Will asked, "Do you hear me?"

"Yeah," Mitch said flatly. "Yeah, I hear you," he repeated, turning toward his friend and adding,

"There are other possibilities, though. She might not be one of the names."

"I never said—"

"You were thinking it," Mitch said, knowing that his friend had every right to arrive at that conclusion. Hell, hadn't he been forced to admit the same possibility? "There are other possibilities," he restated, more for his benefit than for Will's.

"Like what?"

Mitch shrugged. "Maybe . . . maybe she knows one of the women. Maybe one of them gave it to her for safekeeping."

"But I thought under hypnosis she talked as though she were taking the book from someone—perhaps as a means to insure her safety." Before Mitch could reply, Will added, "What was that name she mentioned while under hypnosis?"

"Emily." Mitch anticipated Will's next question. "There isn't an Emily listed in the book."

"Damn!" Will said. "I guess that would have been too easy."

"Apparently," Mitch said, not bothering to hide his frustration. Not only did every question lead to a dead end, but every unanswered question also seemed to spawn a dozen more unanswerable questions. Suddenly, Mitch gave a deep sigh. "Okay, let's assume the worst. She's a call girl. Why does she have the book?"

"Maybe she wanted out of the business, and this was her protection, which raises an interesting question. Who did she take the book from?"

"Her employer is the most obvious answer, right?"

"Right," Will agreed.

Mitch knew that both he and Will had gone to great lengths not to mention one name. Mitch knew, too, that it had to be mentioned, even though it took every ounce of strength he had to do so.

"John Yen Chang," he said finally.

Will studied his friend with a look that said he was certain what saying the name had cost him. No name was more hateful to him, under any circumstances, particularly under these.

The impact of what he'd said struck Mitch. "My, God, do you hear what I'm saying? She might be a prostitute working for John Yen Chang." Bitterly, he added, "Small world, huh?"

Will ignored his friend's sarcasm. "What about the guy who was murdered? Do you think it's possible that it was John Yen Chang?"

"If he'd been found murdered, it would have been front-page news."

"But what if he wasn't found?"

Mitch thought this over, then shook his head. "Surely, with a houseful of servants, he'd have been found. I'd love to see inside his house. I'd love to see if there's a gilt-edged white stairway with a chandelier."

"You're right, his body would have been found—unless, of course, it was disposed of."

Again, Mitch shook his head. "She might be capable of a lot of things, but moving a dead body that had to weigh considerably more than she does isn't one of them."

"Yeah. Unless she had help. Which maybe this Emily person provided?"

Mitch ambled back toward the desk chair and sat down. "I think we're getting carried away. Although," he added as an afterthought, "I guess it would be simple enough to determine if Chang is alive."

As he spoke, Mitch reached for the telephone directory, flipped to the *C*s, and visually ran down the listing. The name he was hunting for jumped out at him like a fiend from a nightmare. He slid his finger over to the address. Yeah, he thought, his stomach recoiling, the address was one of those fancy hillside ones. Forcing himself not to dwell on it, he picked up the receiver, dialed the number and waited for the phone to ring. As it did, Mitch's gaze rose to meet Will's. He allowed himself to be comforted by the fact that his friend was there, hurting for him even as he was hurting.

"I'd like to speak with Mr. Chang," Mitch said when someone answered the phone.

"Who might I say is calling?" the masculine voice asked.

"Just tell him it's an associate of his."

"Yes, sir" came the reply, which was followed by silence.

In less than a minute, an aristocratic voice, which spoke flawless English, said, "This is John Yen Chang."

Mitch's reaction surprised even him. Disappointment washed over him. He'd wanted the man to be dead. As soon as this thought had registered, however, another rose to take its place. No, he didn't want the bastard to be dead. Not before he had a chance to make him pay for what he'd done to him. And he was as sure as the heartbeat inside his chest that this man was responsible for his having lost his job.

"Who is this?" Chang asked.

Mitch replied by hanging up the receiver.

"I take it he's alive?" Will asked.

"Yeah. Very much so."

This time it was Will who dragged his fingers through his autumn-brown hair, sighing as he did so. "So, who was the guy who was murdered?"

Mitch said nothing. He simply buried his face in his hands.

Will, again choosing his words carefully, said, "This is out of your hands now. You have no option but to go to the police. If you don't, you could be charged with being an accessory—"

Looking up, Mitch said, "No."

"Mitch, listen to me, you have to turn over the book, and the woman—"

"No!"

"For heaven's sake, she's possibly a prostitute, possibly a murderer, quite possibly both! Even if she isn't, she's up to her neck in this mess!"

Mitch exploded with a blast that rocked the room. "Dammit, no! And get off my back!"

It was the first time that, as friends, angry words had ever been exchanged between the two men. Mitch instantly regretted his outburst.

"I'm sorry," he said, then added, "You of all people should know that things aren't always what they appear to be. It looked as though you were a murderer, too—even a jury found you guilty—but you were innocent."

"I won't argue with that, but it doesn't change the fact that, given the information you have, you could be charged with a crime if you don't turn it over to the police."

"No. At least, not yet."

Will had opened his mouth to further plead his case when the agency door was suddenly thrown open. Glancing upward, Mitch expected to see the woman who was the subject of their discussion. He did not expect to see Kelly. Certainly, not a Kelly whose face was flushed, whose eyes were bright, with excitement. She was so animated that her few freckles fairly threatened to jump right off her nose. The look on Will's face said that she'd taken him totally by surprise, too.

Will pushed himself to his feet. "Are you all right?"

Kelly, her eyes flashing like green fire, ignored her husband's question. "You're not going to believe this," she said, addressing her remarks to both men. "I mean, even I don't believe it, and I told you she looked familiar."

"What are you talking about?" Will asked.

"I'm talking about the identity of our mystery lady."

This got Mitch's attention—in a big way. "You know who she is?"

In answer to his question, Kelly set down her huge purse, rummaged through it and pulled out a magazine. With a deft flick of her wrist, she tossed the magazine onto the desk. In an action that was pure reflex, Mitch looked down at the magazine's cover. A woman, a beautiful woman, was pictured there. The woman had blond hair and steel-gray eyes. Familiar blond hair. Familiar gray eyes. Mitch looked up at Kelly, his silence, his stunned expression demanding an explanation.

"I was out at the marina, right? I was doing this fashion layout with the boats and yachts in the background—the magazine wanted black-and-white photos with moonlight and all that waterfront jazz—anyway, I had just finished shooting a roll of film. I had one other model to go, but she was giving the hairdresser fits, something about her bangs being too long—" as she spoke, Kelly brushed aside a flame-red curl that had squiggled into her eye "—so, I sat down to wait for Miss Prima Donna." Kelly patted her stomach and smiled. "Junior was getting heavy. Anyway, I sat down and there was this magazine on the chair beside me. One of the models had brought it with her. I picked up the magazine and bam, there she was! I couldn't believe it. But then, I could believe it, because I said all along that she looked familiar."

A self-satisfied Kelly looked at the two men, her expression saying, "Well, guys, what do you think?"

Up until this moment, Will had only viewed the cover from an upside-down position. He righted the magazine. "You're right. It's her."

"Of course it's her," Kelly retorted, her sense of accomplishment growing by the second. "I'm surprised I didn't recognize her immediately, but, believe me, makeup can make a big difference to the way a woman looks. And sometimes they just photograph differently than they look in the flesh."

Mitch looked at Will; Will looked at Mitch. Both men looked at Kelly and asked in tandem, "Who is she?"

Disbelief streaked across Kelly's face. "You don't know who she is?"

"No," both men answered again.

"Geez, guys! This—" Kelly thumped the magazine with the backs of her fingers "—is Jennifer Brooks."

Once more, Mitch glanced at Will; once more, Will glanced at Mitch. Once more, both men glanced at Kelly and asked in tandem, "Who's Jennifer Brooks?"

"Good grief!" Kelly cried. "She's been on the cover of dozens of fashion magazines."

"I don't read many fashion magazines," Will said.

"She's a model?" Mitch asked, needing confirmation. In light of the conversation he and Will had been having, the information that Kelly had just introduced didn't compute. And if what she said was true, how did it alter the facts? Was this Jennifer Brooks a murderer? And what was she doing with a book containing the names of prostitutes?

"Yes, she's a model," Kelly assured him. "I wouldn't say she's the most famous model in the world, but she's definitely up-and-coming. No wonder she knew exactly how tall she was. Any model does."

Mitch turned the magazine back so that he could take a closer look at the picture splashed across the cover. The woman wore a white one-piece swimsuit cut high on the thighs—guaranteed to stop any man's heart in midbeat. Quietly, Mitch let the reality of the woman's identity sink in. A strange giddiness began to capture his thinking. The world no longer seemed real, but rather surreal. Suddenly, he felt like laughing.

It was Will's laughter that ultimately filled the silence. Kelly simply looked at her husband as if he'd lost his mind.

"We thought she was a call girl," he told his wife.

"You thought she was a what?"

"A call girl. This—" Will picked up the little black book "—contains the names of call girls. Or, at least, it most probably does. For sure, it contains the name, address and phone number of one."

"Are you serious?" Kelly asked, easing to the side of the desk and flipping through the book. She took in everything from the decoded names to the word *Chelsea* scratched across the page. "What's this Chelsea?"

"No idea," her husband supplied.

"These are really the names of call girls?" she asked.

"Possibly. Probably," Will said.

"What was Jennifer doing with the book?" Kelly asked.

"Excellent question," Mitch said, the surreal feeling still tugging at him.

Along with everything else, the name *Jennifer* seemed strange, foreign, as though it belonged to anyone but the woman upstairs. Would she be as stunned as he to discover who she was? On the one hand, he couldn't wait to tell her, while, on the other hand, he hesitated to. Would this knowledge jar her memory? Would she remember and return to her old, familiar world? A world that didn't include him?

As Mitch voiced these questions in his head, he heard Will say, "We thought that possibly she'd managed to get the book from John Yen Chang."

It was Kelly's silence that first alerted Mitch to the fact that something was wrong. He glanced up to find her looking directly at him. He saw an apology deep in her eyes. "I'm sorry," she said, "but this is where things get a little dicey, not to mention a whole lot coincidental."

Mitch knew intuitively that he wasn't going to like what she said next.

"Jennifer Brooks is her professional name." A pause, a hesitation, Mitch's missed heartbeat. "Her married name is Mrs. John Yen Chang."

CHAPTER NINE

IN THE END, Mitch told his client nothing, partly because she was sound asleep when he returned to the apartment, partly because he just didn't have the guts for it. Not tonight. Tomorrow, he promised himself. Tomorrow when his mind wasn't a jumble. Tomorrow when he'd know what to say.

If sleep had been elusive the night before, it was nonexistent on this night. Mitch didn't even bother to lie down. He simply sat on the sofa with his head buried in his hands. With all the thoughts racing around in his head, he wasn't certain it wouldn't spin entirely off his shoulders if he didn't hang on to it. His thoughts, all phrased in the form of questions, ran the gamut. Was it possible that Kelly had been wrong about his client's personal life? And, if the woman asleep in his bed was Mrs. John Yen Chang, didn't it constitute the most ironic coincidence that the wife of his archenemy would have chosen to come to him out of all the private investigators in the city?

In regard to the first question, if Kelly was mistaken, she was mistaken on a grand scale. She said that it was common knowledge that Jennifer Brooks was married to John Yen Chang, and had been for two or three years. According to Kelly, photographs of the stunning couple appeared occasionally in the social pages of the newspaper. Apparently, these were often in regard to some social function being sponsored by the local Asian American Art Museum, to which John Yen Chang was a frequent and generous contributor. His client's—he still couldn't think of her by name—knowledge of Asian artifacts suddenly made sense.

What didn't make sense was why he himself hadn't recognized his client, or at least, hadn't thought she looked familiar. Surely he'd seen newspaper photographs of the couple. And why, after investigating Chang with what could only be called an obsession, hadn't he remembered that the man was married to a model? He guessed that the answer to that question might lie in the word *obsession*. He'd been so obsessed with Chang that there had been little room for anyone else. Ironically, right this moment, Chang's wife was of far more interest to him. What *were* the chances of her selecting his agency? He didn't know.

But, damn, he knew he needed a drink!

By morning, Mitch had hatched an idea. Its basis, he knew, might be rooted in cowardice—the idea *did* delay his telling his client anything—but, on the other hand, it would allow her to possibly remember something on her own. Surely that was a more gentle way to allow her memory to return. The plan had one other advantage, an advantage that was important to him personally. It provided an opportunity for someone to recognize her, particularly as the wife of John Yen Chang. Surely, if she was as active with the museum as Kelly suggested, someone there would know her.

"You've learned something, haven't you?" his houseguest asked over a breakfast that neither appeared too interested in.

Mitch looked up from his uneaten cereal, wondering if the long, thick silences had alerted her that something wasn't quite right. And just how much should he tell her? Should he lie entirely or perhaps settle for a half-truth? He decided on a half truth.

"I may have a lead."

She laid down her spoon. "What kind of lead?"

"I, uh, I'd rather not say," he hedged, adding, "But I'd like to take you somewhere, to see if you remember anything."

Disappointment flitted across her face. "You can't tell me more?"

"I'd rather not."

The woman didn't argue. Instead, she asked, "When can we go?"

By midmorning, Mitch's car was slogging its way across the city. As had happened before, the red light indicating engine problems flashed on, but, after a few taxing minutes, it went off and stayed off for the remainder of the drive.

To her credit, the woman didn't ask where he was taking her. Under the same set of circumstances, Mitch wasn't so sure that he himself could have displayed such discipline. He couldn't help but admire her composure. As for his own composure...well, he felt as if a noose had been placed around his neck, and he was just waiting for someone to tighten the rope.

His client continued to say nothing as he parked the car, walked to the passenger door and helped her out. She did glance around her. At the sight of the Asian American Art Museum, she looked up at Mitch, though, again, she said nothing. She simply allowed him to usher her forward and toward the series of steps leading to the building. In seconds, they passed through the door and into the silent, dark, near-fortresslike interior of the museum. The musty, cloying fragrance of antiquity clawed at the air.

The woman stopped.

Mitch halted alongside her, gave her a few seconds to look around, then asked, "Does this look familiar?"

"I—I don't know. For a moment I thought..." Her voice trailed off as she did a complete circle, thoroughly taking in the entryway and all she could see from where she stood.

"You thought what?"

"That I might have been here before." Before Mitch could ask anything more, she asked, "Have I been here before?"

"There's a possibility that you have been," he answered, trying to keep the disappointment from his voice.

If truth be told, he'd wanted Kelly to be wrong. He didn't want this woman to be married to anyone, certainly not to John Yen Chang. He'd prefer her to be married to the devil. Remembering one of the reasons he'd brought her here—namely, to see if anyone recognized her—he looked around for museum staff. He saw no one. He allowed his stomach to uncoil a little, but only a little. He had to find someone to confront before he left. Until then, he'd give the surroundings a chance to work on his client's memory.

"C'mon," he said, "let's look around."

Under other circumstances, Mitch would have found the exhibition fascinating. The museum consisted of five cavernous rooms, which displayed everything from framed art to statuary, from pottery to bronzes. One whole room was devoted to the latter. For the most part, the bronze collection, housed within glass cabinets, appeared to compromise containers of some sort.

"Ritual bronzes," his companion said.

Mitch looked over at the woman who was fast becoming one of the world's top models. He knew that she was extraordinarily beautiful. Even in the simple pair of jeans she now wore, she looked like a million bucks. Her hands planted against the glass, she was studying the bronze display, as though mesmerized by it.

"Bronzes have been cast in China for about three thousand five hundred years, but the Bronze Age was roughly from about 4000-3000 B.C. Most bronzes from this period are ritual vessels. If you look closely at them, you can often find a name inscribed. This vessel was devoted to the worship of an ancestor, which was usually the inscribed name. Sometimes, though," she continued, as though conducting a tour through the museum, "the vessel simply commemorated an important event in the life of the owner. And there were other vessels meant to serve only as heirlooms. These often have inscriptions which end with 'Let sons and grandsons for a myriad years cherish and use.'"

She glanced over at Mitch.

"How do I know this?" she asked.

"Let's look around a bit more and then we'll talk."

"Mitchell, if you know something, please tell me." Her gaze, fastened to his, pleaded with him.

God, how did he tell her that she might be married to a scumbucket? Surely Kelly was wrong. Why would a woman with sensitivity marry a man without an ounce of it?

"Trust me," he begged, his own voice barely more than a ragged whisper.

Without realizing what he was doing, he reached for her hand. He squeezed it reassuringly, taking as much strength as he gave. Somehow, some way, though he would have vowed that neither had intended for it to happen, their fingers entwined. Slowly. Sexily. In that moment, the world receded. There was only now. There was only the two of them. There was only the shattering feeling that she couldn't belong to another man when she belonged to him. Mitch was forced to accept the fact that Susan Simpson and Will were right: He was in over his head. Way over his head. Unless he was sadly mistaken, he was in love with this woman.

Releasing her hand, he said so hoarsely that the sound ricocheted bulletlike off the cool, stone walls, "C'mon."

Again, Mitch looked for someone, anyone, who worked at the museum. For the first time, he noticed a desk located against a far wall. A woman, who he was positive hadn't been there before, now sat at the desk.

"Come with me," Mitch said to the woman beside him. His stomach tightened again, leaving him to feel as if he'd swallowed a shot-put ball. "Why?" she asked, trailing along at his side.

"I want to ask about something."

In seconds, they stood before the desk. The woman, about thirty-five and academic-looking in her black-framed glasses, glanced up from the book she was reading. Not surprisingly, the book was on the subject of Oriental art. Lucy Harrison, whose name was printed on the identification tag, smiled.

"May I help you?"

A swarm of butterflies fluttered through Mitch's stomach. "We—" he deliberately motioned to his client, forcing Lucy Harrison to take a look at her "—were wondering if the museum has any Dogs of Fo?"

"We certainly do," Lucy said, pushing back from the desk and rising. "In fact, we have one of the most extensive collections in the United States." As she spoke, she started off toward one of the rooms that Mitch and his client had yet to look through. "Do you have any particular period in mind?"

"Ah, no," Mitch said, his butterflies easing up now that the woman clearly didn't recognize his client. He forced himself to admit, however, that it didn't necessarily prove anything. The fact that her husband generously donated to a museum and attended gala benefits for that museum didn't mean that she'd be recognized by one and all at said museum. Even so, Mitch couldn't help feeling marginally relieved. "Just show us anything."

The blonde looked up at him as if to say, *Why are we looking at Fo Dogs?*

His look replied, *Humor me.*

As it turned out, the museum did have quite an impressive collection of Buddhist lions, some fifty to sixty, Mitch would have guessed. The museum worker apparently took her job seriously, for, instead of leaving them to browse on their own, she said, "Let me point out some of the more important pieces."

Mitch watched the blonde's reaction as she stepped amid the statuary. For the tiniest of heartbeats, she hesitated, then, with a quick look up at Mitch, she fell in behind the woman.

"Does this look familiar?" he whispered.

"I don't know," the blonde answered back.

"This Fo Dog," said the guide, "is sculpted from amazonite, which is a green microcline. The piece is from the Shang Dynasty. It's unusual because of the complexity and beauty of the carvings here in the base." As the woman talked, she pointed to the intricate designs. They were, indeed, complex and beautiful.

Mitch could have sworn that his client shuddered.

"Okay?" he asked.

"Yes," she answered, though Mitch thought it telling that a dappling of perspiration had formed above her upper lip. While it wasn't cold in the museum, it wasn't hot, either.

"Over here we have a beautiful white marble dog also from the Shang Dynasty."

When the blonde saw the dog, she said, "The Chou Dynasty."

Lucy looked a little taken aback. "I believe the card says Shang Dynasty." As she spoke, she glanced down at the recorded information and said, "You're right. It is from the Chou period." The woman smiled sheepishly. "To be honest, bronzes are my specialty, and I haven't been here at the museum long enough to learn more than just the rudimentary facts about these other areas of Chinese art."

Mitch's butterflies went into flight again. "How long have you been here?"

"Less than a month. I just graduated from UCLA."

Less than a month? Mitch swore silently.

"I have been here long enough to know that you must see one other Dog of Fo. This one is the museum's pride and joy. It's one of a matched pair, donated to the museum just this past year. The other sculpture is in the home of the donor, who, incidentally, lives right here in San Francisco. The dog is carved out of one of the most flawless pieces of jade ever mined. This work of art is priceless." Lucy stopped, then, with a theatrical flourish, presented what she obviously thought to be the pièce de résistance among Fo Dogs.

A sharp intake of air sliced through the silence. Mitch glanced over at the woman who only seconds before had been advancing to his side. She now stood back, as though afraid to step forward. Her breath came unevenly, and, unbelievably, she had turned as white as the marble statue they'd just viewed.

"What is it?" Mitch asked.

The woman said nothing. Instead, she took another step backward. That was followed by yet another.

Mitch grabbed her by the shoulders, forcing her eyes, her frightened eyes, to meet his. "What is it?"

"That's it," she whispered. "That's the one I saw on the floor beside the..." She trailed off, as though unable to make herself finish the damning statement. With that, she turned and walked briskly toward the door.

"Hey, wait!" Mitch called out as he started after her.

Lucy Harrison looked totally perplexed.

If the blonde even heard him calling her, she responded in no way, except perhaps to hasten toward the door. So intent was she on just getting out of the room, away from the dog, that she didn't even see the person stepping through the doorway. Like trains traveling at high speed, the two women collided. The blonde gasped. The other woman apologized.

"I'm so sorry. I didn't see—" The woman, dressed in a red suit and wearing a name tag that identified her as employed by the museum, looked at the individual she'd almost knocked to the floor. Disbelievingly looked at her. "Mrs. Chang, I'm so sorry. I didn't see you."

Mrs. Chang just looked at the woman in red.

"How are you feeling? Your husband said that you'd been ill." The woman smiled. "We've missed your volunteering around here."

Mrs. Chang continued to look at the woman in red. Mitch, who'd heard the exchange, looked at his client. His stomach, his heart, felt as though they'd been gutted.

"Excuse me," the blonde said softly, then brushed past the employee standing in the doorway.

Now it was the woman in red's turn to look perplexed. She watched as the other woman disappeared into the hallway and all but ran for the building's entryway.

Without considering how bizarre his own behavior might appear, Mitch, too, raced out of the doorway, following his client.

"Wait!" he cried.

The woman only hastened her steps. She was now practically running; her sneakers thudded loudly against the floor.

"Jennifer, wait!" He heard himself using the name that Kelly was so certain belonged to his client. He didn't doubt now that it did, just as he didn't doubt that this woman was married to John Yen Chang. He, however, couldn't bring himself to use her married name. He doubted that he ever would.

The woman named Jennifer disappeared through the doorway. Seconds later, Mitch did the same. He half expected her to be gone, but she wasn't. She stood with her face turned upward, as though trying to drink in enough air to satisfy her breathlessness.

Moving to her side, he asked, "Are you all right?"

She looked over at him, her steel-gray eyes meeting his squarely. Instead of answering his question, however, she said simply, painfully, "You set me up."

Mitch didn't deny the obvious, though he might have chosen less condemning words. "I had to see if you recognized anything. I had to see if anyone recognized you."

"Congratulations," she said, adding, "You obviously succeeded."

"WE HAVE TO TALK."

On the drive back to his apartment, neither Mitch nor his passenger had said a word. Mitch had wanted to scream, to shout, "Has your memory returned?" but, when mile after mile had passed in silence, it became easier to postpone the inevitable. The ride home had been very much like the last days of summer. One simply enjoyed what was so fleetingly passing, because one knew that autumn, prelude to grim winter, lay just around the corner. As he stepped into his bedroom and observed his client sitting so regally on the edge of the bed, Mitch knew that summer was gone. Forever.

At his words, the woman glanced up at Mitch. She looked as though she, too, understood that the time had come, that there could be no more postponing of the discussion that had to take place.

"Tell me what you remember," Mitch demanded.

As he spoke, he laid the fashion magazine that bore the cover photograph of Jennifer Brooks on the dresser. He had gone downstairs to his office for both the magazine and the black book. This latter he placed alongside the fashion magazine. If his client noticed either, it didn't register in her expression. To be truthful, Mitch didn't think that she was noticing much of anything, but rather seemed to be in a lifeless stupor. Mitch reminded himself that the outing must surely have been shocking for her.

In answer to his question, she said, in a tone curiously even and controlled considering the emotional subject, "I remember the Fo Dog. It was the exact Fo Dog that I saw lying on the floor by the man's body."

"How do you know it was the exact Fo Dog? You said yourself that they were commonplace."

"Believe me, I know it's the same. It's a flawless piece of jade. No other jade Fo Dog is exactly that shade of apple-green."

Willing to accept that she knew what she was talking about, Mitch broached his next questions carefully. "Have you remembered anything more about where you saw the Fo Dog? Have you remembered the location of the home with the gilt-edged white staircase?''

''No.'' Flat. Noncommittal. With obviously nothing to follow.

''The Fo Dog is all you remember?''

''I sort of remember the museum. It *felt* as if I'd been there before. It would explain my knowledge of Oriental art.''

''And you remember nothing more?''

For seconds she didn't reply, then, casting her eyes downward, she said, ''I remember nothing else.''

Mitch thought it odd that a woman who, up until this moment had been uncommonly forthright, suddenly chose not to meet his eyes. But then, he was probably reading something into nothing.

Surprisingly, it was the woman who spoke next. ''You called me Jennifer. The woman at the museum called me Mrs. Chang. Is my name Jennifer Chang?''

This was the part he didn't want to get into, not so much for her sake as for his. He sighed. ''From the beginning, Kelly thought you looked familiar. You're a fashion model—apparently, a pretty well-known fashion model.'' He nodded toward the dresser. ''She found that magazine with you on the cover.''

The blonde looked over at the dresser, but made no move toward the magazine. Again, Mitch thought her action strange. Under the circumstances, what woman could have resisted taking a look at herself?

Instead, she asked, again atonally, as though inquiring about nothing more than the weather, ''And I'm married to someone named Chang?''

Even if she could be unemotional about the question, there was no way that Mitch could be about the answer. As always at the mention of that name, he felt as if his insides had suddenly gone to war.

"Yeah, John Yen Chang."

"You know him." It was a statement, not a question.

"I know of him."

"You don't like him." Again, it was a statement.

Mitch pulled no punches. "No, I don't."

"Why?"

"I, the police, have reason to believe that he's a gangster, involved primarily in racketeering and prostitution."

To the woman's credit, this announcement took its toll. He noted that she fitted one hand into the other. He wondered if she'd begun to tremble. He wanted to reach out and take her hands in his, to steady them, but he couldn't, wouldn't, didn't dare. He forced himself to focus on the hard cold subject presently under discussion.

He walked toward the dresser, picked up the little black book and announced, "There's a good chance that this contains the names of high-class call girls here in the city. At least one of them has been arrested for prostitution. Though she denies it, a listing of her calls indicates that she phoned John Yen Chang. Your husband," he added, needing to remind himself of this woman's connection with the infamous Eurasian.

"My, God," she whispered, obviously stricken with this information. She stood and walked to the window. Outside, the afternoon sun shone cheerfully, mockingly.

"Jennifer?" Mitch spoke softly, quietly. He'd surprised himself by using her name. It sounded sweet on his tongue, as sweet as the richest candy.

She turned toward him, their gazes meeting and holding.

"You remember nothing of this man?" *Like why in hell you married him,* Mitch wanted to ask, but didn't. He wanted to tell her that he believed this man was responsible for his having lost his job, but he didn't, maybe because he couldn't prove it, maybe because he didn't want to add to this woman's burden.

Again, she lowered her gaze before answering. "No."

Mitch wished that she'd look him in the eye. It wasn't like her not to.

"What is—" she hesitated, then proceeded "—my husband's connection with the museum?"

"He's a patron. I suspect that it was he who donated the companion Fo Dog. The other he obviously kept for himself. Apparently, it was the one used to murder the unknown man."

Mitch expected her to ask two questions: Was the dead man her husband and was she responsible for his death? She asked neither, however, leaving Mitch baffled.

He decided to ask one other question. "You still don't remember anything about someone named Emily?"

"No," Jennifer answered quickly.

Mitch noticed that she seemed agitated again. For the first time, she even appeared close to tears. As if to stem them, she walked to the dresser and picked up the fashion magazine. She gazed down at her image, tracing it with her fingertips, as though to absorb its reality.

Her only comment was, "Maybe that's why my feet weren't too blistered. I'm used to standing on them for long hours."

"That makes sense," Mitch agreed, though it still didn't explain how her nails had survived intact. He pushed the thought aside, not certain now any more than the first time it had occurred to him that the detail had any relevance. Just the way he wasn't certain that his wanting her to look him in the eye made sense when she denied remembering anything. He knew only that he wanted to see her eyes when she made the denial.

He stepped behind her, so near her that his thighs brushed against the backs of hers. The contact shortened both their breaths and forced her eyes to meet his in the smoky, cracked mirror. Each recalled a kiss, a night during which he'd simply held her until the first light of dawn had filtered through the slanted slats of the blinds.

Abruptly, the blonde's eyes misted and her voice was husky when she said, "Whatever happens from this point on, please believe that I never meant to hurt you."

If Mitch thought the comment a bit unusual, he nevertheless did believe her. He saw the truth in her eyes. He also felt her trembling. God, he wanted to take her in his arms!

"Jennifer..." he whispered, uncertain what he wanted to say. It didn't matter, because she halted him.

"Please," she whispered, "give me some time alone. I need to decide what I'm going to do."

He nodded, but, even as he did, he wondered what demon was driving him. Despite the fact that he'd already asked her variations of this question twice already, he needed to ask it one more time.

"You're sure you don't remember anything?"

There was the briefest of hesitations, the briefest fluttering of her eyelashes, before she began to lower her head.

"No," Mitch said, quietly, but firmly. "Look me in the eye."

To her credit, Jennifer did as he'd asked her. Raising her head, seeking him out in the mirror, she leveled her metallic-gray eyes on his.

"I remember nothing," she said.

The cracked mirror distorted her image, leaving the impression that she had become two women. Mitch thought the dual portrait appropriate. On one side he saw a sweet, sensitive woman, a woman who'd believed in him, a woman who'd kissed him passionately, tenderly, a woman who had meant it when she'd said she hadn't intended to hurt him. The other image, ironically darker because of the placement of the room's shadows, belonged to the wife of John Yen Chang. It was this image that had just told him she remembered nothing. It was this image that had just lied to him. On that, Mitch would have staked his life.

JENNIFER LISTENED to the silence swelling around her. In the distance, she could hear Mitchell downstairs in his office. She heard the creaking of his chair and imagined him flopping down in it and leaning back.

He'd reach for a sucker, a detective book and then discard both in a flash. The picture in her mind should have been a humorous one, but it didn't bring even a hint of a smile. Instead, she reached for the telephone sitting on the coffee table. Without hesitation, she dialed the number that was heart-familiar.

The call went pretty much as she'd expected. Hanging up the receiver, she moved quickly—to the bedroom for her purse, then back to the living room to place a second call for a cab. She asked that the cabdriver pick her up at the corner. Like a woman on a mission, she walked to the doorway. Only then did she pause. She took one last look at the modest apartment that had been her home for almost two weeks. A surfeit of emotions rushed through her, chief of which was self-loathing. With one mirthless, rueful smile, she was gone, silently skulking down the stairway like the liar she was.

WITH A FRUSTRATED SIGH, Mitch tossed—no, slammed down—the unopened detective book. Out of nothing more than habit, he grabbed a sucker, unwrapped it and jammed it into his mouth. Before his taste buds had even had a chance to acknowledge the flavor, he whipped the lollipop from between his lips and abandoned it.

Dammit, she had lied to him!

Without question, she remembered more than she'd admitted. That was why she hadn't been eager to look at the photograph of herself. That was why she hadn't asked if it was her husband that had been killed, and if she'd done it. She'd remembered everything. But why had she chosen to lie? Why had she continued to play the charade by asking questions she thought appropriate? Those were the questions he ought to march upstairs and ask her. No, he ought to do more than ask her. He ought to demand answers. Right here. Right now.

Another sigh, this one fractured, filled the silence. He needed the answers to more than those questions, however. In fact, he needed answers to a whole slew of them, chief among which was the one question that troubled him most of all: Why had she chosen him out of all the detectives in the city? Had it truly been coincidence, or had it been a carefully calculated choice? And if it had been the latter, why? What was her game? What was Chang's game? What if the whole amnesia thing had been nothing more than an elaborate ruse? Then again, why go to all the trouble?

Dammit, he had to have answers!

He glanced at his watch. It had been an hour since he'd spoken with her, an hour since she'd politely thrown him out of his own apartment. An hour was enough, he decided. An hour was plenty of time to live in hell. An hour... He stopped, suddenly wondering if her asking to be alone was yet another part of the possible game she was playing. If so...

Mitch pushed himself from the chair with such force that he sent it rocking on its rusty hinges. They seemed to shout, "Hurry, hurry!" Rushing out the door, he took the steps to the apartment two at a time. He hit the door with such speed that he thought he actually heard the wood moan. But that was all he heard. Just as he knew he would. Standing in the middle of his apartment, he didn't even bother to call out her name. He knew she wouldn't answer. He knew she was gone.

Even so, a glimmer of hope forced him to walk to the bedroom. The room's emptiness snuffed out the glimmer. He crossed to the closet, only to find, surprisingly, that she'd left the black dress behind, and the black satin shoes. This raised an interesting question: What about the leather-bound notebook? He quickly looked toward the dresser. There, exactly where he'd left it, was the black book. Had she left it behind on purpose, or had she simply forgotten it in her haste?

One other question coiled serpentlike in his mind: Where was she now? The question was easy enough to answer, however. Ten to one, she'd returned to the sonofabitch she called her husband.

"THERE," JENNIFER SAID, directing the cabdriver to the palatial home discreetly tucked away in the cul-de-sac. In the background, brown- and mauve-colored hills rose in tribute to the canyon that dived off into a majestic, tree-crowded nothingness.

It was just as she remembered, she thought, taking in the perfectly sculpted gardens, the soldierlike figurines, bronze and fiercely militant, that guarded the doorway, the terrazzo steps that gracefully fell away to a terrace in the back. At the sight of the steps, Jennifer touched her head. The injury was healing, though it was still tender to the touch. Tender to the touch. Lots of things were tender to the touch, notably her emotions.

"That'll be $26.75, ma'am."

The cabdriver's announcement brought Jennifer back to the present. "I'll have to get the money from inside," she said, opening the cab door.

"Sure," the cabby said, killing the car's engine and resting his tattooed arm in the open window.

As Jennifer made her way up the walk and to the front door, a breeze whispered around her, singing its euphonious song. "Where have you been?" it crooned.

To hell and back, she answered silently.

Her hand on the doorknob, she turned it and stepped inside the mansion. It, too, was exactly as she remembered. Though unlit, a huge chandelier hung from an exquisitely vaulted ceiling. The afternoon sun peered through a skylight, making the chandelier's crystal sparkle like a psychedelic prism. The color crimson splashed across the imported carpet, dulling the pink-flowered pattern. It reminded Jennifer of the last time she'd stood in this foyer. Red had covered the floor then, too, the red of newly spilled blood. At this remembrance, she glanced toward the long antique table hugging the wall. The priceless jade Fo Dog, an exact match to the one she'd seen in the museum only hours before, sat quietly, innocently in place. The telltale blood had been wiped from it.

Jennifer wasn't quite certain what caught her attention, a sound or maybe the absence of sound. Whatever, her gaze began to travel up the gilt-edged white staircase. Slowly, her gaze swept upward. It stopped short when it reached the man standing midway on the stairs, his hand casually holding on to the delicate railing.

With Oriental features, softened by the genes of his American mother, he was quite literally one of the most handsome men Jennifer had ever seen. His prematurely silver hair, contrasted with his midnight-dark eyes, gave him a wickedly sinful look, a look that never failed to work its magic on the female of the species. He oozed magnetism, strength, sex. The smile he now bestowed upon Jennifer was the single one reason she'd fallen in love with him.

"Welcome home, darling," her husband said. "I've missed you."

CHAPTER TEN

MITCH STARED at the unopened bottle of one-hundred-proof Scotch sitting on his desk. Ever since he'd bought it, right after an Alcoholics Anonymous meeting—he guessed that meeting could be called a failure—the intoxicating contents had beckoned to him.

C'mon, take just one swallow, the dark amber liquid taunted him. *You deserve it, buddy. After all, you've been had. With a capital H.*

"Yeah," Mitch said, studying the bottle as though it were a beautiful, shapely woman. One kiss from her, and he'd be well on his way to forgetting what a fool he'd been.

And he had been a fool. The more he thought about it—and think about it was all he'd done—the more he was certain that he'd been set up. The amnesia had been only an elaborate charade, which would explain certain inconsistencies in her story that had nagged him from the beginning, inconsistencies like fingernails that hadn't been broken, inconsistencies like the absence of a lot of blisters on her feet. She'd explained that one away by suggesting that, as a model, she was accustomed to standing for long hours. Well, there was probably some truth to that, but might it not also be true that she'd been dropped off near his office? Mitch frowned. Of course, if that was true, why would she have had *any* blisters?

Neither was there any denying that she had had a goose egg on her head. Even a doctor had said that she'd been lucky the injury hadn't been nearer her temple. *So what are you suggesting, Brody? That her husband conked her on the head to make it look like the real thing?* Had he then put a run in her stockings and scuffed up her shoe? Had he tossed her out, after making her walk around to get a few blisters, telling her to give the performance of her life?

Put that way, his doubts sounded nothing short of ridiculous, especially the part about her performance. If she'd been acting, it was the best damned job he'd ever seen. Even though he couldn't prove that her dreams had been genuine, even though he couldn't prove that the spaghetti sauce episode and the hypnosis session hadn't been faked, he would have bet his life at the time of each incident that her reactions had been authentic. Her fear had seemed as real as any he'd ever seen. And there was no question whatsoever that she was afraid of someone. Even Kelly had commented on how she spent her time looking over her shoulder. And then there was her kiss... The memory of soft lips moving seductively on his drifted sweetly to mind, a memory far more intoxicating than all the liquor ever distilled. No, no one would ever convince him that her kiss hadn't been the real thing.

So, was it or wasn't it a charade?

Hell if he knew! Just about the time he was ready to concede that it was, he decided that there was no way it could be. This decision was reinforced by his inability to answer one question: If it had been a charade, what had been its purpose? She hadn't even taken the incriminating address book with her, to say nothing of the diamond earrings that had to be worth a small fortune. But she had lied to him at the end, even if he could have sworn that she hadn't been lying all along.

"Whatever happens from this point on, please believe that I never meant to hurt you."

He had believed that, then and now, which was just one more confusing element amidst so many.

Have a drink of me and forget the confusion, the sirenlike whiskey tempted.

Mitch picked up the bottle, unscrewed the cap and brought the exquisite temptation to his nose. He inhaled. A raw tingling burned its way though his nostrils. Mitch imagined a swallow scorching a silken path down his throat and landing, like a fiery ball of flame, in his belly. He didn't like the taste of liquor. Never had. What he liked was the shadowy oblivion that resulted from downing the contents of several shot glasses. There was a blessed peace in those murky shadows, if only for a little while.

Had it been for this same escape from reality that his father had drunk? But what had been so terrible that his father had had to escape? A loving wife? An adoring son? On the surface of things, he had had no good earthly reason to keep turning to the bottle. And yet he had. Over and over, always with the solemn, tear-stained promise that it wouldn't happen again. Mitch had loved his father and had hated him. He'd been ashamed of him and proud of him. Mostly, though, he just hadn't understood him.

That is, until the day he'd buried him. On that morose morning, with friends and family gathered around, all lamenting how Chester Brody had drunk himself to death, Mitch had learned for the first time that his father had never wanted to sell insurance, which, ironically, was something he'd excelled at doing. In fact, he'd loathed being a salesman, yet, because he'd considered himself a simple man, he had lacked the courage to try anything else. In short, Chester Brody had betrayed himself.

Betrayal, self-imposed or inflicted by others, was an excellent reason to drink, Mitch concluded as the whiskey's fragrance caressed him with its simple but sure sensuality. Yeah, he thought, wanting to succumb to its allure, it was just about the best reason he could think of.

"C'mon," the Scotch teased. *"Erase her from your mind. Forget for a while that she lied to you. Forget for a while that she might have been lying to you all along. Forget that she belongs to another man, and forget that that man is John Yen Chang."*

God, he wanted a swallow! What would be the harm in one? Only one?

The phone rang.

Guiltily, Mitch thrust these traitorous thoughts aside. Had he lost his mind completely? He'd worked so hard to stay sober. How could he even consider taking another drink?

The phone pealed again.

Like a man who'd just been in battle and had experienced a close call, Mitch's hand began to tremble. With that trembling hand, he set the bottle on the desk and reached for the telephone.

"Hello?"

"Thank goodness you're home," Kelly started in without preamble. "I tried earlier, but realized that this was the night for AA. I thought maybe Jennifer would answer but when she didn't, I was glad. I'm not certain what this means, if anything, but—"

"Honey, get on with it," Will said, obviously from an extension.

"Okay, okay!" his wife said, and Mitch could envision her swiping back red rebel curls from her forehead. His own forehead was damp with newly formed perspiration. "Remember that I had that nighttime shoot out at the marina?"

"Yeah," Mitch said, wondering where this conversation was going. Wherever it was headed, Kelly was excited about it. "Wednesday night, wasn't it?" *The night I found out Jennifer's identity, the night the world spun off its axis.*

"Right," Kelly replied. "Anyway, I just developed the film and guess what I discovered." Without giving Mitch a chance to answer, she rushed on with, "There were sailboats and yachts moored to the pier. We deliberately chose the spot because of them. Well, one of the yachts was really nice, so I used it in several of the photographs. Guess what the name of it was."

"Tell him, honey."

"Chelsea," she blurted out, adding, "Now, I know the name isn't that unusual, but then again, it's not plastered on everything, either."

"Wasn't that the name in the book?" Will asked.

"Yeah," Mitch replied, his interest suddenly peaked.

"That's not the best part," Kelly said. "Wait until you hear whose name it's registered in."

"Tell him, honey."

Kelly didn't answer immediately, however.

"Will called the Bureau of Statistics, or whatever that department is called that has registration records on seacraft. Anyway, it was after six o'clock when he called and, wouldn't you know it, it was closed for the day. We didn't want to wait until tomorrow to find out, so we went down to the dock and started asking around. It took us almost two hours, but we found someone who knew who the yacht belonged to."

"Tell him, honey."

"This is the weird part," Kelly said.

Mitch's patience was wearing thin. "Just tell me."

"Yeah, just tell him, honey."

"Okay, you two. That's what I'm trying to do. Anyway, the yacht is registered to...are you ready for this?" Mitch wanted to scream. "The yacht belongs—belonged—to Richard Rhincuso."

There was dead silence at Mitch's end. He was recalling the footage he'd seen on television regarding the city councilman's funeral, a funeral attended by the chief of police. Curiously, he'd remembered that same footage when viewing the word *Chelsea* scrawled in the black book. Had they shown the councilman's yacht? They must have. Why else would he have recalled that footage at that moment?

"Hey, are you there?" Kelly asked.

"Yeah," Mitch answered, trailing his fingers through his hair, "I'm here."

"What do you think?" Will asked.

"I don't know," Mitch answered. "Rhincuso's body was never found, was it?"

"No," Will answered.

"Do you think that the man Jennifer killed, or saw killed, was Rhincuso?" Kelly asked. "I mean, I know it's reaching, but, if the *Chelsea* in the book is Rhincuso's yacht, then there is a connection to Jennifer—and to John Yen Chang."

"Maybe Rhincuso was on the take," Will offered. "He wouldn't be the first politician to have gone bad. In fact, we helped put one away. Remember?"

Mitch did, indeed, remember Rodriqué Echieverra, the politician that wanted to be president of Mexico, the man who was now serving hard time for drug smuggling...along with the socially elite Edward Andriotti. Mitch thought of John Yen Chang and of his social standing in the community—Mr. Patron of the Arts himself. No, it wouldn't be the first time that a pillar of the community tumbled from grace, either.

"So, what do you think?" Will repeated.

"I don't know," Mitch said, answering as truthfully as he'd ever answered anything.

"Maybe if you gently prod Jennifer," Kelly suggested.

Kelly's words knifed at Mitch's tender heart. "She isn't here," he heard himself say, and wondered if he was really speaking as calmly as he thought he was. He didn't feel calm. Not by a long shot.

"Where is she?" Kelly asked.

"Probably gone back to her husband." No, he definitely did not feel calm. In fact, he strongly felt the need to punch someone out, and John Yen Chang would fill that bill nicely.

Kelly's voice had softened when she asked, "What happened?"

In as few words as possible, Mitch told her about the outing to the museum and about what had transpired there. He also told them about the silent drive home and, once there, Jennifer's denial of her memory's return.

"She was lying, though," Mitch said. "I'm positive of that."

"She just left?" Kelly asked.

"She asked for some time alone, to get her thoughts in order, and, when I came back an hour later, she was gone."

"What about the address book?" Will asked.

"She left it. I don't know whether it was intentional or she just didn't think about it."

"Are you all right?" Kelly asked, her concern as evident as the night shrouding the city.

Mitch glanced over at the bottle of Scotch. "I'm all right."

No, he wasn't all right, he thought seconds later when he hung up the phone. Rehashing Jennifer's departure had only left him feeling lonelier. Plus, the news he'd just received hadn't helped. The puzzle had just gotten bigger, with more pieces that wouldn't fit together. What in the hell was going on? Maybe he should consider going to the police, he thought. Maybe it was time to forget about Jennifer Brooks Chang, and whatever game she'd been playing, and cover his own rear end. His own sorry rear end, as Speedy would say.

"Yeah, I'll drink to that," Mitch said, recklessly bringing the bottle back to his lips. As he did so, he told himself that every man had his breaking point, and that he'd just found his. Furthermore, what the hell difference did it make if he had a drink? The world wasn't going to stop spinning.

He tipped the bottle and took a long deep swallow. The whiskey spread like wildfire across his greedy taste buds to his starved senses, then raced down his throat with the speed of lightning. It burned his stomach, pledging the forgetfulness he so critically craved. *Yes, yes!* he thought, just a few swallows and he wouldn't care about anything—not about the vow of abstinence he was breaking, not about his friends who'd stood so faithfully by his side, not about fair-haired Jennifer.

From out of nowhere came an image of his father, the man who'd betrayed himself. From out of nowhere came the image of Jennifer telling him that he was strong, that he could beat his alcoholism. From out of nowhere came the need to fight.

"No!" Mitch heard himself cry.

He lowered the bottle from his lips and, once more tilting it, watched as the contents gurgled forward and onto the floor. As the liquid tumbled downward, it splashed the legs of his jeans. Mitch didn't notice. Once the bottle was empty, he threw it as hard as he could against the wall. It shattered, spewing glass everywhere. So loud was the reverberating sound, coupled with his own pounding heart, that it took him a while to realize that the telephone was once more ringing.

He reached for it, assuming that it was Kelly calling back to see if he was really all right. It would be just the kind of caring thing she'd do.

"Hello?"

There was the tiniest of hesitations, then the lone soul-splintering word, "Mitchell?"

Had he not recognized the caller from her voice, he most certainly would have recognized her from the single word she spoke. Other than his mother, only one person called him Mitchell.

"Mitchell?" she repeated.

Mitch thought he detected a note of fear in the second rendering of his name, though he told himself that maybe this call was nothing more than a continuation of the charade. On the other hand, maybe it was the real thing.

"Yeah?"

Another pause, then, "Mitchell, listen to me. You have to help me. The black book—you have to bring it to the warehouse. Tinsung's warehouse. Now. Right now." A meaningful silence followed. "If you don't, he'll kill me."

Mitch noticed that she hadn't bothered to give the man a name, but then, she hadn't needed to. "Mitchell, please," she whispered.

A scrambling of the phone followed, during which Mitch heard Jennifer's sudden gasp. He could easily imagine the phone being torn from her hand, without regard to any pain delivered in the process.

Mitch's hand tightened on the phone. "Jennifer?"

A man's voice answered. The voice was calm, clear, without even a trace of an accent. Mitch would also have sworn that the man was amused. It was the kind of amusement that a cat displays at having at last cornered a mouse.

"She's quite right," John Yen Chang said. "If you don't bring me the book, I will kill her."

"You sonofa—"

"I hardly think you have time for name-calling. If you're not at the warehouse in thirty minutes, don't bother coming at all. She'll be dead at exactly—" Mitch could tell that Chang was checking his watch "—eleven-twenty."

"Chang, listen!"

In response, Mitch heard the dial tone. It sounded loud and ominous. Willing himself to think clearly, Mitch hung up the phone and checked his watch. He gave a mirthless laugh. Chang hadn't given him so much as a minute to spare. The warehouse was a good twenty-five, thirty minutes away, under the best of circumstances.

Don't panic, Mitch cautioned himself. *You have time if you don't waste it.*

As this thought settled in, Mitch began searching his disordered desk for the black book. He shoved papers and folders aside, knocking pens and pencils everywhere. Somewhere along the way, the ashtray full of suckers fell to the floor. The ashtray and the suckers broke, scattering multicolored bits of glass and candy everywhere.

Dammit, where was the book?

In his apartment. On the dresser. It had to be. Mitch had already started for the door when he remembered to get his gun. Dashing back to the desk, he whipped open a drawer and grabbed his revolver. In seconds, he was racing out the door and up the stairs. The book lay exactly where Jennifer had left it hours before. Mitch snatched it up and, jamming it into his shirt pocket, headed back for the door. He took the stairs in three mighty leaps.

The car groaned as Mitch gunned the accelerator and backed the automobile out of the driveway. Before it had come to a full stop, he ground the gears from reverse to drive and tore off at a speed that had the car begging for mercy. Thirty, forty, fifty, the speedometer read, then began to shout sixty, sixty-five, seventy. As always, once the vehicle had exceeded sixty miles per hour, it began to shake, rattle and threaten to roll over dead.

"C'mon," Mitch pleaded. "Just hold together this one time."

The engine light responded by beaming red.

"Ah, man, don't do this to me!"

Mitch checked his watch. He'd already eaten up seven minutes, and he hadn't even made it out of his neighborhood. He had to make better time, he thought, pushing the automobile toward the eighty-miles-an-hour mark. What had been shaking and rattling quickly became nothing short of a mechanical convulsion. Mitch ignored it, and the engine light that continued to burn a bright red. Mitch checked his watch again. It was only a minute past what it had been last time he'd looked.

Surely, the man wouldn't kill his own wife, Mitch thought. Would he? As grim as the possibility was, Mitch realized that he felt a sense of relief. Though he didn't know what was going on, he did know that Jennifer hadn't betrayed him. How could he have doubted her? His own wife had betrayed him by not believing in him. He'd been guilty of the same thing. When the chips had been down, he hadn't believed in

Jennifer. His culpability caused him to edge the car toward ninety miles per hour.

A dozen thoughts filled his mind; the car was pinging and panging notes he'd never heard before, and the smell of liquor—were the legs of his jeans damp?— was invading his senses. Also the traffic light up ahead was about to turn red.

Damn!

Mitch skidded the car to a rumbling stop. The passenger of the car alongside him glanced over, as though to say that the streets were full of careless drivers. Mitch ignored him, checked his watch and wondered where the time was going. He had just under fifteen minutes to make it to the warehouse. A vision of Jennifer lying dead wormed its way into his mind.

"C'mon, change!" Mitch hollered, slamming his fists against the steering wheel.

Miraculously, the light did as ordered, and Mitch again floored the accelerator. The car shimmied, shook and started down the street. It had barely cleared the intersection, however, before Mitch saw the first puffs of gray smoke coming from under the hood. He cursed and kept on driving, not caring one whit if he burned up the engine. If the car would just get him to the warehouse, he didn't care if it ever budged again.

It was clear in minutes, however, that the engine had no intention of cooperating. A few puffs of gray smoke all too soon became a steady, billowing stream of black. And then, the car began to chug and choke. Finally, the engine shuddered and died. With a rabid curse, Mitch steered the deceased vehicle to the curb and started trying to coax the engine into another breath of life.

"Damn!" he blasted when the car defied his every try.

He checked his watch. It read fifteen minutes after eleven. Throwing open the car door, Mitch started attempting to flag down a ride. All drivers looked at him as if he had to think them crazy. People didn't give strangers rides these days. There were too many perverts roaming the highways. Mitch was still trying to catch a ride when the minute hand of his watch eased onto the twenty-after mark.

Surely, the man wouldn't kill his own wife!

At that exact moment, at the warehouse of Tinsung's Oriental Imports, a shot rang out.

BY THE TIME the rattletrap of a pickup truck grumbled to a stop at the warehouse, Mitch had stopped looking at his watch. It was the only way he could survive. Even so, his heart raced at a death-defying rate.

The snaggletoothed farmer who'd finally picked Mitch up, a man carting ripe-smelling cantaloupes to the northern reaches of the city, looked at what appeared to be a deserted warehouse, then over at his passenger. "You sure you ain't made a mistake? This place looks emptier than a nest after the fledglings have flown."

"I'm sure," Mitch said, handing over every last dollar in his wallet.

"Hey, you don't need—"

"Keep it," Mitch ordered, throwing open the truck door.

Without another word, he ran for the warehouse. His footfalls crunched in the pea-sized gravel. It had crossed his mind once already to wonder how Tin-sung's was linked to Chang. It now crossed his mind again as he made his way to the front door of the warehouse. Locked, dammit! Looking around, he started for the back. At the window through which he and Jennifer had peeked, only to discover the Fo Dog, Mitch paused and peered in again. Then, it had been afternoon, with the sun providing the needed light. Now, Mitch could see nothing, only an all-consuming darkness.

No, wait! Was that a pale yellow glow coming from the far interior? Maybe. Mitch stepped around to the back of the building. Just as he'd suspected, there was a door. But was it unlocked? One quick look confirmed that the lock had been jimmied open. As Mitch entered, he pulled the gun from the waist of his jeans. The firearm, which he'd concealed beneath his shirt-tail because no one was going to give a man with a gun a ride, felt reassuring as he stepped into the stomach of the warehouse.

Mitch couldn't believe—he couldn't allow himself to believe—that Chang would kill Jennifer. What would be the point? But then, a man like Chang, if he was the slick mobster, the societal piranha that Mitch believed him to be, made his own rules and had his own reasons for doing every vile thing he did. Maybe Jennifer's fleeing from him was reason enough to snuff out her life. No, he couldn't think that. If he did, he'd go crazy.

"Jennifer?" Mitch called, unable to stop himself.

The name echoed, bouncing off walls and roof beams and coming to rest in far, cramped corners. The sound of silence answered him. Panic flared despite Mitch's resolve to remain clearheaded. He'd been a fool to come here without telling someone, but he hadn't. Now there was nothing to do but brave his way through whatever awaited him. He tightened his hold on the gun, walking resolutely toward what he was now certain was a light. Maneuvering around cartons and crates, some still holding their contents, others emptied of theirs, Mitch stepped into an open area, fringed by cat-gray shadows. It was in these shadows that he saw the body crumpled on the floor. Mitch stopped in midstride.

If his heart had been racing before, it now stopped entirely, then crashed against his chest. That same heart felt empty, as if it were his life that had just ended, as if it were he that lay lifeless on the sawdusty floor. So many questions crossed his mind in the split of a second: Had she been afraid at the last moment? Had she thought of him? Had she known that he loved her? The only thing that didn't cross his mind was to wonder if she were still alive. He'd seen too much of death to question when he was in its presence.

Mitch told himself that he should be filled with avenging anger, but, frankly, he didn't feel anything. He felt as if he'd been shot full of some narcotic. He did acknowledge that he should be wary, that danger might surround him, but something far more potent than fear guided him. He needed to see Jennifer, to hold her close. He moved toward her. From the first step, however, something didn't seem quite right. The way the body lay? Maybe. The seemingly absent shock of blond hair? Perhaps. The way large squared shoulders looked more masculine than feminine? At this realization, Mitch's heart skipped a beat.

Yes, the body was that of a man, Mitch confirmed once he kneeled beside the motionless figure. A man dressed in a white suit. A man shot in the temple. A man facing downward. Slowly, Mitch rolled the victim onto his back. When the man's face came into view, Mitch blinked, certain that he wasn't seeing clearly. Surely, it was only a trick of the faint light that made this man look familiar. Mitch took in the Hollywood tan, the teeth that were grimly bared in a smile despite death, the arrogance somehow still retained in the man's features.

Paul Lerner!

What in the name of all that was holy was the dead body of Paul Lerner, chief of police of the city of San Francisco, doing in this warehouse?

No sooner had the question traipsed through his mind than Mitch saw the gun lying at the man's side. With its scratch on the barrel—Mitch remembered vividly the drug bust that had put it there—it looked as familiar as the man. A creepy feeling crawled through Mitch, a creepy, what-in-hell-is-going-on-here feeling. Out of pure instinct, he started to reach for the gun that had been issued to him when he'd joined the police force, the same one that had been taken from him when he'd been kicked off that same force, but he stopped himself.

Why was his gun here beside the body of Paul Lerner?

The sound of footsteps came to Mitch in the same bleak way as did the realization of what was going on.

He'd been set up. Plain and simple. And quite possibly by the woman he loved. Suddenly, her leaving the incriminating book behind made sense. It guaranteed his being here. Slowly, Mitch turned toward the advancing footsteps. He'd expected to see John Yen Chang. Instead, his gaze met that of Jennifer's. As always, the word *gorgeous* seemed appropriate. There was an aloofness to her, however, that he'd never seen before. An Arctic-cool aloofness.

"Give me your gun," she said softly, authoritatively, as she held out her hand. Her beautifully manicured hand.

For a second, Mitch thought she was referring to the gun lying on the floor, but after following the direction of her gaze, he realized that she meant the revolver he was holding, the revolver presently aimed directly at the woman demanding that he turn it over to her.

"Come now, Brody" came a rich masculine voice from the shadows. Mitch strained to see the voice's owner even though he knew to whom the voice belonged. "Do you really think you can shoot her?" When Mitch made no reply, neither in action or word, John Yen Chang said, "That's all right, Brody. Every man falls a little bit in love with her. Don't they, darling?"

At this, the handsome Eurasian, immaculately dressed in what had to be a designer suit, stepped to his wife's side. He, too, was holding a gun, this one pointed at Mitch. It crossed Mitch's mind that evil often resided in the prettiest places, in the most perfect-looking people. And John Yen Chang was exactly that—perfect-looking. His silver hair was perfect; his facial features, representative of two cultures, were perfect; his smile was perfect.

"Take his gun, darling," he said in a perfectly perfect voice.

Mitch had been trained never to relinquish his weapon. However he had not been told what to do when the woman he loved stepped forward to take it from him. This time, she looked him squarely in the eyes. The hardness in hers froze his heart.

Did the kiss mean nothing to you? Mitch's eyes asked. *Did my holding you mean nothing?*

Nothing, hers returned.

Mitch let her take the gun, telling himself that he had no option. If he resisted, Chang would kill him, which he probably intended to do, anyway. Maybe this way, he could buy some needed time.

"Very good, darling," Chang praised Jennifer as she promptly handed him Mitch's gun.

"You, uh, you want to tell me what all this has been about?" Mitch asked, curious in spite of the heaviness weighing down his heart. "A man ought to know why he's about to die."

"I suppose there's some truth to that," Chang admitted.

"Let me guess," Mitch said. "It all began with Richard Rhincuso's death."

Chang looked genuinely surprised. "I'm impressed. But you know, Brody, that's why you're in the mess you're in. You're too good a cop."

"Is that why you made it look like I'd taken a bribe?"

"Exactly. You were bird-dogging me. You just wouldn't give up. You kept on asking question after question, trying to pin something on me. And you would have, eventually. So, with Paul's help, I got you out of the way."

Mitch was and wasn't surprised to hear that Paul Lerner had been involved in his being ousted. While it was true that Mitch had always felt him culpable, at least in the sense that the chief hadn't supported him, he nonetheless had had no reason to question his boss's integrity. Now, he wasn't surprised to find that the man had come up short in that department.

"I don't get it," Mitch said. "If Paul helped you, why's he dead?"

Chang looked genuinely saddened. "I didn't want to kill him. Having the chief of police in your pocket is always good, but...well, frankly, he just got greedy." The Eurasian's features hardened. "I can't tolerate greed."

"Of course not, Chang. No one would expect you to." From some deep wellspring, a measure of sarcasm had surfaced. It felt good. Damned good! "But what has Lerner got to do with Rhincuso?"

"Ah, Rhincuso," Chang said, as though the name troubled him. "He's going to be missed, but he didn't have the stomach for our line of work."

"What's wrong, Chang? Was he an honest man?"

"Oh, no. He just wasn't a risk-taker. He was always afraid he was going to get caught."

"Yeah, well, some people are funny like that. They just don't much like the thought of doing hard time in the joint. Take you, for example. I really don't think you're going to enjoy incarceration."

Chang gave a slow smile. "I find you amusing, Brody." An arm snaked around his wife's waist. "Don't you, darling?"

Jennifer didn't reply, although she allowed her gaze to merge with Mitch's. Once he thought that he could read her emotions through her eyes. Now he saw nothing. But then, perhaps there'd never been anything there to see...except what she'd wanted him to.

"To answer your question about Lerner's and Rhincuso's connection, Rhincuso came to me wanting out. This wasn't the first time he'd broached the subject. I was already making plans to do away with him. Once a man starts talking about wanting out, he's useless. As I said, I'd already made my plans. I'd already learned the name of his yacht, which I'd recorded in the book, and had hired someone to fake a drowning, but Rhincuso forced my hand. He showed up at the house, demanding that I let him out right then. Regrettably, for him, he overplayed his hand."

"What does that mean?" Mitch asked.

"In short, he thought he could blackmail me. He'd called the police and turned in one of my girls."

"Ah," Mitch said, "Sarah Elizabeth Etheridge."

"Yes, Sarah. Rhincuso made it very plain that other names would follow if I didn't let him out of the operation."

"But you couldn't trust him after that."

"Exactly. I killed him right then and there while his threats of blackmail still hung in the air."

"With the Fo Dog?"

"An unexpectedly admirable weapon."

Mitch looked over at Jennifer. "An unexpectedly admirable performance." It was clear that he was referring to all that had transpired between them from the moment she'd first walked into his life to the moment she'd walked out.

Jennifer was first to glance away. Mitch wished he could have taken more satisfaction from her having done so. Instead, he said to Chang, "So, you faked Rhincuso's drowning."

"With Paul's help. It was easy enough. Bodies are lost at sea all the time and never recovered, especially if weights are tied around the body's ankles."

A shudder ran through Mitch. He was no stranger to death, but being fish food was low on his list of how he wanted to meet his Maker. "I still don't see why Lerner bought the farm."

"Simple. He thought getting rid of Rhincuso entitled him to a bigger cut of the money."

Mitch made a tsking sounding. "Imagine that."

"Precisely."

"Tell me something, Chang. Was that the night this whole little charade was born?" When Chang said nothing, Mitch continued, "Did you see a way of getting rid of both me and Lerner? You needed someone to take the wrap for killing Lerner, and who better than me, right? Everyone knew that I hated his guts. Plus, surely he'd told you that I was still asking questions about you. What could be better than killing two birds with one stone, huh?"

Chang said nothing, but Mitch saw his arm tighten around his wife's waist. Mitch's chest constricted until he didn't think that he was going to be able to draw another breath. It was suddenly important that he hurt Jennifer. Moreover, it was important to remind himself of this woman's duplicity.

"Was that the night you sent your lovely wife to me with the little black book and a sad tale of amnesia?"

This time Chang didn't ignore the question. "More or less."

Mitch thought his answer cryptic, but only for a moment, because Jennifer's gaze had once more found his. Again, however, there seemed no warmth in her cloudy-gray eyes. Only an isolating, chilling coldness that froze both his heart and soul.

"Actually, I think the plan was a rather brilliant one," Chang said, drawing Mitch's attention back to him...and the gun. "It will appear that you lured Paul here, to a quiet, secluded spot, broke in and killed him with your old police gun. Rumor around the station said you'd been asking about Tinsung's."

"Speedy knows why I was asking."

"Speedy can be dealt with."

"I hate to put a crimp in your carefully orchestrated plans, but how would I have gotten my police weapon? I turned it in when I left the force."

"I admit that worried me at first. But Paul himself said that it would be easy to prove that the gun just got lost in the shuffle, that the paperwork indicated that you turned it in, but that you never had." Chang smiled. "Who would dispute the word of the chief of police, especially when he was being honest enough to admit to an error?"

"What cock-and-bull story did you give Lerner to convince him to bring the gun? He suspected nothing?"

"You have to understand the chief of police. He was so full of himself that it never crossed his mind to think that he was expendable. He thought we were staging your death. As for the gun, he agreed with me that there was a certain drama about your using your police weapon to try to kill him. The attempted killing would have to do with your grudge against him for dismissing you from the force."

"And I suppose you have his gun?"

"Of course. You'll be found shot with his, he with yours."

"Isn't that a little too convenient?"

"I don't think so. All sorts of things happen in the heat of a gunfight. A man doesn't meekly accept his death. Surely, Lerner would have fought back. And there's nothing to indicate that either of you died instantaneously."

"I suppose that you'll make certain that the appropriate fingerprints are on each weapon?"

"Of course."

"Mitch had a grisly vision of the hands of two corpses being molded around metal. The vision angered him. The inequity angered him. All the humiliation he'd endured, all the emotional pain he'd suffered, all his fighting to survive would have been for nothing. In the end, everyone—maybe even his friends, maybe even his son—would conclude that he was, indeed, a dirty cop. At best, he was a crazed cop. Bile rose in Mitch's throat. At the same time, some deep-seated instinct for survival kicked in. Chang was right. A man didn't go to his death meekly. Out of the corner of his eye, Mitch measured just how far away the gun lying beside Lerner's dead body really was. A hurl? A rapid roll? A body tuck?

Keep him talking, Mitch thought, taking one tiny step backward. He registered the fact that the handle of the weapon was pointed toward him.

"And how exactly did you talk Lerner into meeting me here?"

"I persuaded him that you had to be gotten out of the way, that it would look like you had set him up, and that he'd killed you in self-defense."

Mitch inched a little to the right. He'd have to dive over the body, grab the gun and shoot before he'd even landed. Could he do it? Probably not. But what the hell kind of option did he have?

His heart hammering wildly, Mitch asked, "What's your connection with Tinsung's?"

Mitch had no intention of waiting for an answer. He had no intention of waiting for anything. Before the question had even left his mouth, he hit the floor. The impact sent a shaft of pain tearing though his hip, but he concentrated only on rolling himself into a tight ball. At the same time, he grappled for the gun. He felt both the cool metal of the weapon and the cool body of Lerner. The latter cushioned his fall, while the former slid into his hand like a familiar lover. He flattened onto the floor.

The world slipped into slow motion.

John Yen Chang, his features now posed in surprise, pushed from his wife. He fired the gun he held. Mitch heard the gun's report, a sharp, piercing sound in a room that had otherwise grown eerily quiet. That was followed by Jennifer's screaming, "No!" as she grabbed her husband's arm. Chang pushed her aside, steadied the gun and prepared to fire again. Jennifer stepped, deliberately, into the bullet's path. The gun went off.

"No!" Mitch screamed, coming to his knees as Jennifer sank to hers.

In reaction, Mitch fired his weapon, striking the center of Chang's forehead. The man died while still standing. Jennifer crumpled to the floor, only inches from where her husband fell. His heart pounding, Mitch scrambled toward her and scooped her into his arms. Bright red blood covered her chest. For one brief second, her gaze found his.

"Mit-chell," she started to whisper, but the word died on her lips.

Her eyes closed. She struggled to breathe. Once, twice, a few pitiful more times. And then the struggle ceased.

CHAPTER ELEVEN

"I HAVE A HEARTBEAT," a male paramedic announced.

"The bullet punctured her lung," said another voice, this one feminine. "We're going to have to intubate her."

Gasping, Jennifer labored to draw precious air into her lungs. Each attempted breath created a hideous hissing in the hole gaping from the right side of her chest. Though floating in and out of consciousness, she was aware of pain—a pain so stark, so all-consuming that there was no description adequate enough to do it justice. Worse even than that were her pathetic attempts to breathe. She was dying. She knew this instinctively, yet she fought not to. She couldn't die before she told Mitchell that she hadn't betrayed him.

"For God's sake, do something!" a panicked voice cried. "Can't you see she can't breathe!"

"Get him out of here," the male paramedic ordered calmly. As he spoke, he took the tubing his partner passed him and expertly began to insert it into Jennifer's throat.

Speedy Talbot placed a restraining hand on Mitch's arm. "C'mon, get out of the way. You're not helping her."

Mitch shrugged out of his friend's tender clutches. "I'll stay out of the way. I promise."

He peripherally noted that the bodies of John Yen Chang and Paul Lerner were being removed from the scene. The warehouse was alive with policemen, while querulous reporters, already gathering like vultures, chattered in the distance. Numb, dazed, his hands red with blood, Mitch watched as the tube, now resting in Jennifer's lungs, was hooked to a bag, presumably of oxygen.

"Give me a hundred percent," the male paramedic ordered.

His female counterpart made some adjustments, then began to manually compress the life-giving gas. The oxygen flowed through the tube and into Jennifer's lungs before rushing forward to make a grotesque bubbling sound around the wound. Even so, Jennifer's struggle abated somewhat.

Though her color was chalky-white, indicative of shock, Mitch nonetheless breathed his own sigh of relief. At least she was breathing better, not the hacking and sucking of seconds before. But he wished she'd open her eyes, just once, so that she could see that he was there.

With the improvement in her breathing, Jennifer's hazy consciousness began to clear, not entirely, but enough for her to hear conversation. Even so, she couldn't will her eyes to open, nor could she will her body to move. All she could do was hear. Two of the voices were unfamiliar to her, but they seemed to belong to authority figures. They issued calm but crisp orders. The only voice she recognized, the only voice she cared about, belonged to Mitchell. But his voice was there one minute, gone the next. Right after she'd first been shot, the terrible pain had ended abruptly, but then she'd come back to the pain, to the racked breathing. More important, she'd come back to Mitchell's voice, pleading with her to live. God, she did want to live! Why? She couldn't quite remember.

What you know about yourself is far more important than what others think they know.

Yes, it had something to do with what she'd told him when she'd heard about his being accused of bribery. The same thing now applied to her, didn't it? She knew that she hadn't betrayed him, but that wasn't enough. She had to tell him that. She had to find the strength to tell him. She had to open her eyes and— Darkness consumed her again, drawing her down, down, to a place where time had no meaning.

"Let's get her hooked up to the heart monitor and get an IV going," the female paramedic said, glancing over at Mitch. It was obvious to any and all that this man cared for this woman. "Come here," she ordered, explaining, "I want you to squeeze this—" she relinquished the task of manually compressing air "—as fast as you can, but with a rhythm. Can you do that?"

Mitch knelt beside Jennifer. "Yeah," he said, taking over the assignment. He was glad that he could do something to help. Anything.

He watched as the two emergency technicians worked with a precision that was awe inspiring. With scissors, they cut every garment of clothing from their patient's body. Her body was perfectly formed, yet at this particular moment, no man would have noticed anything but the hole from which blood still poured.

If she died, Mitch knew that it would be because of him. She had literally, unselfishly, sacrificed her life to save his. The thing that worried him most of all was that, if she did die, she would die without his ever having had an opportunity to beg her to forgive him for not believing in her. This brought such pain that Mitch closed his eyes against it.

Please, God, don't take her! he prayed, pushing air into Jennifer's lungs as though it were a religious ritual.

When Mitch opened his eyes, it was to a flurry of activity. Strategically placed suction pads hooked Jennifer to a heart monitor, which, even as he watched, began to beep with a consistency that was comforting. Even so, there was so much blood. It was all over him, all over the paramedics, all over Jennifer. The sheets of the stretcher, on which she lay, were already stained crimson. The male technician applied a dressing over the wound while the female paramedic started IVs, one in each of Jennifer's arms. Again, working as an experienced team, the man and woman fitted Jennifer's lower body in a pair of thick Velcroed pants. Mitch—any cop—knew enough first aid to know that the pants' purpose was to shift the flow of blood from the legs to the torso.

"Let's transport her," the woman said, drawing the sheet up around Jennifer at the same time as she gathered up the equipment. She placed the heart monitor alongside Jennifer's inert body, while she carried the IVs. Speedy Talbot helped the male paramedic lift the stretcher, while Mitch still remained in charge of the oxygen.

"Don't let up," the female paramedic ordered him.

"No" was his only response.

Mitch moved through the warehouse in a daze, only vaguely aware that the phrase "Out of the way, please" was repeated several times. He concentrated not on Jennifer's pallor, not on her deathlike stillness, not on her continued ragged breathing, but in his sending oxygen to her lungs. In minutes, in hours— Mitch had no concept of time—she, with him at her side, was being placed in the ambulance. The door slammed shut; the siren began to wail.

The movement, the sound—something—called Jennifer away from the pit of darkness where her consciousness had been hiding out. She resented the intrusion because it meant a return of the pain, which was like a fire licking its hot breath along her every nerve ending. She moaned.

"It's okay, baby," Mitch said.

Mitchell's voice. There it was again, Jennifer thought, trying with all her might to open her eyes. There was something she had to tell him. Something about betrayal, something about loving him, something about Emily. She had to tell him to find Emily.

Suddenly, the timeless pit pulled her down again. Yesterday was today; today, yesterday. Yesterday had no perimeters. What had happened weeks before was just as memorable as what had happened within the hour. She heard all kinds of voices from this murky land of remembrance.

"I'd like to speak to Emily," Jennifer could hear herself asking. She'd made the call from Mitchell's apartment when her memory had returned, praying that she wouldn't be discovered. She was afraid, afraid

of what the administrator of Holy Angels would tell her.

Holy Angels?

Was that why she'd dreamed of Emily with a bright, halolike light wreathing her head? Yes, Emily was an angel, a sweet angel. What else could you call a woman with the mind of a child?

"She's not here, Mrs. Chang," the administrator had replied, clearly confused. *"Your husband removed her from the home days ago."* There was a pause, then, *"Is everything all right?"*

"No," Jennifer had wanted to reply, but instead she had said, *"Yes. We, uh, we just decided to move Emily closer... closer... closer..."*

Jennifer moaned. She had to find Emily.

"Easy," the unfamiliar, feminine voice said. "Just take it easy!"

"It's okay, baby."

It was *his* voice again. *Mitchell,* she wanted to call out, but she couldn't find the strength. She wanted to tell him again that, when he was near, the emptiness that dwelled inside her disappeared. She wanted to tell him that his presence made her feel full, that his gentleness, which she could hear in his voice, made her feel like weeping. She tried to speak, to tell him that he was nothing like her husband, but the darkness, like a sinister current, was towing her farther downstream.

"Please give me a divorce," she'd begged a hundred times.

A hundred times, John Chang had answered, *"Never, my love."*

"Never, never, never," the voices of darkness chanted.

And so, she'd devised a plan. *A plan,* the darkness echoed. *Bide your time, then, when the circumstances present themselves, take the little black book from the safe and flee, along with Emily. The book is important . . . important . . . you can use it to negotiate yours and Emily's, safety.*

Book? Did Mitchell say that it contained the names of call girls? Yes, yes, he did. She remembered now thinking that it must.

The ambulance began to speed off into the night, the male paramedic at the wheel. As he drove, he radioed to the hospital.

"We're transporting a white female, approximately thirty years old. She's been shot once in the chest. The bullet is internally lodged. Her heart stopped once, but she was manually resuscitated. Have a trauma team standing by. Her vital signs are as follows . . ."

"Here, darling." The male's voice blended into that of her husband's. Eerily, Jennifer heard him above the wail of the ambulance, once more in a macabre blending of the past with the present. *"Wear these earrings. They're perfect for the black dress, perfect for the symphony."*

As always, he'd ordered her, not asked her. She loathed all the jewels he bought her. She especially hated her diamond-encrusted wedding ring, a symbol not of his love, but of his need to possess. She wore it only when she had to.

"Have you forgotten your wedding ring again, darling? Run on upstairs and get it."

Before she could, however, an unexpected commotion had sounded in the hallway that night. Or maybe the commotion was in the ambulance.

Ambulance?

Was she in an ambulance?

Yes, someone had been shot. Look and see...

"Lie still, Jennifer," the female paramedic said.

"Can't you give her anything for pain?" Mitch asked, the question harsh and impatient.

"No, I've given her all the drugs I can," the woman replied.

"Dammit it to hell!" Mitch cursed.

"What in hell do you mean showing up here at my home?" Jennifer heard her husband ask his unexpected visitor. She recognized the voice as belonging to Richard Rhincuso. He occasionally called the house, but his doing so always made her husband angry.

"Because you won't take my telephone calls."

"That's because you're talking nonsense."

"I want out... I want out... I want out..."

Jennifer's darkness ran red with blood, the blood of Richard Rhincuso. She could hear the thud, see the green Fo Dog covered in blood and a dead man lying on a carpet of pink flowers. Pink flowers. Like the ones in the field of her dream? Yes, a field of pink flowers. But she could feel her fear blossoming, for, like in her dream, the green dog was searching for her, the green dog that would rip out her throat.

Reaching into the safe, she'd taken the black book and fled. *Run, run... don't get the blood on you... run, run... don't let the dog catch you... run,*

*run...don't fall on the terrace...run...run...
run...*

The heart monitor went crazy.

"We're losing her," the female paramedic said just as the ambulance pulled into the emergency area of the hospital.

In seconds, Mitch was unceremoniously shoved aside and told in no uncertain terms to stay out of the way. He tried to disobey, but to no avail. The emergency room doors slammed in his face with a frightening finality. All he could think of was that he hadn't had the chance to apologize, to beg her forgiveness, to tell her that he loved her.

THERE WERE phantoms who lived in the night that lived nowhere else, Mitch thought as he sat in the hospital waiting room. These phantoms toyed with men, taunted them, teased them, told them that the greatest sins were not those acts committed, but rather those uncommitted, those should-have-been-dones, those should-have-been-saids. Mitch checked his watch, hoping to God that the night would be over soon, so that, hopefully, the phantoms would steal away if only for a little while.

"What time is it?" Kelly asked.

The redhead sat on the sofa next to Mitch, whose hair was a shambles and whose eyes were shaded with fatigue. He had managed to cleanse his hands of the blood, but he hadn't been able to remove it from his clothes, with the result that he wore grim reminders of what had transpired earlier. For most of the evening, beginning the moment she and Will had rushed to their friend's side, Kelly had held Mitch's hand. With a total lack of embarrassment, he'd allowed her to do so. His friends were holding him together, Kelly with her gentle touch and Will with his quiet strength. At his wife's question, Will turned from the window, as though he, too, needed to have an answer to the question of time.

"Almost five o'clock," Mitch replied, adding, "She's been in surgery nearly four and a half hours."

Once during that interminably long time, a kind-faced nurse had told them that Jennifer was still alive, still clinging to life with an admirable courage. She'd also told them that someone from the police department wanted to talk to Mitch. Speedy Talbot and the assistant chief of police had asked their questions as quickly and quietly as possible. Mitch had told them what had happened at the warehouse, and what had led up to his being there, then had given them the black book containing the names of the call girls. As he was leaving, Speedy had informed Mitch that the news about famous Jennifer Brooks was spreading like wildfire, but that he'd personally see that reporters were kept at bay. Mitch had thanked him. That had been hours ago. Maybe even a lifetime ago.

"It's good that the surgery's taking so long," Kelly said. "We know that the doctors are being thorough. We know she's still fighting."

"I guess," Mitch said.

Kelly squeezed her friend's hand. "You listen to me, Mitch Brody. Don't you dare believe anything but that she's going to make it. You hear me?" When Mitch didn't answer, she pressed, "You hear me?"

Despite the heaviness of his heart, he smiled wanly. "I hear you." The smile faded, however, and he laid his head against the back of the vinyl sofa. He closed his eyes. He knew that he should tell his friends to go home, that Kelly needed her rest, but he couldn't bring himself to be alone right now.

"You want some more coffee?" Will asked.

"Not unless you're going to pour some whiskey in it."

"There's not enough whiskey in the world to ease your pain," Will said.

Opening his eyes, Mitch found those of his friend and said, as though confession would somehow absolve the act, "I went off the wagon tonight."

Quietly, Will returned, "I know."

Mitch couldn't contain his surprise.

"You smell like a brewery," Will explained.

Mitch had forgotten about the liquor that had splashed on the legs of his jeans, liquor now long dried. Again, he smiled faintly. "Well, there's good news and bad. The bad news is that I went off the wagon, the good news is that it smells worse than it was." Mitch didn't bother to explain why he had turned to the bottle. The why never mattered. If an alcoholic wanted a drink, he'd find an excuse.

"How bad was it?" Will asked, but there was no condemnation in his voice. Only concern.

"One swallow." Mitch saw his friend's relief. "One swallow or the entire bottle, it's still going off the wagon." Tearing his hand from Kelly's, Mitch came to his feet abruptly, as though he could no longer sit still. Tears threatened his eyes. He fought them as he walked to the window to stand by Will. He braced one hand against the sill. "It scared the hell out of me! I don't want to turn out like my old man, go through that endless, pathetic cycle of on-again, off-again drinking."

"How come you smell like a brewery?" Will asked.

"I poured the contents onto the floor."

Will grinned.

Mitch didn't. "I'd pay a hundred bucks right now for one more swallow. And I'd have no compunction about licking that floor to get it."

Will laid his hand on Mitch's shoulder and squeezed. "I know."

With the first pastel rays of the sunrise, Mitch said, as though he needed to confess one more crime, "I didn't believe in her. When push came to shove, when the moment of truth was at hand, I believed she betrayed me." Mitch laughed harshly. "I, who've lived with betrayal, became the consummate betrayer."

"Under the circumstances, you were justified," Will said. "The whole thing looked like a setup from the get-go."

"I should have believed in her."

"Good Lord, after she lured you to the warehouse, anyone would have believed he'd been set up."

"I wasn't just anyone," Mitch said, knowing that there were still so many unanswered questions. If she didn't make it, he might never know why she'd chosen his agency, what significance Tinsung's warehouse had, who Emily was. The thought that she might not make it filled him with despair. It also filled him with anger. If she died, he would lose her before he'd ever found her. This thought hurt so badly that he slammed his hand hard against the windowsill. "Dammit, why did she step in front of that bullet?"

Will, the man of few words that he was, said simply, "She did it for the same reason that you would have stepped in front of it for her."

The two men stared wordlessly at each other. An implication hung in the air, the implication that Jennifer cared for Mitch as much as he cared for her. The thought lifted his despair, but only momentarily. If she did care for him—he avoided thinking any stronger word—it only made his culpability greater. Wasn't it hell on earth to have someone you care for doubt you? Wasn't—

"Mr. Brody?"

The doctor, his feet encased in green surgical slippers, had entered the room quietly. A mask, which he'd freed from his nose and mouth, hung haphazardly around his neck. To any eye, observant or not, the surgeon looked tired and worn.

Mitch's mouth went sand-dry. He had to literally shove the words out. "How is she?"

"She's in recovery now and will be for a while. From there, she'll be moved to ICU."

"How is she?" Mitch persisted. He was vaguely aware that Kelly had moved to his side and had once more taken his hand in hers.

"She's stable, but critical."

"What does that mean?" Mitch asked.

"Just that. You know that her heart stopped once and began to race once. I believe that both times it was due to her inability to get enough oxygen, which leads me to her lungs. The bullet entered the right side of her chest, shattering several ribs in the process, then punctured her right lung before lodging itself near her spine. We've done what repair work we could. We've removed the bullet. We've given her blood."

"Is she conscious?" Mitch asked. *God, please just grant me the chance to apologize, to beg for her forgiveness.*

"No." The doctor apparently saw how important this was to Mitch because he added, "I'm sorry."

It took all the courage that Mitch had to ask the question, but he was left with no choice. He had to know the truth. "Is she going to live?"

"Mr. Brody, I make it a point to always be honest with my patients, their families, their friends. I honestly don't know if she's going to live. I do know that I've done everything I can. It's in higher hands now. In a very real sense, it's in the hands of the lady herself. In the next few days, we'll see just how badly she wants to live."

THE WORST THING about vigils is that they don't seem structured out of ordinary time. Seconds blend into minutes, while minutes blur into hours. Hours, on the other hand, don't merge into the normal pattern of days, but rather into some endless, meaningless, timeless succession of sunrises and sunsets. On the whole, vigils batter the heart and wear the spirit thin.

For two sunrises and two sunsets, Jennifer lay in ICU. Mitch was allowed to see her only at prescribed times, and then only for a short while. At all other times, he could be found hanging out in the hallway, sleeping on an uncomfortable sofa, existing from one cup of coffee to the next. Occasionally, he'd slip down to the cafeteria for a quick bite, then hasten back to

Jennifer's side... or as close to it as he could get. He lived only for the time he spent with her.

Though the tube in her nose, the needles in her arms, the bags dripping life-sustaining liquids into her body, frightened him—as did the deathlike way she lay—he would always sit by the bed and take her hand in his. Ignoring her hand's lifelessness, he'd entwine their fingers with a fierce tenderness. And then he'd talk to her.

"Hey, sweetie, it's me again," he said on the evening of the second day. "I'd come in more often, but the nurses guard you like you're royalty, which is kind of funny because I always thought you looked like royalty. Not that I hobnob with kings or queens, you understand, but... Anyway, how about if I sneak in some night and kidnap you? Would you like that?"

He pretended she'd answered him.

"Yeah, I'd like that, too." His voice thickened. "There are a lot of things I need to tell you—things like I'm so sorry I didn't believe in you, things like I know how that hurts, things like..." His voice choked and he fought tears. Gently, he stroked the back of her hand with his thumb. Her nails were still remarkably intact, a fact Mitch couldn't explain now any more than he could the first time he'd met her. Now, unlike then, he didn't give a damn. He cared only about one thing. "Forgive me, Jennifer. Please."

The only sound in the room was the beeping of the heart monitor.

"Please, darling. Open your eyes and tell me you forgive me."

Again, nothing but the sound of remorse.

Weary with a bone-deep fatigue, Mitch laid his forehead on their clasped hands. He closed his eyes and muttered, "It's okay, darling. You don't have to forgive me. Just know that I'm here."

FROM HER drug-induced state, Jennifer listened to Mitch's voice. No, she did more than listen to it. She clung to it. It came regularly, but all too infrequently. She always felt safe when it was near, though she felt frustrated, too. Whenever it asked her to open her eyes, she always tried to, but never could manage the act. That simple task had grown into an impossibility.

But she did know that he was there. How could she not? Especially when he held her hand so tenderly, so gently. Hadn't it been his tenderness that she'd first noted? He was so unlike her husband. *Husband.* What had happened to him? *Please, God, let him be dead.* No, he mustn't be dead. He had to tell her where Emily was.

Emily. Where are you, Emily?

Jennifer tried to rouse herself. She had to tell Mitchell to find Emily. She had to tell him that she hadn't betrayed him. She had to tell him that she loved him. She had to... She fell back into the bottomless sleep from which she couldn't awake. She wondered if she was dying. She wondered if the green dog would be the victor after all.

"YOU LOOK LIKE HELL," Speedy Talbot told his expartner on the third day of Jennifer's hospitalization.

"Wow, Talbot," Mitch said, drawing his fingers across the scratchy stubble on his chin, "you're going to turn my head with talk like that."

"C'mon, I'm taking you home. I want you to freshen up." Mitch started to object. "Then I want you to go somewhere with me." Triumphantly, he added, "I think we've found Emily."

Two hours later, Speedy pulled the police car from the home for the mentally retarded. Mitch was grateful for Speedy's silence. It gave him a chance to put his thoughts in order. More important, it gave him a chance to try to deal with what he'd just seen.

The administrator of the home, a smartly dressed man with a compassionate disposition, had shown the two men to a private room. He explained that this client—he refused to call the people staying in the home "patients"—had been there only a couple of weeks. She'd been transferred from Holy Angels, another well-respected institution for the mentally impaired. He'd been told that she was being relocated so that she could be nearer her family. He had then thought it odd that none of her family had been to see her. He'd told them that the young woman kept asking for Jenny. Did they have any idea who she could be?

"How did you find out where Emily was?" Mitch asked.

Speedy glanced over at his friend, then back at the tree-lined street.

"Naturally, we tried to find Jennifer's family to notify them that she was in the hospital. It became clear pretty quick that she had none here in the city. She had come from New York City, so we tried there. We talked to her agent, who informed us that Jennifer's real last name is Mauritz, that her parents were dead, but that she had a younger sister who was retarded. A younger sister named Emily." Speedy pulled the car into traffic, headed back for the hospital. "From there, we started calling institutions in this area. We talked to Holy Angels first, and they said that Emily Mauritz had been removed from their home recently. By John Yen Chang. The staff had thought it a little strange because Mrs. Chang had always been the one to deal with them."

"It all makes sense," Mitch said. "Under hypnosis, Jennifer said that some man—my guess is that the man was Chang—was ashamed of Emily. Jennifer also seemed protective of her."

"When Jennifer split with the book, Chang split with the sister. Jennifer was probably going to use the book as her insurance policy—'Leave me and my sister alone or else'—but she lost her memory before she could get to her sister. Chang then took the sister as his own insurance policy. After all, he had no idea what had happened to his wife. I'm quite certain that the very last place he expected her to be was with you. In the end, of course, you turned out to be even better bait than Emily, especially since he wanted you out of the picture permanently."

"Yeah," Mitch said.

He tried to focus on anything that would take his mind off how Jennifer was paying dearly for the game that Chang had so callously played. He let his mind drift back to Emily. If the sight of her had been sobering, it had also been humbling. This child-woman, who'd looked so much like Jennifer that Mitch had wanted to cry, had smiled at him so trustingly. She'd then offered her doll to him. He'd rocked the doll, waiting to rock Emily, wanting to tell her that everything would be all right, that Jenny would be coming to see her soon. But he couldn't tell her that, because he didn't know if it was the truth.

"You okay?" Speedy asked.

"Yeah," Mitch lied, changing subjects. "What's it like at the precinct?"

"The chaos you'd expect after discovering the chief of police was corrupt. I never did like that son of a bitch. He smiled too much. By the way, they're investigating the whole city council. They're going to see if there are any other bad apples besides Rhincuso."

"From what Chang said he'd been planning to get rid of Rhincuso for a while—bumping him off, then making it appear a drowning."

"Rhincuso just forced his hand by coming to his home when he did," Speedy said. "I'm sure he would have preferred something neater, tidier than murder in his own foyer."

"What about the call girls?" Mitch asked, thinking of how Rhincuso's turning in Sarah Elizabeth Etheridge as a show of his own power, a power that turned out to be pitifully weak, had guaranteed the councilman's death.

Speedy grinned. "All looking for lawyers. Chang had quite an operation going."

When the car pulled back into the hospital parking lot, Mitch immediately threw open the door. "Thanks for taking me to see Emily."

"You're welcome. Hey," Speedy called out as Mitch slammed the car door and impatiently started for the hospital. Mitch pivoted toward his ex-partner. "My money says Jennifer's going to make it."

AT HIS NEXT VISIT, Mitch once more took Jennifer's listless hand in his. With delicate, loving strokes, he tried to breathe his own life into her. Again, he spoke to her, as though she could hear his every word.

"Hey, babe," he said softly. "How's it going?"

No answer.

"I saw Emily today. I wanted you to know so that you wouldn't worry about her. She's fine, but she misses you. She asked me when Jenny was going to come see her. I'll take you to see her as soon as you're better. Would you like that?"

No answer."

Mitch studied Jennifer's face. She looked so incredibly pale that it sent prickles of alarm scurrying through him. Her face was drawn, with lines pinching both the corners of her eyes and the corners of her mouth. Her cheeks, ordinarily high and round, had sunken until they looked frighteningly concave, and her hair, usually a wild, sexy tangle, just appeared in desperate need of a brushing. He'd try to remember to bring a brush next time he came...and maybe some perfume...and a pretty gown.

"Oh, Jenny, Jenny," he pleaded. "Please come back to me."

Mitch closed his eyes at the same time that he lowered his lips to the back of Jennifer's hand. He kissed her slowly, softly, the single act one of devout worship.

Fight, he willed her. *Fight...fight...fight...*

His lips stilled. Had her hand moved? Or had he only imagined it? Raising his head, his eyes found hers. Though bleary from sedation, her silver-gray eyes were still beautiful. In fact, they were the most beautiful eyes that Mitch had ever seen—simply because they were open and staring at him.

For long moments, neither spoke.

Finally, Jennifer whispered, her voice barely more than a choked whisper, "You look awful."

Mitch tried to respond, but couldn't. He couldn't get the words around the lump in his throat.

CHAPTER TWELVE

"DOESN'T SHE look pretty?" Kelly asked as Mitch walked into the hospital room two afternoons later.

Pretty? That was hardly the word Mitch would have used. Sensational, fantastic, gorgeous—those words seemed far more appropriate. He and Kelly had gone shopping that morning, with the result that Jennifer now wore a lacy cinnamon-colored nightie instead of a drab hospital gown. Her hair had also been brushed until it shone like sun-spun gold. Plus, the flowery fragrance of a perfume that Mitch had bought wafted around the room—the private room, not a room in ICU. In those moments when Mitch had trouble believing that Jennifer was better, that maybe he'd only dreamed that she'd opened her eyes and spoken to him, the room was proof that he was wide-awake. That, and the removal of all of the frightening tubes, with the exception of one IV.

"Yeah, she looks pretty," Mitch muttered hoarsely as he stepped forward.

Braced against a pillow, her hair fanned out around her, Jennifer smiled faintly, tiredly. "There's nothing like begging for a compliment."

Mitch grinned. "You really have to beg. Thank goodness, I know how to lie big-time."

Jennifer and Mitch just stared at each other, grins nipping at their lips. Actually, neither felt that jovial. With the return of Jennifer's memory, with the return of her consciousness, had come concerns that had not been anticipated. In short, did the two of them have a future? Was what had happened between them—the kisses, the attraction—the result of mere circumstance? Had it occurred simply because they had been confined to their own little world?

Even more unsettling was Mitch's realization, after observing how the press kept hounding her, that he and Jennifer belonged to very different worlds. To put it bluntly, she was on her way to becoming a famous model; he was a nobody. She was rich; he was poor. She was elegance personified; his idea of elegance was clean underwear. There was absolutely no reason that a woman like her would want a man like him—which she probably didn't now that she'd discovered her identity. And then, there was also John Yen Chang. No matter how he tried to ignore the fact, no matter that she'd sacrificed herself to save his life—she probably would have done that for anyone—the truth was that she'd been married to Chang.

That marriage concerned Jennifer, too. How could Mitchell ever forgive her for being married to a man who'd so callously wronged him? Could she make him understand how she'd ever come to be married to such a man? For that matter, could she make herself understand? She tried to console herself with the knowledge that Mitchell had sat diligently by her bedside, that he'd come to see her regularly, that he'd bought her the beautiful gown, but none of that meant anything more than that Mitchell Brody was a nice man.

Tell him you love him! Jennifer ordered herself. Isn't your love for him what kept you fighting when death threatened to claim you? Yes, she had to answer, but still she hadn't spoken of love since returning to consciousness. Maybe she'd read more into their relationship than had actually existed. If so, she didn't want to embarrass herself and Mitchell. After all, being physically attracted to someone was hardly the grounds for a lifetime commitment.

Tell her you love her! Mitch told himself at the very same moment that she was thinking about him. Isn't that what you promised you'd do if she survived? Yes came the immediate reply, but still he said nothing, simply because he didn't want to put Jennifer on the spot.

"Are those for Jennifer?" Kelly asked after a few seconds. "Or are you planning on keeping them for yourself?"

Mitch followed the path of Kelly's gaze, which was directed at the forgotten bouquet he was carrying, a simple bouquet he'd bought from a street vendor.

"Yeah, sure," Mitch answered, handing the flowers to Kelly.

"I'll put these in water and then I've got to scoot. Will is picking me up to take me to the doctor for my checkup." Here, Kelly patted her rounded tummy.

"How is my godchild?" Mitch asked.

"Active. Without question, he or she is going to be a punt kicker. By the way," Kelly added, "I think our patient is tired. All this beautifying is hard work."

Concerned, Mitch looked over at Jennifer. "I won't stay, then."

"No! I mean, please stay. I'm just a little tired."

"I could come back—"

"No, please," Jennifer said, indicating a nearby chair.

"Just a little while, then," Mitch said, dragging the chair to the bedside.

Kelly smiled discreetly into the posies she was placing in the water pitcher she'd turned into a makeshift vase.

"Thanks for the gown," Jennifer said.

"You're welcome," Mitch answered.

Unnoticed by either of the room's other occupants, Kelly placed the bouquet on the table by the bed.

"Thanks for the perfume."

"You're welcome. I didn't know anything about the brand. I just thought it smelled nice."

"It's very nice."

Kelly gathered up her purse and started for the door.

"You shouldn't have spent so much money on me. I know how tight your budget is."

"Don't worry about my budget. Besides, a few clients decided to pay their bills."

"Bye," Kelly said from the doorway. No one noticed her.

"You, uh, you really do look great," Mitch said, trying not to gawk like the teenager he suddenly felt like. He wanted to take Jennifer's hand in his, the way he had while she'd been unconscious, but now that she was conscious he suddenly felt that doing so might be presumptuous. Maybe she didn't remember the long hours they'd held hands, their fingers entwined as one.

Kelly cleared her throat. Again, no one noticed.

"Thank you," Jennifer said, thinking that Mitch, in his simple jeans and white shirt, looked pretty great himself. She wanted him to take her hand in his, the way he had innumerable times over the past few days, but he didn't. What would he do if she reached out and took his?

"Hey, you two," Kelly called.

Both Mitch and Jennifer glanced toward the door. They seemed surprised that they weren't alone.

"Bye," Kelly said, wiggling her fingers in the air and fighting another grin.

Mitch and Jennifer looked embarrassed as they chorused, "Bye."

"Thank you," Jennifer added.

"You're welcome," Kelly said. "See you later."

When the door closed, and it was just the two of them, a thick awkwardness set in. There was so much that both wanted to say, but neither knew quite where to begin. Since her sister was the only thing they'd discussed, it seemed a safe enough subject.

"I, uh, I talked to Emily this morning," Jennifer said.

"Did you?"

Jennifer nodded. "She's a little scared in the new home, but she's fine. I told her I'd come to see her soon."

"I'll take you," Mitch said, then hastened to add, "If you'd like me to."

"I'd like that."

"Then I'll do it."

More awkwardness.

Take her hand, you idiot! he told himself, but he didn't.

Take my hand, she thought. *I feel lost without it.*

More silence, followed by two abrupt statements.

"I want to talk . . ."

"We have to talk . . ."

Both looked relieved.

Jennifer was first to repeat, "I have to talk to you."

"I know. I have to talk to you, but maybe we should wait until you're stronger."

"No, I want to talk now." There was the slightest of hesitations before she said, "Kelly told me that John is dead."

Mitch suddenly felt as if the rug had been pulled out from under him. This wasn't exactly where he would have chosen to start the discussion, but then perhaps it was as good a place as any. There was one inescapable, harsh reality that had to be dealt with.

Looking her straight in the eye—she deserved no less—Mitch said, "I killed him."

"I know," Jennifer said softly. "You had no choice. He would have killed you."

Remembering how he'd threatened to shoot Mitchell on the spot if she didn't cooperate, she shuddered. Visibly. This time, Mitch's need to take her hand was so strong that, to keep from doing exactly that, he stood and walked to the window. As Mitch watched the antlike traffic crawl the streets, as Jennifer lay quietly in bed, both relived what had happened that tragic evening in the warehouse. He heard the deafening silence, saw the lifeless body of Lerner, saw Jennifer step from the dark shadows. She recalled the event only in terms of the overwhelming sense of helplessness she'd felt. Never had she hated anyone as much as she'd hated her husband. God forgive her, but she'd always regret not having killed him herself.

At long last, Jennifer said, with not a hint of an apology, "I'm not sorry he's dead. I haven't even tried to be." Mitch turned, his gaze going to hers. "My husband—" Mitch had the feeling that she was punishing herself with the selection of this word "—was a terrible man. He hurt a great many people."

"I know," Mitch replied, suspecting that John Yen Chang had hurt this woman most of all. Mitch was relieved that Jennifer didn't harbor any illusions about her husband, that she obviously wasn't holding fast to some emotional attachment. What Mitch didn't understand was how she had ever been enticed into marrying such a man.

Jennifer heard this unspoken question as surely as if Mitch had whispered it in her ear. Heaven only knew she'd asked the question of herself countless times.

She smiled, although it was obvious that the smile never reached her heart. "When you're a model, people expect you to be worldly. I was far from that. In fact, I was very naive." The smile turned self-derisive. "Incredibly naive."

Mitch saw her exhaustion and knew that he should tell her to rest, but he wanted desperately to hear what she had to say.

"I was raised in Iowa, with traditional heartland values. My marital role models were my parents, whom I never heard raise their voices at each other. I believed in the basic goodness of everyone." The scornful smile returned. "I wasn't prepared for John Yen Chang."

"When did you meet him?"

"Ironically, my first evening here in San Francisco. That was almost three and a half years ago now."

Jennifer wondered if her tone betrayed how difficult, how nightmarish, those years had been. There had been times when she hadn't known if she could last another day. She hoped that telling Mitchell about her pain would ease some of it. From the very first time she'd seen him, he'd made her feel physically safe. Surely, such a man could ease her emotional hurt as well.

"I'd been modeling for a couple of years," she continued. "Mostly in New York and Paris, but I'd never been to the West Coast. I was sent out to do a shoot for a swimsuit company—my agent thought it would be good for my career—and the public relations people wanted me to attend some bigwig's private party that night. John was at the party."

At that, Jennifer hesitated, as though seeing the party in her mind's eye. Sights and sounds came rushing back with a disturbing precision. She heard laughter and the tinkle of fine crystal; she saw guests dressed in their expensive finery, all wearing their very best social smiles.

"I take it you heard the proverbial bells that evening," Mitch prodded, wanting, yet not wanting, to proceed with the discussion.

Jennifer pulled herself from her inner world, forcing herself to concentrate on the man who stood at the window. Mitchell Brody had substance, emotional substance, while her husband had had none. She knew that now. In answer to Mitch's comment, she said, "With John it was difficult distinguishing between what one actually heard and what he made one believe one heard. There was no question that I'd never met anyone quite like him. He was uncommonly handsome, with women flocking to him in droves. His smile was enough to make a woman swoon right on the spot. It was so...exclusive. It made you feel as if you were the only woman on the face of the earth. But it was more than his looks that attracted me. He was dynamic, charismatic, so in control of his life. This last quality appealed to me because my own life was in such chaos."

Mitch knew that it was petty, but he hated the thought that Jennifer had found Chang handsome, though he could understand why she had. The man *had* had the kind of charisma that had women hanging off of him, the kind of polished good looks that made his own raw features appear crudely Neanderthal by comparison. Mitch told himself that making a comparison was juvenile.

"What kind of chaos?" he asked, reining in his wayward thoughts.

"My mother died when I was in high school, my father only six months before I met John. I was all that Emily had. Worse, I was our sole support. I was making a lot of money, but it took a lot of money to keep Emily institutionalized. I didn't want to keep her in institutions, but I had no choice. I had to work and that meant traveling. I felt I had to make the money while I could, because modeling is such an unstable profession. The very people who can't get enough of you today won't touch you tomorrow." She smiled sadly. "Aging isn't permitted in this business."

Mitch knew what Jennifer obviously didn't, that nothing, certainly not something as feeble as time, could destroy her beauty.

"And so John Yen Chang promised to take care of you and your sister," Mitch said.

Jennifer looked sheepish. "Is the story that sadly predictable?"

Mitch shrugged. "You were vulnerable. Chang was a man who knew how to ferret out human weaknesses, human frailties."

Sighing, Jennifer said, "There've been times when I've told myself that I got what I deserved. In my heart, though, I don't think that's true. I never would have married him, no matter what he'd promised me, if I hadn't thought I was in love with him."

Mitch *knew* that he didn't want to hear this part of the discussion, but he had no choice. "Go on."

"No one had ever courted me the way he did. He made it clear from the very night we met that he wanted me, and he did everything he could to convince me that I wanted him. He sent me flowers, not just a bouquet, but a dozen bouquets at a time. He once sent me every orchid in the city, which turned out to be so many that they filled my hotel room and left all the hotel employees talking, mostly the women, who thought it all terribly romantic. And then there were jewels—a diamond bracelet, an emerald ring, a ruby brooch. One evening, after a month of this kind of lavish treatment, he flew me to Acapulco for dinner and asked me to marry him. He promised me that we'd bring Emily to California immediately and that she'd live with us. What I remember most about his proposal was the sincerity in his eyes."

Jennifer's eyes clouded with memories, dark and painful. Mitch, too, felt pain, again the crippling pain of comparison. His simple bouquet of summertime flowers suddenly looked woefully inadequate, and he doubted that he could have scraped together enough money for one orchid, much less a city's worth of them. And as for jewels . . .

"Emily never lived with us," Jennifer said, breaking though Mitch's troubling reverie. "Not for a single day. We brought her to San Francisco, but John insisted that she needed constant care, which he assured me I couldn't give her. I argued that I could, but he maintained that I wouldn't have time. As his wife, I had certain social obligations. It took me a while to figure it out, but the truth was that John was ashamed of Emily. He told me never to mention her to anyone." Jennifer laughed—mirthlessly. "I was just supposed to sweep her under our pretty pink-flowered carpet."

Though he loathed himself for doing it, Mitch couldn't help but make another no-win comparison. Though he'd never seen Chang's home, he was nonetheless certain that it was palatial. It was everything that his apartment, seedy and second rate, was not. Hell, he was doing well if he had electricity!

"It didn't take me long to realize that John wasn't what he appeared to be. The sincerity in his eyes was nothing more than cold manipulation, his smile nothing more than a sham. And he didn't love me. He was incapable of loving anyone. All he really wanted was to possess me, to show me off."

How could Chang not have loved this woman? Mitch thought. *Sure, any man would be proud to show the world she was with him. But not love her? The idea was incomprehensible.*

"In the beginning I wanted to have a baby," she said, ensnaring Mitch's attention once more, "but he wouldn't let me. He didn't want to share me with anyone. That's when I realized that John could be selfish and cruel. That's when I realized that I was ashamed of my husband, ashamed of myself for having married him."

"Is that when you started trying not to be photographed with him?"

Jennifer looked surprised. "How did you know?"

"As soon as I found out you were Chang's wife, I wondered why I hadn't recognized you. I'm usually pretty good with faces. And I knew that I'd seen photos of you and your husband in the paper. So, I went to the library and looked through some back issues. In the dozen or so I looked at, I couldn't find a good clean shot of you. You always managed to turn away at the second the shot was snapped."

"As I said, I was ashamed. I meant nothing more to John than the Oriental art that decorated his home."

Mitch didn't trust himself to say what he wanted to, which was that anyone who considered Jennifer a mere object was clearly a bastard of the first degree. Instead, he moved on to a safer topic. "He liked Oriental art."

"Yes. Oriental art was a passion with him. In fact, he imported so much of it—a lot of which he donated here and there because it was a tax deduction and made him look generous in the bargain—that he had an agreement with Tinsung's to use their warehouse for temporary storage. He even had his own key."

"Which he didn't use that night, because he wanted it to look as if I'd broken into the warehouse."

"Yes."

Mitch frowned. "But the woman at Tinsung's didn't recognize your photo."

"There was no reason she should have. Though I went to the warehouse a couple of times with John, I never met anyone at Tinsung's. Which was typical of how our married life evolved. There were whole sections of John's life that I knew nothing about. I grew suspicious of phone calls that had to be taken in private, of locked desk drawers, of the black book that always remained in the safe. I was afraid to admit to myself what I increasingly thought he was involved in."

Here, Jennifer paused, as though it was too emotionally painful to go on.

"Did you suspect what was in the book?"

"Let's just say that when you told me that it contained the names of call girls, I wasn't really surprised. Nor was I surprised to learn that Sarah Etheridge was involved. She called the house occasionally and always managed to show up at the same social events that we did. At first, I thought that she and John were having an affair, and maybe they were, but more likely their relationship was just business. I think that the other girls answered to her. It's possible that Sarah Etheridge was the only one of the girls who knew that John was behind the operation."

"Did you know that Rhincuso and Lerner were also involved?"

"Rhincuso, I suspected—he showed up at the house several times—but I had no idea about Lerner. As awful as this sounds, I'll always be grateful to Rhin-cuso. His murder allowed me to escape. I'd promised myself that I would the first chance I got.''

"It was your plan to take the black book as a guar-antee against yours and Emily's safety?''

"Yes, but I had to bide my time. I didn't know the combination to the safe. He always stepped between me and the safe when unlocking it.''

"What happened that night? Did John know you'd witnessed the murder?''

"He suspected it. After I disappeared, along with the book, he had no choice but to take Emily. He knew he could buy my silence with her absence. He had no idea that I couldn't remember Emily, the book, or the murder.''

"What happened that night to make you lose your memory?''

Jennifer smiled, the fatigue of talking weighing down her words. "I fell. On one of the terrace steps. They're terrazzo and uneven. I caught my heel, I guess.''

A visual montage played through her mind. She re-membered falling, and forcing herself to stifle a cry, lest she attract her husband's attention. She remem-bered how loudly her heart was pounding. She re-membered the pain that had shot through her head. And then, she'd blacked out.

"I remember coming to down at the warehouse, but I still don't remember how I got there. I obviously walked, but why I even went to the wharf area I'm not sure. Maybe I chose it simply out of proximity. Once there, maybe I recognized the name of Tinsung's.

Then again, maybe it was merely the sheltering overhang that drew me."

"And what brought you to my agency?" Mitch asked, the answer to this question of paramount importance.

"I think I may have recognized your name as I was checking the yellow pages." At Mitch's surprised look, she continued. "I must have overheard a conversation in which John had mentioned it and maybe somewhere in my lost memory I reasoned that, if you weren't a friend of John's, maybe you'd be a friend to me."

Images sprang to two minds, images of how they'd become more than friends. Far more than friends. Friends didn't kiss, at least not longingly. Friends didn't admit to a physical attraction.

"When did your memory return?"

"When the woman at the museum called me Mrs. Chang, everything came rushing back, but I couldn't admit it. I was too ashamed of being his wife, too frightened of what he'd done to Emily. And so I lied to you about remembering. Mostly because I was afraid that you'd believe I'd made up the amnesia story. I left you the book because I thought you could use it to implicate John and clear yourself. In the end, though, the only thing I managed to do was make myself appear guiltier." Tears glazed her eyes as she remembered the look on Mitch's face in the warehouse. "I didn't betray you, Mitchell. I swear it. He told me he'd kill you if I didn't cooperate."

The tears were Mitch's undoing. If an army had stood between them, he'd have fought his way to her side, or died trying. He took her hand in his. It felt soft and silky-smooth to Mitch. To Jennifer, his felt warm, deliciously rough, and capable of filling that deep emptiness that always dwelled within her when he wasn't near.

"Please, don't cry," Mitch said, his voice ragged with emotion. He tilted her head, brushing aside a tear with the pad of his thumb. "I know you didn't betray me, but I did betray you." At her questioning look, he added, "I didn't believe in you."

She sniffed slightly. "Under the circumstances, what choice did you have?"

"One always has a choice, but I give you my solemn vow it'll never happen again."

His words implied a future. Perhaps he'd selected those words because he wanted to test the waters, she thought.

Which was exactly what he'd done. Did this woman want a future with him? He knew that it was unfair of him to pursue the future at this point. What she needed now was time, time to heal both physically and emotionally. Right this minute, she needed to rest, a fact her pallor attested to.

"You're exhausted," Mitch said. "You need to get some sleep."

"No."

"Yes," he insisted, noticing how heavy her eyelids were growing.

"Stay with me," she whispered, adding, "Hold me." As though in explanation, she said, "Sometimes the green dog comes back."

If she'd asked him to cut off the hand she presently held, he would have done so. Twice over. The bald truth was that he needed little coaxing to comply with her request. He wanted nothing more than to stay with her. And as for holding her, he'd sell his soul to do that. Easing to the edge of the bed, he gently scooped her into his arms.

Jennifer sighed, closed her eyes and settled against his chest. She remembered vividly the nights he'd held her, chasing away her demons by his very presence. The width of his shoulders, the breadth of his chest could so easily become the perimeters of the only world she cared to know.

As for Mitch, his world had been reduced to the gentle swells of two breasts rising seductively from the confines of the cinnamon-colored gown. He could feel them push against his chest. There was nothing prurient about her body seeking out his, nothing lewd in his body searching for hers. In truth, nothing had ever seemed quite so right, quite so spiritual.

"Mitchell?" she whispered, feeling the same heady emotions.

"Yeah?" he said, thickly.

"Are we friends?"

"We're friends."

As he spoke, he allowed instinct to take over. Angling his head, he placed a kiss to her forehead, a slow, tender kiss that made Jennifer sigh soulfully. It also caused her to react instinctively. With a slight arch of her neck, she raised her face, nuzzling her nose against Mitch's. The act was innocent, yet irresistibly intimate. The act made both want more.

"Good friends," he muttered, doing what any red-blooded male would have done. He nuzzled her nose, then sent his lips downward in search of hers. When he unerringly found them, he molded his mouth to hers. The kiss proclaimed them far more than good friends.

Jennifer moaned.

Mitch groaned.

Abruptly, Mitch ended the kiss and hauled her closely to him. His arms tightened around her in a grip that was almost painful. Jennifer could feel the panic coursing through him and wondered at its source. She soon found out.

"You scared me out of ten years of my life when you stepped in front of that bullet." He shook her gently, lovingly. "Why did you do that?"

Jennifer angled her head just enough to find Mitch's eyes. "I couldn't let him kill you."

"But he almost killed you, you little fool!"

"At that point, I didn't much care. I thought he'd probably kill you, anyway, and, if so, I didn't want to go on living." With a tenderness that brought tears to Mitch's eyes, she palmed his cheek. With the forthrightness he'd come to expect from her, she added, with a small smile, "I love you, Mitchell Brody."

Over the years, he'd had his share of women declaring their love for him. No declaration had ever moved him more deeply. Mitch closed his eyes, wanting to savor the honeylike warmth lapping around him.

"You don't have to say you love me. You don't have—"

"I love you," Mitch whispered.

At the lengthy silence that ensued, Mitch opened his eyes. A single tear streamed down Jennifer's cheek.

"Shh," he whispered, drawing her back into his arms where he simply, uncomplicatedly, held her.

"Where do we go from here?" Jennifer asked.

"We'll take it one step at a time, babe, and see where it leads." He tightened his hold. "Right now I just want you well and out of this damned hospital."

CHAPTER THIRTEEN

TWO WEEKS TO THE DAY that Jennifer entered the hospital, she was released. She refused to return to the mansion she'd shared with her husband, the site of so much unhappiness, of Rhincuso's murder. At Mitch's invitation, after storing most of her belongings—Mitch and Will had collected them from the Chang residence—she again moved in with him.

Because Jennifer needed to heal, both physically and emotionally, and because their relationship was still so new, so tentative, Mitch slept on the sofa. The truth was that he needed time, too. His emotions were every bit as fragile as hers. Killing a man, even in self-defense, and standing vigil once more at Jennifer's bedside, waiting for her to live or die, had stripped him of his strength, a strength that time alone could restore.

After an investigation, he'd been exonerated of both Chang's murder and accepting a bribe. Curiously, having his innocence finally proven had further exhausted him emotionally. He'd waited so long for it to happen that he'd begun to doubt it ever would. When it did, it seemed unreal, and suddenly, much else in life seemed unreal. Sunsets looked like pastel paintings of sunsets; sleeping and waking seemed brand-new, as though he'd never done either before.

The attraction between him and Jennifer was definitely alive and well—kisses and I-love-yous were commonplace—but each was content to see where their relationship would lead. And, if it meandered en route to wherever it was headed . . . well, that was all right, too. Day by healing day passed until July, firecracker-hot, came and went. Then August, with a few cooling breezes, arrived with all the authority of the last ruler of summer.

Surely, the soon-to-come change of seasons was what was causing her antsiness, Jennifer often thought as she lay awake at night, unable to sleep, unable to do much of anything but think of the man in the other room. Thoughts of him caused a restlessness, the likes of which she'd never experienced before, a kind of jump-out-of-her-skin feeling that bordered on painful. Kissing him had become torture because it always left her feeling as though something had been begun but not finished. Deep in her heart, deep in her feminine body, she knew what that something was, but thought it best not to put a name to it.

Mitch, too, blamed his restlessness on the seasonal change that hovered in the air. That and the uncertainty of his life at present. The investigation of the city council was still going on—even the mayor had been checked, but found clean. Apparently, Lerner had cozied up to the mayor more than the mayor had cozied up to him. Rumor had it that another couple of councilmen might be forced to resign. Each time Mitch heard this rumor, he was reminded of his own forced resignation. Another rumor, this one whispered to him by Speedy Talbot, said that Mitch was on the verge of having his old job offered to him, along with a mayoral apology. What would he do if this rumor proved true? Mitch wondered as he tossed and turned on the sofa night after night.

Mostly, though, as he remained wide-awake, he thought of the woman in his bed. He wasn't exactly sure when it had happened, but somewhere along the way, he'd grown weary of not knowing where they were headed. A sojourner without a destination was a testy traveler. He knew the one direction he *wanted* their relationship to take. His masculine body was presenting him with the road map it wanted to follow. It was a straight-arrow shot that would take him from the sofa to the bed, from lying alone to lying with the woman he loved.

By the time the last day of August arrived, both Jennifer and Mitch were fit to be tied. The day had been a particularly exhilarating one. A lot of loose ends had suddenly come together, beginning with that morning's announcement that two councilmen would be leaving office. As though he had waited to settle this issue before righting the injustice done Mitch, the mayor called and offered Mitch his old job, plus a public apology. Mitch found himself agreeing to return to the force, realizing that he'd never really had a choice. Being a policeman was all he'd ever wanted to be, and he knew that he was damned good at it. So with a job on the horizon, he and Jennifer had gone car shopping. Since his old one had died, never to be resurrected, he'd been using Jennifer's car. In short order, they found a secondhand car that was both affordable and in good condition. The day had ended with Mitch calling his son to tell him the good news about his reinstatement. From there, after a celebratory dinner, he and Jennifer retired to their separate beds.

Their lonely beds.

Mitch sighed into the darkness. He really didn't want to be alone tonight. A day that had begun with something special happening ought to end that way as well. Actually, what he wanted was nothing more than he'd wanted for days—weeks—now. *So, Brody, why not just march right into the bedroom and tell her what you want?*

Yeah, sure, he thought, jabbing the lumpy pillow. *Just burst right in and tell her that you want to sleep with her. Better yet, just break down the door and take her. Just strip back the cover, throw yourself atop her and—*

Go to sleep, Brody!

He was uncertain what the sound was when it first awakened him. He was also uncertain where it came from. An intruder! he thought, his heart beginning to pound. The assessment made sense since he didn't exactly live in a prime section of the city. He'd just reached for his gun, which he kept under the sofa bed, when the sound came again—from the kitchen. He glanced toward it just in time to see the dim light of the refrigerator come on. Jennifer, dressed in the cinnamon-colored nightgown, stood before it. With the light behind her, Mitch could see right through the satin fabric. He could see a well-rounded behind and two legs just long enough to wrap around a man. At the sight before him, at the thought tormenting him, his pounding heart slammed against his chest. He just stood there and stared. . . .

Meanwhile Jennifer reached for the jug of water, then closed the refrigerator door. Maybe if she had a cool drink, she'd be able to settle down and sleep, she thought. Yeah, and maybe she'd be able to do a swan dive off the Golden Gate Bridge. If one more image of Mitch imprinted itself on her wide-awake mind, she was going to scream. She hadn't been ready to say good-night, not after the special day they'd had. In fact, she could think of only one way that would have properly concluded this kind of day. And think of it she had, over and over. She'd imagined Mitch, wearing only his pajama bottoms, knocking down the bedroom door and quickly taking her in a frenzied state of passion. She could still imagine the blistering kisses, the feel of his hands moving over her body, the feel of his body slipping into hers. She could still imagine—

She gasped when she realized that someone stood near her.

"You scared me," she said, the jug thudding to the countertop as her heart thudded a wild beat.

If possible, her feathery breathlessness excited Mitch further. "I'm sorry," he said, his own voice barely more than a whisper. "I thought we had an intruder. I was ready to pull my gun."

As ludicrous as it was, this last comment sounded rife with sexual innuendo, which gave Jennifer a clue as to just how ready for the nut ward she was. Even so, she heard herself—no, maybe this wasn't her at all!— say, "That sounds . . . dangerous."

This remark sounded far more dangerous than any drawn gun. At least as far as Mitch was concerned. "Yeah," he said, "I guess it could be."

With the closing of the refrigerator door, the room had been plunged into darkness. Slowly, though, both Jennifer and Mitch, aided by the moonlight generously streaming through the window, began to grow accustomed to the shadowy lightlessness. Jennifer could easily make out the fact that Mitch wore only pajama bottoms, slung gunslinger-low on his hips. Equally as interesting was his chest, bare except for a thick covering of dark hair. Mitch, too, could see enough to make out the sexy tangle of Jennifer's hair and the sexier curves of her body. So much for the theory that models were flat-chested.

"I, uh, I was thirsty," Jennifer said into the silence that had come between them.

Funny, Mitch thought, she sounded far more hungry than thirsty. Hungry for maybe the same thing he was hungry for? Wordlessly, he padded over to a cabinet, opened it and picked up a glass. He set it down beside the jug.

Strangely, the placement of the glass on the counter seemed very much like a challenge. Jennifer could swear he was saying, "Prove that you're thirsty."

Uncapping the jug, she poured out half a glass of water.

"I thought you were thirsty," he said.

She filled the glass to the top, then, her eyes on his, she brought it to her mouth. His gaze lingered on hers before dropping to her lips. He could imagine their being icy-cold from the water. The idea appealed to him, maybe because his body was beginning to burn hotter than a bed of coals.

Drawing the glass from her mouth, she held it out to him. "Want some?"

The question, which they both knew had absolutely nothing to do with her offering him any water, jabbed at his stomach with such force that he wouldn't have been surprised to find himself flat on the floor.

"Yeah," he answered, but he made no move to take the glass.

At the sound of his voice, which reminded Jennifer of scratchy sandpaper, at the realization that he wasn't going to play coy, the breath caught in her throat.

Setting the glass on the cabinet, she asked, "Are we flirting?"

"Is that what you think?"

"Yes."

"I think you're right."

She closed her eyes. Slowly, he stretched out his hand and gently brushed back some strands of hair from her cheek. His touch was softer than starlight and sent tingles of desire shooting through her.

Mitch felt her shiver of anticipation. "Why couldn't you sleep, Jenny?"

"I, uh, I just couldn't."

"Why, Jenny?"

She opened her eyes, her gaze merging with his. She could feel the intensity of his stare. The sexy intensity of it. It—and the delicious way that his hand lingered at her cheek—caused a brazen recklessness to roam through her. She blamed that brazen recklessness for what she said next.

"I was having this fantasy."

Her very tone indicated that she was making the most intimate of confessions. That fact ignited new fires in Mitch's burning belly.

"What kind of fantasy?"

"A wild fantasy."

"That's the only kind worth having," Mitch said thickly, the pad of his thumb grazing the corner of Jennifer's mouth. "Tell me about it."

His thumb at her mouth produced the most decadent thoughts, the most delicious sensations. Was she really going to tell him what she'd been fantasizing in the dark, in the depths of her heart?

"I, uh, I wouldn't want to shock you too badly," she said, continuing to flirt simply because it felt daringly good.

Mitch liked the idea of drawing out the sexy game— at least up to a point. He fought a grin. "So, you think your fantasy might shock me?"

Jennifer, likewise, struggled with a grin. "It might."

"Well," he said, still playing with her delicate lips by brushing them ever so slightly, ever so occasionally, "we wouldn't want that. I mean, it could be so embarrassing, your trying to explain to the paramedics why I just keeled over. And then, there'd be the doctors at the hospital and, if I didn't make it—people do die of shock, you know—then the preacher would announce it at the funeral. And, of course, my tombstone would read: He Died From Jennifer's Fantasy."

Jennifer tried to keep the smile from growing, but couldn't. "Do you think I'd be arrested for murder?"

"Oh, yeah, you can't go around killing people like that in a civilized society. Of course, my guess would be that every policeman in the city would want to bring you in for questioning."

Jennifer couldn't help but laugh.

No sound had ever been more pleasing to Mitch's ear. Her laughter was real—that is, it came from sheer happiness.

"I'll just keep my fantasy to myself, then," she said.

"No, no!" Mitch hastened to say. "Let's don't be so hasty."

"Then what should I do, Officer? I'll put myself totally in your hands."

Again, the innuendo was so thick that Mitch could hardly breathe.

"Why don't you tell me just a little bit of your fantasy? Sort of ease me into it."

"That makes sense," Jennifer said. "Maybe I could begin with the part where you kick in my bedroom door."

"Oh, yeah," Mitch said, hoarsely, "that's a good place to begin. A real good place."

"Well," she said, breathlessly, "you kick in my—actually, your—bedroom door. Then you move to-ward the bed—slowly, but with a steely purpose."

"What am I wearing?"

"Pajama bottoms—with a string that can easily be untied. Is that last part too shocking?"

"It's terribly shocking, but I'm surviving."

"Good," she whispered, wanting to place her hands on his chest, but knowing the game would end the minute she did. She could hear Mitchell's breathing. It was as unsteady as hers.

"What are you wearing?"

"Nothing," she answered.

Mitch made a *whooshing* sound.

"Shall I call the paramedics?" she asked.

"Not just yet. Why don't you tell me what happens next . . . in the fantasy, of course."

"You lower yourself to the bed and . . ."

"And what?"

"Kiss me . . . kind of soft, then real hard."

His breathing was coming so quickly—as was hers—that his words sounded clipped and sharp.

"Yeah, then what?"

"You touch me . . . everywhere." The last word suddenly sounded like the sexiest word in the English language.

Mitch's *whooshing* was back.

"Paramedics?" she asked.

"No, just call the undertaker. I'm a dead man."

Again, Jennifer laughed, pure notes of joy.

"Actually, this sounds a great deal like the fantasy I was having," Mitch admitted.

"Really? You were having a fantasy, too?" Jennifer whispered, thinking that this kind of love-play was totally foreign to her. With her husband, there had never been any playing, any teasing. There had only been his possession of her. In the beginning, she'd pretended to like his touch. Soon, however, she'd stopped the pretense and had only tolerated his nearness.

"Yeah," Mitch answered, wondering what her relationship with her husband had been like. He couldn't imagine John Yen Chang flirting. No, he was a man who wouldn't have been bothered with such subtleties. He was a man who'd have been interested only in his own pleasure. He was a man who'd have had no time for games. "Want to know what happens next in my fantasy?"

Jennifer said nothing.

Mitch drew his thumb across her bottom lip.

Jennifer's breath rushed forward, a tiny gale lashing his hand.

"What?" she whispered.

"You're sure you won't be too shocked?"

"Tell me."

Mitch could tell from the urgent tone of her voice that the fantasy had just about played itself out.

"As I recall, I sat on the edge of the bed and whispered all kinds of decadent things that I was going to do to you." At this, he leaned forward and filled her ear with a sampling.

Jennifer said nothing, and Mitch thought that she'd been overcome suddenly by a maidenly shyness. He liked the idea. In the end, every man liked his woman to be an enticing combination of innocence and out-and-out brazenness.

"You're shocked," he whispered so softly that the accusation could barely be heard.

"No," she returned. "Just curious as to how this decadence begins."

"Simple. Like this," he whispered, slipping his hand to the back of her neck and drawing her forward.

Jennifer's heart skipped a beat in anticipation of his kiss. She knew instinctively that this man would always give more than he took. This fact was proven the moment his lips touched hers.

His mouth settled over hers warmly, with all the tentativeness of a butterfly lighting on a perfect rose. Like a spirited butterfly, his lips stayed only teasing seconds before they lifted from the perfection of her mouth.

Jennifer moaned in protest.

"Was that the kiss in your fantasy?" Mitch whispered, the words warm against the mouth that his lips hovered above.

"Yes . . . no," she whispered, her unsteady breath mingling with his.

"No? Then, how about this?"

With just the exertion of his thumb on her cheek, his fingers at her neck, he angled her head. This time he took her mouth with a tender aggression, an aggression that tilted her head back even as it parted her lips. His tongue slid forward, tasting the sweetness of her mouth before engaging her tongue in an erotic game of tag. When Jennifer moaned, he deepened the kiss.

Her lips tasted cool from the water she'd drunk.

His lips tasted hot with desire.

When her hands eased forward to settle on his hair-dusted chest, it was Mitch who moaned. The hand at her neck slid under the bulk of her hair, making its way over her back and onto the flare of her satin-covered hips. Splaying his hand wide, he pulled her into him. At the same time, she slipped her hands upward and around his neck. Her breasts nestled against his chest, while his manhood thrust against her stomach. At the feel of his need pressed so evidently against her, Jennifer experienced a rush of the purest passion.

"Shocked?" Mitch asked, a blatant reference to his arousal.

"No," she said, just as blatantly.

She trailed her hands down his shoulders, his back, the curve of his spine, then eased them inside the waist of his pajama bottoms. She stopped them just short of his hips.

"Shocked?" she whispered.

He wondered anew why her nails—now digging into him—never seemed to break, why they always seemed lush and long. Someday he'd tell her how her unbroken nails had troubled him. Someday he'd tell her how he'd been forced to accept the fact that coincidences do happen, even if he wasn't inclined to believe in them. Now was not the time, however.

"No," he answered, trailing kisses down the column of her neck. From there, he delivered a kiss to the hollow of her throat, then bestowed a kiss to the curve of her breast.

At this last kiss, Jennifer whimpered. The whimper turned into a groan when Mitch lowered the strap of her gown, exposing one breast to the sweet savagery of his mouth. Cupping the fullness in his hand, he bathed the nipple with his tongue, then pulled it into his mouth. At the white-hot fire flaming through her, Jennifer lowered her cheek to his bent head, causing her hair to cascade around them both like a silken waterfall.

Raising his head, Mitch found her lips with a hurried hunger. At the same time, he scooped her up into his arms and carried her to the sofa bed, where he gently laid her amid the rumpled sheets.

"I'm tired of flirting," she whispered breathlessly as she reached to pull him to her. "I'm tired of playing games."

"Funny, so am I," he said, rushing his mouth back to hers.

This kiss was long and deep, promising the intimacy that both had dreamed of and longed for. As the kiss deepened, Mitch shoved the other strap from her shoulder. Rolling to his side, he pulled her to him, caressing her back with his hands, snuggling her breasts against his bare chest. It was then he felt the scar, now healing, but indelibly etched into her delicate skin. Forever, it would remind him of what she'd been willing to sacrifice for him: namely, herself. He then, inch by slow inch, kissed the scar, wondering as he did so if he'd ever be able to repay the debt he owed her.

The kiss ended at her mouth with a passionately proclaimed, "I love you."

"I love you," she whispered back, slipping her hands between their bodies and untying the drawstring of his pajama bottoms.

Yeah, Mitch thought, a man liked a woman who could be both shy and brazen. At this moment, he particularly liked the brazen side of this lady.

"Why don't you show me how your fantasy ends?" he said huskily.

Slowly, like a sultry she-witch, Jennifer maneuvered her hand into the now-loosened waist of Mitch's pajamas. At her bold, but gentle touch, Mitch hissed.

"So far, it's not bad," he managed to say.

Her mouth eased onto his, tasting, teasing, tempting, at the same time that her hand performed its wondrous magic. Both her mouth and her hand worked at a languorous pace. Which was fine for all of about two glorious minutes. His blood heating, heating, heated—God, he'd never felt so hot!—Mitch had had all he could withstand. Taking control, he rolled Jennifer onto her back and, latching his mouth to hers, he tried to wrestle the gown from her. Hiding beneath her hips, coiling around her long legs, it resisted him. He gave a lover's curse of impatience, yanked the gown free and shoved it to her waist. Shedding his pajama bottoms without ever leaving her, he whispered, "I've wanted you for so long."

"I want you, too," she said softly, raggedly, as she adjusted her body to meet his.

There was to be no more waiting. From the moment he entered her, from the moment he tenderly, fiercely moved inside her, Jennifer knew, unequivocally, that this was how the binding of man and woman should feel. And how did it feel? As though she were tumbling from the highest mountain, falling down, down, down into the softest of grass-covered fields. As though she were worshiped and adored. As though she had been filled in such a way that she could never again be empty.

Mitch, too, felt the rightness of their union, the consummate perfection of their bodies' merging. But it was more than a physical conjoining. Their hearts had been bound as well. Forever bound. He called her name, wanting to tell her this, but the moment of rapture was at hand. Pulling her tightly to him, he poured himself into her, just as he poured his heart and soul into loving her.

A while later, tucked cozily into the crook of his arm, Jennifer glanced up at her lover. "Well?"

"I'm positively shocked...that I survived your fantasy."

Jennifer grinned. "Not a bad fantasy, huh?"

"Not too shabby."

Jennifer frowned. "What do you mean 'not too shabby'?"

"Well, to be honest, for all that your fantasy was shockingly great, mine ended better."

"Oh?"

"Yep," he said, trailing his fingers in a lazy pattern across the arch of her shoulder.

When he said nothing more, she prompted with, "Well?"

Feigning surprise, he asked, "Oh, you want to hear my ending?" She jabbed him in the ribs with an elbow. "Okay, okay!"

Repositioning himself until he loomed above her, he looked down into her night-shadowed face. When he spoke, his voice had turned serious. It also quivered, just as the hand that caressed her cheek trembled. He asked but a single question.

"Will you marry me?"

"THE WOMAN IS crazy to be marrying me," Mitch said as he struggled to knot the navy-and-red tie at his throat.

"Yeah, she's crazy all right," Will agreed, holding the baby bottle under the faucet of warm water.

The two men, Will already dressed in a gray suit, Mitch still agonizing over the uncooperative tie, stood in the kitchen of the Stone home. Nearby, in the cradle that Will himself had carved, lay an auburn-haired, blue-eyed baby, who on that fair October day was exactly six weeks old. As though adding her two cents to the discussion, the baby cooed.

"Even Kelly Marie agrees that she's crazy," Will said.

"Thanks, K.M., you're out of the will."

The infant gurgled, then, growing impatient for the food promised but not yet delivered, she began to whimper.

"Okay, puddin', Daddy's gonna feed you," Will said, tying a bib around the baby's neck. Picking the child up, he cuddled her in his massive arms in a manner suggesting that she was made out of the purest gold. When he had settled her in, he said, his voice, usually so rough and masculine, now as soft as snowflakes, "That's a good girl. Let's have some dinner so we won't make a scene at your godfather's wedding. Of course, we can't guarantee that, even fed, we're not going to make a scene, can we, sweetie?"

"Good. Make a scene, K.M., and stop your godmother from making the biggest mistake of her life. Oh, God," Mitch lamented, "what in the world do I have to offer her?"

"Let me guess," Will said. "Nothing?"

"You're right. Absolutely nothing."

"That's what I thought."

"Well, it's true. You saw Chang's home. It makes Buckingham Palace look like a slum."

"Yeah, it was pretty impressive," Will agreed. "Nothing to compare with the new home you two just bought."

Mitch thought of the modest two-story dwelling that they'd recently purchased. It was only a couple of streets over from the Stone home and, like many of the dwellings in the city, was Victorian in style. Like the Stone home, it, too, needed to be renovated. Though he'd had little experience at remodeling, the idea rather appealed to him. Jennifer seemed excited at the prospect, too. They'd already spent long hours studying paint chips and swatches of fabric and wallpaper.

"Of course, once we get the house fixed up, it's not going to be too bad. In fact, it'll have its own quaint charm."

"Yeah, but it'll never be the Chang mansion."

The image in Mitch's head, one of a newly painted white-and-blue Victorian two-story standing pristinely behind a picket fence, shattered. In its place appeared the Chang residence, which personified elegance.

"Yeah, you're right," Mitch said. "And I can hardly give her the jewels he could. Hell, I couldn't even afford to give her an engagement ring."

"No jewels," Will chimed, adding, "Although, as I recall, Jennifer wanted only a simple gold wedding band."

"Yeah, well, but I couldn't have given her an engagement ring even if she'd wanted it."

"No, he couldn't have, could he, sweetie?" Will asked his daughter who slurped voraciously on the nipple. "He couldn't have given her even the tiniest little diamond."

"Nor tons of flowers," Mitch said, warming to the depressing subject. "And I sure can't give her every darned orchid in the city!"

Will glanced over at his friend, who was still fidgeting with his tie. Will's look said that he was certain Mitch's comment about the orchids meant something, but he wasn't exactly sure what.

"Why would you want to give her every orchid in the city?"

"I don't—I think it's a gauche display—but Chang obviously didn't."

"So, why worry that you can't afford to give her what you really don't want to give her?"

"You've missed the whole point."

"Obviously."

"I couldn't give them to her even if I wanted to."

"Ah," Will said, still looking a little confused. "Do you understand that, Kelly Marie?"

"Of course, she understands it. She's quite possibly the smartest child ever born."

"Well, as her father, I won't argue that."

"And to make matters worse," Mitch ranted on, "I'm an alcoholic."

"A real boozer," Will tossed in.

"I'm on the wagon right now, but there's always the chance I'll fall off. Look at my father. Look at what I did several weeks ago."

"You're right," Will said. "You could topple at any moment."

"I do have my old job back. At least I *am* gainfully employed." Mitch sighed. "But then, Jennifer makes more at one photo session than I make all month."

"True," Will said. He set the empty bottle on the table and, after placing a cloth on his shoulder, he hoisted his daughter up and began patting her back.

"So, I repeat," Mitch said. "The woman is crazy to be marrying me."

Kelly Marie burped.

"I guess that about sums it up," Mitch said, then uttered an expletive as he gave up on the tie. He thought of the wedding that was scheduled to occur right there in the living room of this very house in less than an hour. He thought of the guests who would be arriving soon. He thought of his son who'd made the trip to see his father remarry. He thought of Jennifer who was upstairs with Kelly getting ready for the event....

"Are you through?" Will asked. Before Mitch could answer, Will continued, "For your information, you've been bad-mouthing a friend of mine—the godfather of my child. Do you think I'd entrust that position to the guy you've just been talking about? To the *loser* you've just been talking about?"

A small grin claimed one corner of Mitch's mouth. "Geez, for a man of few words, that was quite a speech."

A similar smile jumped to Will's lips. "I'm rarely that provoked." Will sobered. "You're right about one thing. You can't give her what her husband did. You can't give her a grand home, jewels, bouquets by the dozen or every orchid in the city. She loves you, though, for what you don't give her. You don't give her pain and heartache. What she wants from you are the things that money can't buy, the things that John Yen Chang never could give her, because he didn't have them in his heart to give."

Mitch glanced over at his goddaughter, a delicate bundle of pink. He recalled Jennifer's confession that she'd wanted a child, but that Chang had denied her her wish. God willing, that he could give her. He could think of nothing that he wanted to do more.

"And you're not an alcoholic," Will stated with defiance. "You're a *recovering* alcoholic. There's a big difference in the two. Don't make more out of one swallow than it deserves. One swallow is just that— one damned swallow. You could have drunk the whole bottle. There was no one there to stop you—except yourself."

Again, Mitch couldn't help but grin. "Mercy me, that's two long speeches in one afternoon."

"Well, there won't be another," Will said, standing and gently laying the baby back in her downy-soft bed. He then turned and fixed his gaze on Mitch. "The way I see it is that you have only one thing you need to be worrying about."

"And that is?"

"How to tie that darned tie."

CHAPTER FOURTEEN

"HERE, LET ME," Kelly said.

Jennifer gladly relinquished the job of trying to anchor the rose to the shoulder of her suit jacket. Only minutes before, the florist had arrived with the corsage and a bridal bouquet, both sent by Mitchell. Each was the ultimate in simplicity, something she had insisted upon from the beginning. All she wanted this time around were blossoms given from the heart and not from the pocketbook.

"There, that looks sensational," Kelly announced after the deft placement of a couple of pearl-headed pins.

Checking the dresser mirror, Jennifer had to agree that the rose looked perfect anchored to the shoulder of her ivory silk suit. Absolutely perfect. As did her hair. She'd wanted to wear it up in some casual but elegant style, but Mitchell had put his foot down. He wanted it flowing around her shoulders just the way it had been the first time he'd seen her. Yes, she thought, picking at a couple of curls, there was something appropriate about wearing it down.

"You look great," Kelly announced.

Smiling, Jennifer said, "Thanks. So do you."

Jennifer knew that Kelly's beauty was more than the emerald-green dress that matched her eyes to a T. It was marital happiness, motherhood, that she wore so beautifully. In less than an hour, Jennifer would be married to Mitchell. Even the prospect of being Mrs. Brody made her happy, to say nothing of the future that lay before them. With any luck, she'd have the family that her first husband had denied her.

"Thank you," Kelly answered, running a brush through the multitude of curls that clung to her head like a cap. Kelly frowned. "If only I could do something with this hair."

"It couldn't look better."

Kelly laughed, saying, "Hey, what are friends for, huh?"

Friends. Yes, Jennifer thought, Kelly was her friend. No, she was more than a friend. She was the sister she might have had had Emily not been born retarded. During the last few months, Jennifer had come to owe Kelly Stone a great deal. Far more than she could ever repay.

Suddenly turning serious, Jennifer said, "Thanks for everything. There were times when I wouldn't have been able to make it if it hadn't been for you and Will."

Before either woman knew quite what was happening, they were embracing. Tears stung two pairs of eyes.

"Okay," Kelly said, dabbing at her eyes, "enough of this sentimentality, or we're going to miss the wedding while we reapply our mascara."

As Jennifer rescued her eyelashes, she asked, "Are you sure you'll have time to check on Emily next week?"

"Absolutely. Will and I have already planned to go on Tuesday and Friday. We thought spacing our visits out would be best."

"If she's afraid—"

"We have the telephone number of the hotel where you're staying in Cancun. We'll call and let her talk to you. Okay?"

Jennifer grinned sheepishly. "I know, I know, we've been over this before."

Kelly took her friend's hand and squeezed. "Look, Jen, just have fun and let us take care of everything here. And look on the bright side—when you return, Emily will be moving in with you."

Yes, Jennifer thought, that was without doubt something to look forward to. The fact that Mitchell had insisted upon it had only made her love him more. If that were possible. In their absence, two bedrooms in their newly purchased house would be readied so that they could move in after returning from the honeymoon. A sitter would be hired to help give Emily the care she would need. That would also free Jennifer to begin remodeling the house, a task she was looking forward to with some anxiety—she'd never remodeled a house before—and a lot of enthusiasm.

"By the way," Kelly said, "Emily adores Kelly Marie. She calls her 'her baby.'" Kelly grinned. "I think Emily's going to make a wonderful aunt."

Jennifer grinned, too. "Will you let me get married first?"

Kelly looked surprised. "Hey, did I say anything? Although now that you mention it, Kelly Marie could use a playmate."

Jennifer's grin eased away. "I'm going to have my hands full trying to win over Mitchell's son."

"Are you crazy? The kid adores you. The only time he's taken his eyes off you is to settle them on his daddy."

An image of father and son came to Jennifer's mind. It had been a rare privilege to see the two together—laughing, scuffling, playing ball. Yes, Scott was a loving son, Mitchell a loving father. In the future, she would do what she could to see that they spent more time with each other. This led to thoughts of Scott's mother.

"I can assure you that Connie Brody doesn't adore me," Jennifer said.

Kelly made a sound of pure dismissal. "I guess not. You probably remind her of what a fool she was. She gave up a darn fine man and, in the process, hurt Mitch badly."

"I know," Jennifer said, thinking that it was going to take a long time to heal her future husband's wounds, but that it would be a labor of love each step of the way. For that matter, she herself had wounds that needed to heal. There was no question in her mind that Mitchell could do the job.

A knock on the door halted the conversation.

"Come in," Kelly called.

The door opened and Will's head appeared. His gaze went to his wife's and, as always, something warm passed between them. "Could you come downstairs a minute?"

Kelly frowned. "What's wrong?"

"Mitch can't knot his tie, Kelly Marie spit up on her dress and the caterer just arrived with the wrong cake—unless we're about to celebrate a bar mitzvah."

With a groan, Kelly headed for the door. There, she glanced back at Jennifer and said, "Don't worry. I'll get the cake straightened out."

But Jennifer couldn't have cared less what message was printed on the cake. As long as she married Mitchell, the cake could read "Happy Bar Mitzvah," "Happy Birthday" or "Welcome to Disneyland."

FORTY MINUTES LATER, as Jennifer descended the staircase carrying the simple bouquet of colorful flowers, a dozen or so pairs of eyes glanced in her direction. She tried to take in the wedding scene so that she would forever remember it: the white lighted tapers glowing on either side of the fireplace; the white satin ribbon flowing in frothy swags from the mantel; the white ribbon clumped in billowy bows; the white roses peeking out from here and there.

She also tried to notice the guests. There were several of Mitchell's police buddies, including Speedy and Joan Talbot, who had thoughtfully picked up Emily and brought her to the wedding. Mitchell had insisted upon her being present, a fact that had touched Jennifer deeply. Beside Emily sat towheaded Scott. Jennifer tried, too, to notice Will, who stood so handsomely at Mitchell's side, and Kelly, who stood waiting to execute her matron-of-honor duties. Finally she tried to focus on the minister.

Tried was the operative word, for the only thing, the only person, she could truly see was Mitchell himself—Mitchell standing so tall and handsome, Mitchell looking so eager, Mitchell looking so sexy. Part of her noticed that someone—Kelly?—had gotten his tie knotted, while another part of her thrilled at the prospect of unknotting it later—perhaps as they were standing on the beach in the dying rays of the Mexican sun. Perhaps they'd even go for a midnight swim in the warm salty sea waters. Perhaps...

Mitch watched as his bride stepped forward. If she wasn't the most gorgeous woman on the face of the earth, he was at a loss to say exactly who was. And he knew for a fact that no woman, at least none that he'd ever known, was so memorable a lover. She combined innocence with a sexy audacity that left him breathless and unfailingly wanting more. The most he could hope for, the most he prayed he could ever hope for, was a temporary satiation of the hunger that she caused in him. Even now, he wanted her. Even now, he could feel her bare body standing next to his on the ivory-sanded beach. Even now, he could feel her lips on his.

Those lips smiled at him. He stretched out his hand in invitation. The second that her hand entwined with his, a curious thing happened. As though by magic, all his doubts disappeared, as though they'd never existed. In their stead came the certain knowledge that he was doing the right thing. He wasn't perfect, but he could bring her a perfect love. And there was no bottle of booze that could intoxicate him the way she could. What a fool he'd been to even entertain the notion. The only temptation he now felt was the one of giving her a houseful of kids. Their kids. Mitch squeezed her hand, physically communicating his assurance to her.

The ceremony passed, a sweet lover's litany recited by minister, bride and groom. The bride would always remember the sweet smell of flowers, the husky promise of her soon-to-be husband's "I do," the slipping of the simple but priceless band of gold onto her finger. The groom would always remember the way his bride's hand trembled slightly in his, how her lips clung to his when the minister pronounced them husband and wife, the tears of happiness that glazed her eyes, making them look like flawless diamonds.

A whirlwind of activities followed. Congratulations flowed from one and all, along with endless rounds of ginger ale, which Jennifer had insisted upon instead of the usual champagne. Next, the giddy couple cut the wedding cake that had arrived at the eleventh hour. One bite went to Mitch and one bite to Jennifer; creamy icing coated two pairs of lips, and the newlyweds kissed yet again. Everyone laughed and applauded.

Then came the throwing of the bridal bouquet, followed by endless good-byes. Scott gave both his stepmother and his father a hug, and, though he was returning to his mother's home that evening, it was already settled that he would spend the Thanksgiving holidays in San Francisco. That left only Emily to say goodbye to. When she looked as though she might cry, Kelly saved the day by placing Kelly Marie in the young woman's arms.

"Don't you worry about her," Kelly admonished the couple as they headed for the waiting cab, their suitcases in tow.

"Thanks," Jennifer said, giving her friend a quick hug.

At the same time, both Mitch and Will gave each other a hearty handshake that ended up in an unselfconscious embrace.

"If you need us..." Mitch began.

"We have your number," Will finished.

The next few hours flew by on the wings of happiness. Later, all the newlyweds could recall about the flight to Mexico was holding hands and stealing kisses and making incredibly wonderful plans for the future. The plane landed as the day was ending. Another ride in a cab and the couple was shown to their hotel room. The first thing they did when the door was closed was to tumble into each other's arms. They made love, sent for room service and made love again—shocking love, Mitch teased her—as their dinner grew cold. Somewhere around midnight, they slipped from the room and went down to the silken sea.

Jennifer lifted her face to the balmy breeze that blew landward. Beneath her feet, sugary granules of sand played between her toes, while overhead the moon, looking like a nugget of silver, beamed down its seeming approval. Never had she felt so happy, never had she realized that happiness could be so painful. It filled her heart until she felt as if it might actually burst in two. Like right now.

Taking Mitch's hand, she placed it over her heart, saying, "I love you so much that it hurts."

His wife's honey-sweet words reached Mitch's ears over the gentle roar of the ocean, a sound as old as time, as magic as life itself. Beneath his palm, her breast swelled, her heart beat.

"I know," he said. "I hurt, too."

As he spoke, he slid his arm around her waist and drew her to him. The only way he could survive these days, the only way he could ease the sweet pain that filled his own heart, was to have her close.

Jennifer sighed, as if his nearness helped to alleviate a little of her pain as well. She wanted more, though, so much more, and in pursuit of that something more, her lips found his. The kiss was slow, sweet and simple.

At its end, she said, "Do you remember the day I walked into your office?"

"Oh, yeah," he replied, knowing that it was a day he'd never forget, not if he lived to be a hundred.

"Well, I know you're no longer a private investigator, but I have one more job I want to hire you for.

Mitch grinned. Jennifer could see his white teeth flashing in the moonlight. She knew that his mouth was still wet from her kiss. That thought excited her.

"Well, since you have some clout with Mitchell Brody, PI, I suspect he'd hire on for one more job."

"Good. Although in all fairness it's going to end up being a lengthy job."

"What is it?"

"I mean, it's going to last for—" she shrugged "—oh, years."

"What is it?" Mitch asked, as equally intrigued by Jennifer's request as he was by the way the moonbeams frolicked in her hair.

"For the rest of our lives."

"What is it, Mrs. Brody?"

"Ah, what a nice name."

"Are you going to tell me?" he said, impatient to hear her request, impatient to feel her beneath him once more.

"All right. Well, you remember that I first hired you to help me recover my memory?"

"Yes."

"Well, I want to hire you this time to help me make memories—a lifetime's worth."

Her entreaty wrapped itself around Mitch's heart like silken chains, chains he hoped never to be free of. When he spoke, his voice was husky.

"I think that can be arranged. In fact," he added, as his hand eased to the small of her back, as his head began to lower, "why don't you punch in my time card right now?"

"Consider it punched," Jennifer whispered, her head tilting upward.

And then his lips took hers, commandingly, demandingly, in a way that she would, indeed, remember for the rest of her life.